Deathmaker

BOOK TWO

Lindsay Buroker

DeathMaker

by Lindsay Buroker

Copyright Lindsay Buroker 2014

Cover and Formatting: Deranged Doctor Design

No part of this book may be reproduced, scanned, or distributed in any printed or electronic form without permission. Please do not participate in or encourage piracy of copyrighted materials in violation of the author's rights. Thank you for respecting the hard work of this author.

This is a work of fiction. Names, characters, places, and incidents either are the product of the author's imagination or are used fictitiously, and any resemblance to locales, events, business establishments, or actual persons—living or dead—is entirely coincidental.

Foreword

I would like to thank those of you who checked out Balanced on the Blade's Edge and have come back for more. Readers left over a hundred reviews around the web in the first month it was out, and thanks to your help, it hung out as the #1 steampunk novel at Amazon for several weeks. That meant I could justify doing something I wanted to do as soon as I finished working on BotBE: write another story in this world.

This adventure features a couple of new characters, but Ridge and Sardelle will be playing a role in the second half. I hope you'll enjoy the novel, and I would like to thank those who helped me get it ready for the world: my enthusiastic beta readers Cindy Wilkinson and Sarah Engelke, my tireless editor Shelley Holloway, and the cover art specialists at Deranged Doctor Design.

Chapter 1

Cas didn't like her new cell. After having spent two weeks jammed into a dark locker on a Cofah warship, the space so confining that she couldn't stand up or stretch out straight, she probably should have considered this an improvement. But she wasn't one of those irritatingly cheerful optimists. She hadn't liked the last cell, and she didn't like this one either. The window might let in the ocean breeze, but it was too small to climb through, not to mention barricaded with iron bars. The cries of parrots and the yowls of monkeys beyond it were a reminder that she was in a strange land, far from home, without hope of rescue.

Heavy footsteps and the jangle of weapons sounded in the hallway.

Cas bared her teeth, hoping the guards would only stroll past on their way to attend to another prisoner. It had been scarce minutes since her welcome-to-the-Dragon-Spit-prison-and-here's-a-thorough-beating-to-make-you-feel-at-home greeting. She was still lying on the floor and recovering, so she flinched at the idea of another round with those bone cudgels. For all her vows to stay strong, she had spent most of her first beating curled in a ball on the ground, clutching her gut, and doing her best not to whimper. Whimpering wasn't expressly forbidden in the "Survival, Evasion, and Recovery" chapter of the army field manual, but the line about the "inherent stoicism of soldiers" seemed to discourage it.

The footsteps stopped, and the door opened. Yellow lantern light spilled in from the hallway, making Cas realize that twilight had fallen outside. Not that the time of day mattered much.

A guard scurried inside carrying a stool. He set it down, the legs scraping against the hard sandstone floor, then he stood beside the door. Thanks to the shaven head, scarred face, and broad shoulders, he would have been ominous and forbidding even without the bone cudgel and short sword secured on either hip and the shotgun gripped in his hands.

Another shaven-headed man walked in, this one older and wearing a tiger fur cloak over his brown uniform. It didn't look particularly climate-appropriate. The man wasn't carrying any visible weapons, but Cas assumed he was in charge. If the Cofah military was anything like her own, only important people got to tinker with the dress code. For a moment, she thought of her own commander, Colonel Ridge Zirkander, and the way his non-regulation cap was always tilted at a rakish angle, but she hurried to push the image away, lest tears form in her eyes. She could be tough while they questioned her, but only as long as she didn't let herself think of comrades—*friends*—back home... and whether she would ever see them again.

"Lieutenant Caslin 'Raptor' Ahn," High Lord Cloak said, settling on the stool. "Wolf Squadron."

Cas searched for something cocky to say, something to show that she wasn't intimidated by him or this situation—Zirkander would have had a witty riposte for this statement of the obvious—but all she got out was a muffled, "Yeah?" Her lips were split and swollen from the beating. Even that single syllable hurt.

"Raptor?" Cloak made a point of eyeing her up and down, or rather, since she was on the floor, forward and back. Then he smirked. "Truly?"

Cas would have liked to stand up and tower threateningly over him, but she had to wear her thick-soled combat boots to brush the five-foot-two mark on a measuring wall. So far, she hadn't managed to tower over anyone older than ten. It would have hurt too much to climb to her feet anyway.

"I didn't give myself the nickname," she grumbled. Not that she minded it; *most* of the squadron had embarrassing nicknames, especially the other young lieutenants. Pimples and Snuggles came to mind.

"Well, *Raptor*, our latest intelligence confirms that your people know your damaged flier sank during the skirmish in the Seven Tides Strait. They believe you're as dead as the other pilot."

The other pilot—Dash. Her eyes threatened to water again. She had seen the fire in Dash's cockpit, seen him burning, his skin charred, his mouth open in a scream of pain right before his flier plunged into the ocean. There was no chance he had swum away as she had, having survived by clinging onto a piece of a wing until someone pulled her out of the water hours later. The *wrong* someone.

Cloak leaned forward, his elbows on his knees, his hands clasped as he regarded her. "That means nobody's coming for you."

A monkey howled in the distance. Cas wouldn't have minded making a similar screech. She muttered a, "No kidding," instead. Maybe she shouldn't be saying anything. But if she responded to him, she might get a scrap or two of information in return. Though she wasn't sure how she could manage it at the moment; escape had to be her priority. That *was* specifically mentioned in the field manual. Escaping and reporting back, that was her duty.

"That means we can keep you here as long as we need to." Cloak smiled. Someone who found joy in his job. What a soul to be treasured.

"Oh, good," Cas said. "I was afraid I wouldn't get to thoroughly appreciate this hot, humid-as-spit climate before getting shipped somewhere else."

"We'll interrogate you, of course," the man continued, as if she hadn't spoken. Maybe he was used to talking to himself. "I doubt you know much. What are you, a year out of the academy?"

A year and three months, thank you, but she kept the thought to herself. No need to start giving away intel before they began the interrogation; no matter that they already seemed to know more about her than she would like.

"But you *are* Wolf Squadron," Cloak went on. "If you've served under Zirkander for a year, my emperor will want whatever information you can supply on him."

Cas had been beyond proud when she had been selected

for Wolf Squadron straight out of the academy—she had done her best to live up to the prestigious unit's reputation—and she would never regret that choice. But, for the first time, she realized her position might not serve her well. Everything that made her commander a lauded hero in Iskandia would make him a loathed enemy here.

"Zirkander?" she asked, licking her lips—odd how dry her mouth had suddenly grown, humid air notwithstanding. "His favorite color is green; his favorite meal is pot roast; he prefers beer to straight spirits; and, when winter comes, he'll throw a snowball at anyone, even officers who outrank him. If that's enough intel, you can leave my cell door open, and I'll be happy to show myself out."

Neither the guard nor Cloak seemed to find her sarcasm amusing. Given how much saying all that had made her mouth hurt, she shouldn't have bothered.

Cloak pulled a dagger out of a sheath that his furry garment had hidden. Cas tried to draw back, or at least manage a sitting position, but he moved quickly for an old prison commander. The blade came up beneath her chin, the sharp point digging into tender flesh. She froze, but that didn't keep a drop of warm blood from welling and dripping down her throat.

"I've sent a communication to the emperor," Cloak said. "It's possible he'll simply want to hurt Zirkander by sending him your head. As a sign of his failure."

Cas lifted her chin, part defiance, and part an attempt to put some air between her and that blade. "The colonel wasn't even in command of the squadron at Seven Tides. *He* didn't fail at anything." Although Cas couldn't help but feel that *she* had failed. Due to her inability to dissuade a Cofah diplomat from groping her, the colonel had stepped in and punched the man, a move which had resulted in disciplinary action. It was Cas's fault the colonel hadn't been flying with the squadron that day. The man who had taken over, Major Pennith, was a good officer, but Zirkander never would have accepted the mission, one that ultimately cost the squadron four fliers and Dash's life. The colonel would have known the odds were too poor and would have pushed back against the general, maybe even the king, or he would have changed the situation, changed the odds somehow. As he always did. As Cas should have done in facing that diplomat. She shouldn't have needed rescuing. Her father would have been embarrassed for her. Rightfully so.

"Yes," Cloak purred, "we've heard that he hasn't been flying of late. Care to tell me *where* he's been?"

"Not that I would tell you anyway, but I have no idea. You're right that lieutenants fresh out of the academy don't get told much by generals and colonels."

Zirkander had barely had time for more than a goodbye wave to all of them before disappearing to who knew where. Reassigned, he had said, his face almost ashen. Cas had never seen that expression on him before, and it had alarmed her. But he'd told them he couldn't say more, simply giving everyone pats on the back and encouraging words before collecting his lucky charm from his flier and walking out of the hangar.

"You're sure you're not anyone's bedroom confidant? You're young and pretty enough. Under the blood." Cloak traced her jaw with his dagger, his dark eyes growing thoughtful.

For a moment, rage replaced fear, and Cas spat at his face. It was stupid, but it felt good. She found the strength to pull away from him, too, not that she could go far. All he would have to do was get off that stool. If he couldn't corner her on his own, the guards surely would.

Cloak snorted and wiped his face. "It's unfortunate there are rules against jailers raping prisoners. If the Iskandians are stupid enough to put women in their military, they're asking for it, after all. Besides, after all of our men your flier squads have brought down—*killed*—you deserve it." He looked at the soldier standing next to the door.

Cas gripped the sandstone bench lining one cell wall, pushing herself into a standing position, bruises and pain notwithstanding. Rules were good, but if Cloak wanted to break them, she meant to face him on her feet.

"If you want me to shut the door and see nothing, I will, sir," the guard said.

Loyal to his commander, was he? How sweet.

Cloak's thoughtful expression returned to her. There was far too much consideration on his face.

Cas dug through her mind, looking for a way out of this mess. To distract them, if nothing else, and make them forget about her for the night. "Since you seem to know quite a bit about me, you might have heard of my father. He wouldn't have been so quick to dismiss me as dead when he heard the news. He could be over here, hunting for me already."

"Yes, I've heard of your father, and my research tells me that he hasn't spoken to you in three years. I understand he didn't approve of your decision to join the army and serve the king instead of going into the family business."

Cas swallowed, disturbed by how much intelligence the Cofah had on specific Iskandian personnel. They couldn't know this much about every soldier in the army, could they? Maybe the flier pilots had been singled out because they were particularly irksome.

"I doubt he'll be looking for you," Cloak finished. "No, you'll stay here with us for a while. We'll break you and get every iota we can out of you while waiting for word from the emperor."

Break you. That did not sound promising.

More footsteps sounded in the hallway.

"Any chance that's dinner?" Cas asked, hoping this chat was over. "They didn't feed me regularly on that glorified tug. As you can see, I'm getting a little waifish."

"You missed dinner. I'll be sure to tell Captain Trivolt that you called his warship a tug though. I'm sure that will make him more hospitable to the next prisoner he captures."

A guard jogged into the cell and whispered something into Cloak's ear. Cas took the opportunity to move farther from him and his dagger. She put her back to the window wall, her canvas prison smock little insulation from the cool, coarse stone against her shoulder blades. Coarse or not, she liked having it behind her and putting as much distance between her and the men as she could.

"Yes, I'd heard about his capture," Cloak said when his

man straightened. "An even more intriguing prisoner. Yes, I'll question him immediately."

As he stood up, Cas allowed herself a hint of relief. Good, someone else for the commander to harass.

Cloak paused before walking out the door though. He looked thoughtfully back at her, his hand on the door jamb. Then he threw back his head and laughed, a deep hollow laugh that reminded her of the big bell clanging in Sky Tower back home.

"Sir?" the new guard asked. Judging by the way his mouth dropped open, his commander didn't laugh like this often.

Oh, good, that meant he had come up with something special. Cas prayed it had nothing to do with her. Would the seven gods hear her prayers over here in enemy territory? Or did they think her dead too?

"Bring him here, Corporal," Cloak said, his lips still stretched with mirth. Mirth Cas couldn't help but find alarming, especially when he turned that smile toward her. "I believe we'll save space by having our two new prisoners share a cell."

The guard's brow wrinkled. "But there are plenty of empty cells, sir."

"Ah, but nobody hates Zirkander and Wolf Squadron more than the Deathmaker."

Cas stared for a stunned moment as the words sank in. Deathmaker. Cas closed her eyes. She would have liked to scoff at the overly dramatic name—pirates couldn't ever call themselves Thon or Jed, could they?—but she had been to Tanglewood Peninsula, seen the memorial there, the graves. Six years earlier, the entire village—every man, woman, and child—had been slain by a horrible biological agent that melted their lungs and other organs, killing them from the inside out. There was nothing about the Deathmaker that should make one scoff. The evil scientist belonged to the Roaming Curse, one of the biggest pirate outfits flying the Targenian Sea. Wolf Squadron had battled with them just that past summer, taking back a pair of dragon-flier energy sources the pirates had stolen during a raid. Zirkander hadn't been lenient, and Cas had been along on that mission. She had helped bring down their flagship. She shouldn't be surprised that Deathmaker had gotten away. He was one of the few pirates who had a reputation even more horrendous than that of his bloodthirsty leader, Captain Slaughter.

But what would he be doing *here*? Why would a nefarious pirate scientist be roaming about where he could be captured?

"But won't he kill her, sir?" the guard asked after scratching his head a few times.

"Possibly. Though I'm hoping he'll want to prolong her torment a bit." Cloak turned his unfriendly smile back onto Cas. "The rules say nothing about what prisoners may and may not do to each other." Cloak laughed again. He even wiped tears from his eyes. What a dung flinger. "If nothing else, she'll be less lippy in the morning, I'm sure."

"Yes, sir. I'll get him."

Cas stared at the floor, trying hard not to feel defeated... and failing.

Deathmaker. Fate was hating her this month. When she had gone to flight school and joined Wolf Squadron, she had known she would make enemies. Even if Iskandia merely defended its homeland and rarely looked for trouble beyond its borders, the Cofah believed her people were rebels who should be reconquered. Hundreds of years may have passed since her ancestors had killed their externally imposed rulers and cast the Cofah off their continent, but the empire had a long memory. The Cofah had never stopped wanting Iskandia, and they would always believe themselves the righteous ones. When Cas had started shooting down their dirigibles and attacking their ocean warships, it had been inevitable that she would become a target herself.

Well, she didn't have to be an easy target.

Cloak and the new guard had gone.

Cas eyed the remaining guard. He was watching her right back, his shotgun aimed in her direction. Surprising him and escaping would be difficult, but the door was still open, and he was alone. This might be the only chance she got.

She subtly slid her hands along the wall behind her, hoping to find some crumbled piece of rock that she might hurl as a weapon. There were such chunks in the corners of the floor, but he would notice if she bent to pick one up. Oh, what she would give for the powers of the sorcerers of old, the ability to convince one of those noisy parrots out there to swoop through the window and claw this man's eyes out. She would have to settle for a more personal attack.

She shifted her weight and found one of those rocks with her toe. She nudged it away from the wall, thinking to kick it across the room. If she could distract him for a second, maybe she could wrestle that shotgun free from him. She might not be much more than a hundred pounds, and little more than salt and vinegar in a fight, but with a projectile weapon in hand, the odds should shift in her favor.

The footsteps returned in the hall. Out of time. She cursed under her breath.

The guard glanced toward the doorway. Cas kicked the rock.

It skittered across the room, banging him in the toe. Not much of an attack, but he looked down, and she leaped across the room. Her wounds protested the sudden movement, but her nerves flooded her limbs with fire to compensate. She grabbed the barrel of the rifle, trying to yank it free before he recovered.

He snorted. His eyes met hers, and there wasn't a glimmer of concern in them. He lunged at her, bowling her off her feet, and slammed her into the side wall so hard that it knocked her breath away. She tried to knee him, but he thrust her against the wall again, the back of her head thumping the stone this time. Blackness rimmed her vision, and dots of light floated through the air before her. She was vaguely aware of her feet dangling several inches off the ground.

"Women make pathetic soldiers," the guard said. "That you're here is a sign of how desperate the Iskandians are." He rammed her against the wall again.

"That's enough, Sergeant," Cloak said from the hallway.

He had returned, along with more guards, a *lot* more guards. And another man.

Cas blinked, trying to clear her eyes. The man standing in the doorway, his hands shackled before him, appeared more warrior than scientist, with a hide vest leaving his muscular arms and part of his chest exposed. She had expected a crazy old man with spectacles or magnifying goggles and white hair sticking out in all directions. The figure in the doorway appeared to be about thirty, and his long black locks fell down his back in matted ropes. In contrast to the tangled hair, his mustache and goatee were trimmed, and his bronze Cofah skin was clean of grime, but nothing about the dark scowling eyes, the shark-tooth necklace, or the spiked leather wrist cuffs invited one to venture closer. Amazing that the guards had been able to get his shackles on over all that pointy metal.

They were watching him now, far more warily than they had watched her. No less than four pistols were aimed at the pirate.

"Deathmaker," Cloak said, extending a hand toward Cas, who was still pinned by the guard. "Allow me to introduce your new roommate."

The guard stepped back, letting Cas drop to the floor. She braced herself against the wall. Her heart was beating a couple thousand times a minute, and she needed the stone for support. So much for her grand escape attempt.

The pirate stared at her. Full darkness had fallen outside, and she doubted he could see much in the shadowy cell, but she didn't see how that helped her.

Out of some sense that she shouldn't let him know she feared him or that he had any power over her whatsoever, she said, "How come you got to keep your trendy pirate clothes, and they forced me to put on this potato sack?"

The prisoner turned his dark glower onto Cloak. If he found anything amusing about her question, it didn't show on his face.

"Ah, are introductions in order?" Cloak grabbed a lantern from the wall and hung it from a hook in the cell—Cas eased back into the shadows near the window again. "Deathmaker, this is the Iskandian, Lieutenant Ahn. From Wolf Squadron."

That got a reaction. The pirate's nostrils flared, and his head jerked back toward her, his hair whipping about his face.

Cloak waved to one of the guards. He stepped forward warily and unlocked the pirate's shackles. The metal fell away, clanging to the stone floor. The pirate lunged inside, springing toward Cas like a lion taking down its prey.

She could only take a step before her back smacked into the wall. She tried to duck and dodge away, but even in the darkness, he anticipated which way she would go and grabbed her. Much as the guard had done, he slammed her into the wall. Her already battered body betrayed her, and a gasp of pain slipped out. She wanted to fight, to spit curses if nothing else, but a calloused hand wrapped around her neck.

Cloak's dark chuckle came from the hallway, then the door thudded shut, leaving Cas along with the pirate. The hand about her neck tightened.

Chapter 2

Tolemek stood unmoving, his hand around the woman's throat, listening for the footsteps to recede in the hallway. There was a guard still standing outside, he was sure of it, but Commandant Searson was leaving, along with his hairy-knuckled team of brutes. He didn't know if they knew who he was—who he had been before becoming a pirate—but they had relished going over him with their cudgels either way.

While he waited, he noted the window, the breeze stirring the muggy air, and the way he could see the prison's rampart from the cell. That was good. If that kid came through, this might work out after all. Whoever his "roommate" was, this location was superior to the windowless holding cell he had originally been placed in.

He was about to let go of the woman—though there was a big part of him that wouldn't mind ridding the world of one of those cursed Iskandian fighter pilots, his attack had been a ruse to get the guards to leave him alone for the night—but she had recovered from the surprise of being grabbed. She twisted, trying to jam a knee into his groin. Hands clawed for his face. Fortunately, she wasn't very tall, and his longer arms kept him out of her range.

"Enough woman," he said and released her. "Leave me be, and I'll do the same for you."

He took a step back and waited in a fighting stance in case she came after him—she seemed livid enough to take on a pack of wolves barehanded—but she backed away, too, not stopping until her shoulder blades bumped the door.

The commandant had left the lantern hanging on the wall, and the light illuminated the side of her head. Her short hair hung in wisps about what was likely a cute, impish face when it wasn't bruised. She had endured at least one round with the guards and their cudgels too. Her swollen cheekbone, and the blood smearing her chin and upper lip made him feel guilty about manhandling her, show for the commandant or not. He reminded himself that she was an enemy. Her pale, freckled skin and red-blonde hair couldn't be anything except Iskandian. If Searson was to be believed, she was a *mortal* enemy. She scarcely looked old enough to be out of her basic military training though. It was hard to imagine she had been on many flier runs. And just because Searson had said she was in Wolf Squadron didn't mean she was; the commandant had clearly wanted to manipulate Tolemek into something. Something designed to hurt her? Or a trap for him? If he murdered some other prisoner, they might have an excuse to shoot him without a tribunal.

He shook his head. He could muse upon it another time, after he escaped from this cell.

He propped a boot on the stone bench and tore off the hem of one of his trouser legs. The material wasn't bright, so he would have to trust that his helper out there was paying attention. He tied the strip around two iron bars in the window, making a cheerful bow.

Tolemek sat on the bench to wait, his back against the wall. He pulled up a leg and propped his arm on his knee. Nothing except the woman's eyes had moved. They were round and green. Innocent was the word that came to mind, and he wondered again at Searson's assertion. A fighter pilot? Truly? And if so, how had she gotten onto Colonel Zirkander's team? They didn't have any rookies flying with them. After last summer, Tolemek could say that for certain. He rubbed scars on his lower back that still itched—three bullets had been extracted from his flesh. The doctor had sworn he should have died and proclaimed his organs the toughest in the outfit. Another dubious accolade that, for good or ill, added to his reputation.

The girl—Ahn?—was considering the strip of cloth. She glanced at the lantern hanging beside her, and he wondered if she was thinking of burning his little flag. Well, she wouldn't have much luck if she tried.

"Got friends coming?" she asked softly, her Iskandian accent lilting, almost singsong to his Cofahre-born ears.

He didn't answer her. The last thing he needed was for her to alert the guard to the fact that he was trying to escape—*and* failing to menace her, as Searson had so clearly wanted. At least she had kept her voice low—it shouldn't be audible to the man standing in the hallway. He thought of keeping quiet, of saying nothing at all to her, but his curiosity got the best of him.

"You really a fighter pilot?"

It was more than curiosity that prompted the question; he wanted to know if he should let her go when he escaped, or make sure she stayed put in her cell. Though his loyalty to the Cofah had faded after his expulsion from the army, he still had family on the mainland. He worried from time to time that her people would one day shift their strategy from defensive to offensive. The size of the Iskandian army, and their population as a whole, might be laughable when compared to the empire's, but with those fliers, they could dance circles around imperial dirigibles and easily engage in guerrilla attacks on the mainland.

This time, the woman was the one who didn't answer. Tolemek kept his amused snort to himself. There wouldn't be much of a conversation if neither of them answered questions. It was just as well. The silence suited him. He looked at the starry sky beyond the window, listening for quick feet on the rampart that might not belong to the guards. At least he tried to. The howler monkeys made it difficult. They ought to be sleeping by now, surely? Maybe some predator out there had them roused.

A soft clink sounded outside. A pebble thrown at the wall.

Tolemek sprang to his feet, at the window in an instant. As soon as his face was pressed against the bars, a small irregularly shaped object lofted over the outer wall and sailed in his direction. Right away, he knew the trajectory was off. It wasn't going to land anywhere near his window.

He knew it would be in vain, but he stuck his arm out anyway. He would only get one chance.

The small bundle struck the roof overhang twenty feet above. Tolemek stretched his arm out as far as he could, hoping luck would bless him, and he could catch it as it fell. The packet shifted, but caught on some crevice or drainpipe on the edge. He stared, disgusted. This was what he got for enlisting the aid of a twelve-year-old boy.

A whistle blew on the rampart, then two guns fired. Monkey howls blasted from the jungle. Tolemek didn't see the target, but the guards were aiming toward the rocks beneath the wall. He cursed and hoped the boy had been able to scramble away quickly or knew how to swim and had dived for the deep water beyond the rocks. The kid had known the risk of helping him, but he had volunteered anyway, his eyes gleaming at the promise of a silver round before and a gold one after, but Tolemek hadn't expected the guards to shoot at a kid. That was the reason he had enlisted someone young instead of talking the captain's men into helping. That and the fact that, should his mission prove fruitful, he didn't want to share the find with any other pirates.

"Problem?" the woman asked.

Yes. "No," he said and patted along the window ledge, hoping he might pull out some cracked piece of sandstone to use as a projectile.

"There are some rocks on the floor."

He eyed her. She hadn't moved, but had clearly deduced his problem from his wild lunges. Without saying anything, he patted around on the floor. He found a few chunks, then stuck his arm out the window again. Ridiculous angle, but he had to try.

He threw the first rock. It clanged off the roof eave, several inches from the pouch. He grimaced at the noise, but the monkeys were still complaining about the gunshots, so he doubted anyone would hear it. Still, his grimace grew deeper as he tried three more times. The last time, the rock sailed past the pouch, six inches away. Curse the awkward angle—the bars made it impossible to make a decent throw, and he had limited ammunition.

"Need help?" the woman asked.

Tolemek snorted. "What are you going to do?"

"Hit whatever you're trying to hit, I imagine."

"Uh huh." He knelt to grope around for more rocks. "Can you even reach the window?"

"I'm not *that* short."

Though he was loath to waste even one rock, he wasn't having much luck himself. And she sounded oddly confident. Maybe she had a secret rock-throwing skill. Who knew?

Tolemek extended an arm toward her, a rock on his palm. She hesitated a moment before walking over, then visibly steeled herself before coming close enough to pluck it from his grasp. He wasn't surprised. His attire choices were more about convincing bloodthirsty pirates to leave him alone than scaring off women, but they had a dual effect. He backed away, so she wouldn't feel uncomfortable with him breathing on her neck—or the top of her head. She was barely five feet tall. Didn't the Iskandian army have height requirements?

Rock in hand, she looked out the window and located her target. She had to stand on tiptoes to stick her arm between the bars. He snorted again. If the angle had been awkward for him...

She stuck her tongue out of the corner of her mouth and threw the rock upward. A second passed, and she jumped and flung her arm out as far as she could.

Tolemek's mouth dropped open as she caught his pouch and landed back on the floor. He recovered his usual grim expression before she turned in his direction and was ready when she tossed the sack to him.

"You have dragon blood or something?" he asked.

The flash of surprise—and horror—that crossed her face told him that suggesting such was as much of a faux pas in Iskandia as it was in Cofahre, maybe more so. He lifted a hand, his instincts urging an apology, but she spoke first.

"I shoot things all day for the king. Hitting a target that close isn't much of a challenge." She strode to her spot against the door, folded her arms across her chest, and resumed watching him.

"Even when you're bleeding?"

At some point, her nose had started trickling again. She must have felt it, but she only sniffed. "It's not the first time."

These words were the admission she hadn't voiced before, and Tolemek found himself starting to believe the commandant's claim. Zirkander wasn't his quest, not now, but he wouldn't mind paying that man back for all the lives he had ended. And for the military career he had ruined.

Tolemek splayed his fingers and looked down at his hand, a hand that had once held a sword for the Cofah army, a hand his father had once grasped with approval. If he brought one of Zirkander's people back to the captain, maybe the Roaming Curse could use her to lead them to him. To set a trap for him. To *kill* him. Goroth loathed Zirkander even more than Tolemek did.

He lifted his head and met the woman's eyes. He didn't smile—he didn't want to be too obvious that he wanted something from her—and forced a casual disinterest into his tone as he hefted the bag in his other hand. "I know the layout of Dragon Spit, above ground and under. And I aim to escape. Want to come with me?"

"Why'd you think I helped you with that pouch? I'm hoping you have something in it to handle the door."

"I was thinking beyond the door. I have a ship waiting in the harbor. You help me get what I'm looking for here, and I'll get you off Cofahre."

"Sure, Deathmaker. Sure, I'll hop right into your ship with you. With your chivalrous reputation, how could I go wrong?" While he was considering a response—his reputation might not be flattering, but he didn't think it had anything to do with being unchivalrous toward ladies—she surprised him by shrugging and adding, "I *will* happily get out of this monkey-kissed dungeon with you."

He wasn't surprised she didn't embrace his offer wholeheartedly—even if she couldn't guess at his ulterior motives, she had to be thinking that she would be, at best, trading one imprisonment for another—but it was good enough for now. He felt fairly certain she wouldn't shoot him in the back at the first opportunity, not if she believed he knew a way out. It was after they stepped into the jungle that he would have to keep an eye on her, lest she slip away and he lose his chance to get Zirkander. But that was something to worry about later. He had a stop to make before leaving the ancient fortress.

*　*　*

Cas moved out of the way so the pirate could approach the door. He was untying his pouch and eyeing the hinges.

"You can call me Tolemek," he said.

Oh, first names? He was schmoozing her now, eh? She would use it, but only because Deathmaker was on the unwieldy side.

"Ahn," was all she gave him. Maybe it was too much, but Cloak had already spilled the beer all over the table. He knew who she was, and he had to be thinking the same way Cloak and his people were—that she was a route to the colonel. Let him think whatever he wanted, if he got her out of this prison.

He glanced at her, but she couldn't read his face. Probably because all that shaggy hair was hanging in front of it. What an animal. Wait, no, she had better not think of him like that. After all, Deathmaker was supposed to be a scientist, even if this man didn't look the part, a scientist who made horrible, horrible disease-filled devices that could kill legions of innocent people.

She leaned against the wall and watched him unwrap a couple of items from the pouch while wondering what kind of reward she might get for bringing him back to Iskandia in chains. Or maybe she could just bring his head. But decapitating people was gruesome, even by her standards. Growing up as her father's student had somewhat inured her to death, but there were levels of beastliness that a human being should never descend to.

Tolemek opened a glass vial with a glass stopper and used a slender brush to smear dark goop onto the hinges. He removed the lantern from the wall. "I have matches, but I might as well save them, since our guards were thoughtful enough to supply ambient lighting for our evening."

The casual tone and chatter didn't fit in with his look or his reputation, so she assumed he was trying to win her over. Like a hunter laying salt out in the woods for the goodly deer to enjoy, all the while waiting with a rifle in the trees. Even if he wasn't, she wasn't going to be anywhere around when he beelined for whatever ship he had in the harbor. She would find a freighter and take her chances stowing away.

Tolemek held the lantern up to the hinges. Cas lifted her brows, thinking he meant to light the substance—though that would be tough with the glass sides protecting the flame, but he was merely observing his work. Soon, the goop burst into a white flare.

The intensity of it made Cas blink and look away. Something clanked to the ground. By the time she looked back—it couldn't have been more than a second—Tolemek was tearing the door off and thrusting it sideways into the hall. The edge rammed into the startled guard's chest. Even though the man had been turning, swinging his weapon toward them, he didn't get a shot off. Tolemek used the door to shove him against the opposite wall. The man's grip loosened on his weapon.

Seeing an opportunity, Cas jumped through the door and caught the guard's rifle before it hit the ground. She leaped back, checking in both directions—and checking her pirate as well. He wasn't so busy bashing the guard into the wall that he didn't notice her grabbing the firearm. Nobody else was around, so she trained it loosely on the guard, but the man's eyes were already rolled back into his head, the result of a few palm strikes from Tolemek.

Cas waited to see if he would argue over the rifle—or try to take it from her. He did *eye* it briefly, but he simply took the guard's sword belt, tightening it a few holes so he could hang it, complete with sword and cudgel on his own waist. Like he needed weapons to look fiercer. Cas gave him an insincere smile and risked getting close enough to slip the extra bullets out of the ammo pouch. She stayed on her toes, feeling like the deer watching the hunter, ready to dart away at any moment. Tolemek's eyebrows flickered, but he didn't say or do anything. After she had fished out the bullets, he headed down the hallway. *Not* in the direction that would lead to the stairs and the offices Cas had been led past on the way to her cell.

She eyed the lantern, but it had struck the floor hard in the melee, and oil was spilling from its dented cache. The gas lamps on the wall couldn't be removed, so she hoped he wasn't taking her anywhere dark. She jogged to catch up with him.

They hadn't gone more than twenty steps, passing several other closed oak doors, when he stopped before an intersection and raised a hand to halt her. "Don't fire unless it's an emergency," he whispered. "It'll be too loud. They'll sound an alarm, and there won't be time to... escape."

She resisted the urge to point out that he was stating the obvious. Besides, she was busy noticing that little hesitation. Escape wasn't the first thing on his mind, not when he seemed to have let himself get captured so he could get in here.

The sound of rustling clothing somewhere around the bend reminded her to focus on the moment. Without warning, he burst into a sprint, disappearing around the corner in a blink.

Startled, Cas hustled to the intersection. There were three guards in the hallway he had charged into. The closest one was on the floor, clutching his stomach; the farthest one was staggering backward, grabbing at his face with both hands—something dark and blotchy covered his eyes and nose. Tolemek was trying to take the middle one down, but this opponent had clearly had time to react. He had his sword out and swung it at the pirate's head.

Though shooting would have been a quick way to end the fight, Cas was as reluctant to make noise as he was. She grimaced as sword struck sword, the clash echoing in the hall. She raced to the man on the floor, who had recovered enough to get to his hands and knees. She kicked him in the side of the face. His head cracked against the sandstone wall hard enough that the thump rang out as loudly as the swords. The colonel would have found a way to take these men out with more honor—or at least without kicking them while they were down—but her size didn't get her far in fisticuffs, and her mission was escaping, not sparing the lives of enemy soldiers. Fortunately, the crack against the wall dazed the man enough that she could remove his weapons without hurting him further. In addition to the standard cudgel and short sword, he had a pouch of Cofah throwing stars at his waist. She plucked it off with relish, glad for a projectile weapon that didn't involve gunpowder explosions.

She palmed one of the stars and stood, seeing if her pirate needed help. But the guard he had been trading sword blows with was down, his eyes rolled back in his head. The last man hadn't figured out how to remove whatever was sticking to his eyes, and he could only flail ineffectively with his sword. Tolemek dodged the swats, ducked under his arm, grabbed it, and twisted his wrist so the man dropped the blade. After shoving him against the wall, Tolemek grabbed a key ring off the guard's belt. He kicked open a door and thrust the man inside. Tolemek locked the door before his foe could recover. He grabbed the unconscious sword fighter and thrust him into another cell. It crossed Cas's mind to help manhandle the last guard inside, but she couldn't begin to lift one of these big men. Besides, Tolemek was handling the situation fine. He hoisted the last man into a cell and locked that door too.

Interesting that he hadn't killed anyone, given his reputation. Or maybe not. Even if Cloak had locked him into a cell, she was fairly certain he was Cofah and that these were his people or at least had been at one time. If this were an Iskandian prison, his choices might be different. No, given his record of killing her people, she was certain they *would* be different. She wondered if he knew there was a memorial on the Tanglewood Peninsula and that kin of the three hundred people who had died in that village made pilgrimages there every spring to pray for the souls of their lost loved ones.

With the last door locked, he faced her. Cas had the rifle in one hand and the throwing star in the other. A good fifteen feet separated them. Enough for her to throw one of the stars if she were of a mind to. If she did, could she get out on her own?

For a moment, they stared at each other, and she suspected he knew exactly what was on her mind. There was a wariness in his stance, like he was prepared to spring away if he needed to, but he didn't look that worried. He probably didn't think she was that dangerous with some enemy weapon native to his continent and not hers. She thought about showing him how dangerous she was, but what would that serve? Only to warn him that he had best keep an eye on her.

Cas waved at the hallway behind him. "What's the plan? There another set of stairs that way?"

"Yes." Tolemek held her eyes for another long moment before turning his back on her to lead the way.

She watched the target area between his shoulder blades for several seconds before following. She hoped a moment wouldn't come when she regretted not taking the opportunity to plant a bullet or throwing knife there.

Another turn took them down another hallway of cell doors. On the positive side, it was devoid of guards. On the negative side, it was devoid of stairs or other exits too. That didn't keep the pirate from striding down to the end. There wasn't an interesting tapestry, decorative plant stand, or slyly placed lever that might suggest a secret door, but he rested his ear to the stone and thumped the blunt tip of the cudgel against it. Whatever he heard satisfied him, for he delved into his pouch, pulling out the vial again. He dabbed the goo on the sandstone, making a circle with it this time.

Cas leaned against a side wall so she could watch him as well as the way they had come.

"What is that stuff?" she asked, wondering where he had gotten it. The burning of the metal hinges had been handy, and if it could also burn holes in a six-inch-thick sandstone wall, that would truly impress her. She could think of a few useful applications for it back home.

"It doesn't really have a name." Tolemek kept dabbing at the wall, trying hard to stretch what little paste he had to complete his circle. They better not get locked up again, because he didn't look to have enough for another set of hinges.

"How can it not have a name?" Cas tried to imagine shopping for it in some exotic market by simply describing its properties.

"The creator didn't come up with one. Though I hear it's recorded as Brown Goo Number Three in his journal."

Oh, so this was something he had invented. Even though it had proven nothing but handy thus far, the admission, however oblique, chilled her. It was as if, in admitting to creating this little concoction, he had admitted to creating every horrible thing she had heard of the Roaming Curse using on its enemies—its *victims*.

"Chastor?" someone called from the hall around the corner, the hall with all the guards locked in cells. "Ponst?"

"Better hurry," Cas murmured.

"The wall is thick. This will take a minute."

Cas fingered the rifle, then decided on the throwing star. She bent her knees, readying herself in case a guard ran around the corner.

An acrid scent lit the air. She had been too busy running out to grab that first guard's weapon to notice it before, but she knew it was the goop burning. When she glanced back, the wall was charred and smoking, but it was intact. Brown Goo Number Three might not be strong enough to help them escape again this time.

The guard in the other hall didn't call out again, but his footsteps echoed ahead of him. He was walking their way.

A grinding came from behind Cas, followed by a couple of grunts, then a crash as loud as a rifle shot. So much for not warning the whole fortress.

She started to cuss at Tolemek, but the guard ran around the corner. He halted so quickly he skidded as he gaped at the end of the hall. That didn't keep him from whipping his rifle butt to his shoulder. Cas was already hurling the throwing star. She trusted her aim and knew it would hit, but ducked anyway—she was the closest to the intersection, and that rifle had been pointing toward her.

It never went off. The throwing star lodged in his throat, slicing into his jugular. Blood spurted from the severed artery, and the rifle tumbled from his fingers, clacking onto the floor. He crumpled soon after.

Aware that beige stone dust had flooded the hall, Cas faced her pirate again. He had to have seen her take down the guard—so much for not showing him she was dangerous—but he didn't say a word. He stood by a circular hole in the wall, the gaping orifice opening into utter blackness, and extended a hand toward it, like a man holding the door open for a woman at a café. So much for her hope that they weren't going anywhere dark.

"No, no, you go first." Cas batted at the dust in the air, almost coughing when she spoke.

Tolemek slipped through the hole and disappeared. He looked like he had dropped down. She supposed it was too much to hope that he was simply leading her into some nice forgotten tunnels that would deposit them on a beach below the fortress.

Wishing she had kept the lantern that had been in their cell, Cas walked to the lip of the hole and peered inside. Her estimate of a six-inch wall had been off; it was more like a foot thick. That goo was powerful. The edges of the hole still smoked, and she wouldn't have touched them if she hadn't already seen Tolemek do so.

"How far of a drop is it?" she whispered.

She didn't want to stall—someone would have heard that noise, and the dead guard would soon be missed, too—but she couldn't see more than two feet into the gap. She had the sense of a vertical shaft dropping away and didn't see any stairs.

Tolemek didn't respond. He hadn't done something stupid like falling to his death, had he? For a moment, she thought she would have to go back the other way and hope she could avoid notice, but his voice finally drifted up from below.

"Fifteen feet to a landing. Then there are stairs. Sort of."

Well, didn't that sound promising?

He didn't sound farther down than his estimate, so Cas took his word. She ought to be able to land from that height without breaking anything. She stuck her feet through the hole and slithered over the edge. For a silly moment, she wondered what the view looked like from below. She might be an expert marksman, but nobody had ever accused her of amazing athleticism.

She lowered herself down, probing with her feet, though logically, she knew she would never reach the floor without letting go. Also, her boots pressed against some squishy substance growing on the wall. Maybe it was better without the lantern.

"You out of the way?" she asked before letting go.

"Does that mean you don't want me to catch you?"

"It means I don't want to kick your ear off as my legs flail around on the way down."

"Thoughtful." His voice had shifted—he'd moved to the side.

He hadn't truly been thinking of catching her, had he? Having the Deathmaker's hands wrapped around her waist sounded a lot more creepy than it did thoughtful or pleasant.

A gong reverberated somewhere in the distance. Alarm. No more dawdling.

Cas released her grip and fell into the darkness, her heart in her throat. Without any light, she couldn't gauge the distance to the bottom, and could only guess when she needed to soften her knees for impact. The landing jarred her nonetheless, though a hand caught her arm, steadying her. Tolemek released her almost as soon as he touched her.

"Thanks," she said grudgingly.

The air was warm and close, smelling of the jungle, of plants and decaying matter. The gong was barely audible from down in the well, but she heard it nonetheless.

"You're welcome," Tolemek said. "The stairs are behind you. I'll lead."

"Good, because I wasn't going to volunteer."

He didn't light a match. She supposed his stash would burn out quickly if he did. She found a wall with her palm, grimacing at the bumpy algae—or whatever it was—growing on the old stone. It was on the stairs too. Her boots squished with each step. At least they were going down. Down was good. There should be a way out to the beach or the jungle from below the main fortress.

The stairs, beneath the inch of algae, felt old and worn. More than that, in several spots, the edge crumbled beneath her boot.

"What is this place?" she whispered as they continued to descend. Their cell had been on the second story of the three-story fortress. Though there were no landings to help judge it, Cas already felt as if they had descended three or four floors.

"Long ago, there was a dragon rider outpost in the base of

this cliff," Tolemek said. "*Real* dragons, not little mechanical fliers designed to look vaguely like dragons."

"Should you be insulting my people's aircraft when I'm walking behind you with a gun?" She said it lightly, though his tone had miffed her.

She expected some dismissive comeback, but he descended a few more steps before responding with, "Probably not. Are you as deadly with a rifle as you are with a throwing star?"

"I've had more practice with firearms."

"I thought you were too young to be what the commandant claimed, but I'm beginning to believe that Zirkander would have recruited you."

His tone didn't drip malice when he said the colonel's name, but the alarm gongs that went off in Cas's head rang far more clearly than those in the fortress above. She didn't want to discuss Zirkander with him, or her work at all. The last thing she wanted was to slip up and give away some useful intelligence, especially to someone who could make explosive goop and only the gods knew what else.

"Were you with the squadron last summer?" Tolemek asked in the same conversational tone, but there might have been the faintest edge to it. A were-you-among-those-who-fired-on-our-dirigibles-and-nearly-killed-the-captain-and-me-last-summer edge.

"Where I am is watching your back until you get me out of this dungeon, and I think we can leave it at that." Another throwing star had found its way into Cas's hand. The cold steel was reassuring against her thumb. Maybe she would leave it there until the fresh jungle air was upon her face and Tolemek had taken off in his ship.

CHAPTER 3

THE STAIRS ENDED AT A wide corridor with the stone floors pockmarked with age. Some of the holes were deep enough to be considered craters, sizable obstacles in the darkness. Tolemek walked near the edge, fingers following the wall, taking care to test each step before he committed to it. He wasn't expecting booby traps in the centuries-abandoned fortress, but crumbling floors could drop him into a pit as easily as an ancient architect's whims. And then there was the woman walking behind him, making his shoulder blades itch. Thus far, she had been helpful, but it didn't take some telepath of yore to sense that she believed she would be doing the world a favor by getting rid of him.

They came to the first intersection, the wall disappearing and his fingers brushing air, so Tolemek concentrated on the route. He had memorized the old map he'd found before coming, but it would be easy to grow disoriented down here in the dark. The few matches he had wouldn't do any good without a lamp to light, and he doubted he would find one down here that still had oil in it. Or whatever they had used back then. There were tales that said the halls in the sorcerers' homes were simply alight with their magic.

Something rustled through the algae on the floor, whispering past his boot. Not magic, but a snake. Whatever sorcerous power had once imbued this place was gone, leaving nothing but ruins. He wondered if he was a fool to believe he would find anything here.

At the third intersection, Tolemek said, "Left," and turned down it.

Lieutenant Ahn grumbled something under her breath, but kept following.

"I *do* have a couple of likely escape routes in mind," he said.

"After I find what I'm looking for, I believe I can get us to the jungle."

She didn't answer promptly. He admitted *likely* and *believe* weren't the most encouraging words he could have used. Since he had only studied the fortress from a distance, he was reluctant to promise more. He feared that at any moment, the route would be blocked by rubble from some hundred-year-old cave-in. He had memorized a couple of routes to the library, just in case, but so far the only obstacle was the musty air. Possibly the snakes.

"How does this stuff grow down here without light?" Ahn mused.

"I've wondered that. Perhaps some residual energy left in the walls from those ancient sorcerers. Plants are highly adaptable, and most ecological niches get filled, given enough time."

Her grunt suggested she wasn't that interested in his theories. Or that discussions of sorcerers made her uneasy. Or maybe she was imagining sinking her throwing stars into his back again.

Tolemek was counting doors, or rather doorways since the wood had long since rotted away, and didn't speak again. He wondered if the books and scrolls he hoped to find had rotted with age too. He hoped the ancient scribes had used their magic to preserve some of them.

"This is it," he whispered when they reached the fifth doorway.

"The treasure room?" Ahn guessed.

Was that what she thought this was? Some quest for gold? He supposed it was as plausible a theory as any. "In a manner of speaking. This was their library."

He slipped inside, forgetting some of his caution. He almost didn't notice the long pause before she asked, "You planning to study some ancient magics?" She had stopped at the doorway. "To help you make better... goo?"

Her tone was full of wariness. She knew his name, the rumors surrounding him. She had to be uneasy down here with him, understandably so. He wasn't sure how to settle that unease. He also hadn't figured out how he was going to get her to his ship, short of overpowering her and knocking her out. As long as they were close, and she didn't have the range to throw something sharp at him, he figured he *could* overpower her, but that seemed a poor reward for the help she had provided so far. If she hadn't been there when that guard had rounded the corner, he would have aimed at Tolemek instead of her. Waiting for his goo to work at the end of the hall, he had been too far away to do a thing about it. But simply letting her escape into the jungle? He didn't know if he could do that either.

"I prefer science to magic when it comes to my goos," he said. "Not that I know enough about magic to know if it has any useful applications, regardless, but this—what I seek here—is to help another, not myself."

"Some lover or relative sick?"

"What?" he blurted, almost tripping into one of the pockmarks in the floor.

In the darkness, he couldn't see the shrug, but he heard it in her voice. "They say some of those old sorcerers were healers."

Tolemek's first reaction was to stop talking or to brush her off. Her guess had been a little too close—not even the captain knew what exactly he was searching for and why. But maybe he could lessen her wariness by talking about his family, making her believe that no matter what she had heard, he was simply a person.

A person who wanted to entrap her for his own gains. He grimaced at himself. Why was he even worrying about her when he had reached the room he had been scheming and planning to reach for the last three months?

"Not a lover," he said by way of completing the conversation. "My little sister."

"Oh."

Tolemek fished out a match from his pouch and found a wall to scrape it on. The flame flared to life, revealing walls full of stone bookcases, *empty* stone bookcases. A few old tables had been pushed to the sides of the big room, and an expanse of mostly bare floor lay before him. The mold wasn't growing on it, but piles of fine gray dust undulated across it. Rat and snake tracks disturbed it in places, but there was so much that it hadn't been scattered completely by time or visitors.

Frowning, he crept forward and crouched, touching his finger to one of the piles. His match burned down, searing his flesh and going out, at the same time as he realized what he was looking at. Not dust. Ashes.

He snarled and slammed his hand into the hard floor. He couldn't see them now in the darkness, but he felt the ashes stirring and rising into the air, tickling his nostrils with the scent of ancient books and scrolls long destroyed. Oh, he didn't know how long it had truly been, but it didn't matter if it had been a year or hundreds of years. He was too late.

* * *

Cas waited in the darkness beside the doorway. She wanted to get going—this far under the main fortress, she couldn't heard the alarm anymore, but she wagered it was still going on, and it wouldn't take long for guards to find that huge hole in the wall. Still, she suspected Tolemek would want to search further, if he had made the journey here specifically for this. Whatever this was. That room hadn't looked promising from what she had seen in the handful of seconds the match had been lit, but maybe there was more to it.

"We can go," he said scarce seconds later. He hadn't even bothered to light another match.

Cas thought about telling him she was sorry he hadn't found what he was looking for, but she wasn't sure she believed his story about wanting to help his sister. For all she knew, he was looking for something to turn into a weapon. "I'm ready."

He took the lead again, and she followed him through the dark passages, using a hand on the wall to feel her way along. She tried not to feel uneasy about the fact that she would be lost down here without him. Usually, she had a good sense of direction, but they had taken a few turns, and the darkness made it hard to note landmarks.

"Right turn," Tolemek said, "and a tight squeeze."

She found the gap in the wall, using both hands to get a feel for the opening. It wasn't tight by her standards, more like the width of a closet door rather than a wide corridor. But as soon as she turned after him and bumped into his back, she understood what he meant. Maybe it *was* a closet.

"You can pick your hole," Tolemek said, shifting to the side, "though my understanding from the blueprint I studied is that they all come together into a single vertical shaft that drops eighty feet before joining with the current sewage removal system."

Cas stuck her foot forward, trying to find whatever hole—or holes—he was talking about. But she smacked her toe on a wall. No, the base of a shelf or bench. It took a moment for her to realize where they were. Not quite a closet. "Is this a latrine?"

"Yes. A centuries-old one. There shouldn't be any biological contaminants left, if you're concerned about cleanliness."

Cleanliness? Please. "The eighty-foot-drop you mentioned is more problematic for me. Unless you've got a coil of rope hidden in that little pouch of yours." She was beginning to see why he'd arranged to have himself captured instead of simply using his concoctions to infiltrate the ruins from below.

"Rope would have been impractical for someone to throw across the courtyard to my window."

"Maybe so, but it would have made a much bigger target to aim at with a rock."

He snorted. "The walls are somewhat slippery, making climbing up the shaft difficult, but I think we'll be able to slow ourselves down enough to land on the bottom at a reasonable, unlikely-to-break-bones speed."

How comforting. "I'm going to refrain from making sarcastic comments or telling you to stuff your head in a latrine, but only because I could be stuck back in that cell and waiting for my next beating right now."

"And because I *will* be stuffing my head in a latrine?"

Huh, her pirate had a sense of humor. How odd for someone named Deathmaker. "Yeah, that too."

Tolemek lit a match. "So we can see what we're getting into."

Between his description and her time feeling around, Cas already had an image of the place in her head, and it proved fairly accurate. Three holes in a sandstone shelf were all that remained of the latrine. The rims of the openings had crumbled away, so they were larger than they would have originally been. She could squeeze through one, yes, and he probably could, too, though it would be a tight fit.

When he held the match over one of the holes, she peered inside. If there was an opening at the bottom, it was too far down to see. He dropped the match inside, and for a moment, she had a good view of those walls before the flame went out, long before it got close to the bottom. The important thing was that the shaft appeared narrow enough for her to climb slowly down, bracing herself with her arms and legs. The stone was stained with time—or something more visceral—but wasn't cloaked in algae and hadn't appeared that slick in the light.

"I'll go first," Tolemek said.

"All right, but do me a favor, will you?"

"Such as?"

"If you slip and fall to your death, try to crash down in a way that won't leave those spiky bracers pointing up for me to land on."

"I'll keep your request in mind." He climbed into one of the holes, grunting as flesh smacked against stone.

Cas waited for the curses, scrapes, and bumps to fade away before she stuck the pouch of throwing stars into her mouth and climbed onto the shelf. She almost left the rifle there, but thought she could make something of a lap as she descended, her legs out and her back against the wall, and keep it from falling. She thought about waiting long enough for him to climb down the entire eighty feet, so that if she fell—or dropped the rifle—she wouldn't knock him loose, but there had to be guards searching in the ruins by now. She imagined one running in, looking down, and shooting her while she was helpless. She didn't want to die in some latrine drainage shaft.

With that cheery thought, she lowered herself into the hole, pressing her back against one side and her legs against the other. She lowered one hand, then the other, from the rim of the hole and placed them on the walls to either side.

"A promising start," she murmured when she didn't slip, then inched her way downward.

It didn't take long for her to find the slick spots Tolemek had mentioned. When that happened, she slipped inches—or feet—before catching herself on coarser material. Each time, her heart tried to leap out of her chest, doubtlessly searching for a less insane place to reside. She almost lost the rifle a couple of times too. Tolemek would not be pleased if it cracked him on the head, but maybe those thick ropes of hair would offer padding.

Without being able to see a thing in the blackness, it was hard to judge how far she had gone, but she guessed she was halfway down when her butt bumped into something. That gave her heart another jolt. It turned out to be a bend in the shaft. The passage curved in one direction before returning to vertical, and maneuvering past the hump, which was slick of course, was scarier than her first time upside down in a flier had been. At least she didn't pee on herself—a couple of her classmates at the academy had done that on some of their early flights. Although, if one were to have such an accident, this would be the natural place for it, she supposed.

"Ahn?" a soft call came from below.

She had lost track of time, so it surprised her. "Yeah?" she asked around the pouch of throwing stars, her voice as tense as the rest of her body.

"I'm on the ground. We made it." Tolemek sounded like he was about ten feet down and standing right under the hole. Lucky for him that she had managed to keep bodily functions under control.

"Are your bracers out of the way?" she asked.

"Yes." He sounded amused. Maybe deep down, pirates knew their wardrobes were silly.

Cas's heart got one more jolt when she ran out of wall to brace herself against, and one of her feet slipped, dangling into emptiness. Her hands pressed against the side walls like immovable anchors. She didn't say anything, but Tolemek must have heard her suck in an alarmed breath, for his hand came up to touch her leg. "You've got a seven- or eight-foot drop, and then it's flat down here."

She didn't want to admit that his touch reassured her, but since she couldn't see a thing, it did. She let herself drop, twisting in the air to land facing him and grabbing him as she fell—just in case he was on a ledge and there happened to be another hundred-foot drop for the foolish girl who missed it. Her feet landed on solid stone. She released a long, relieved breath.

"Are you trying to undress me?" Tolemek asked mildly. She had a death grip on his vest, her fingers clenched in the thick hide, and he was probably missing a few chest hairs too. "Or just admiring the feel of my clothing?"

As soon as he spoke, Cas released him and took a step back, glad for the darkness. An embarrassed blush heated her cheeks. She pulled the pouch out of her mouth and strove for a nonchalant response. "It *is* an upgrade to what they gave me to wear."

Fortunately, he didn't make any more jokes about her grabbing him—or mention that he'd noticed that the climb down had scared her. "Getting out should be easy from here," he said, turning away from her. "This way."

Cas followed him down a new passage, this one with water trickling down the middle—water that didn't smell all that fresh—and was relieved when a warm breeze touched her cheeks. Finally.

They turned around a bend, and the blackness faded to gray, the bumpy green walls growing visible. The end of a tunnel came into view beyond a grid of rusted iron bars. The alarm gongs were audible again, and Cas wondered how many guards would be out there, searching for the escaped prisoners.

"You have any more of that metal-burning goo?" she murmured as they walked toward the bars.

"No, but I already applied it." Tolemek strode toward the grate. "Last night, when I was hoping I could get into the ruins without having to deal with the dungeon or its guards."

That meant Cas never would have met him—and would still be in her cell—if not for a thousand-year-old latrine. Fate was a capricious spirit.

Tolemek lifted a hand to stop her and dropped into a crouch near the wall. They were still twenty feet from the bars but close enough that she could see hinges, identifying it as a gate, and a shiny new steel lock securing it.

"Looks like someone noticed your sabotage," Cas said.

"Annoyingly efficient of them."

The sounds of foliage being snapped and trampled drifted in from outside. Someone in a uniform jogged past the entrance. The figure glanced in their direction, but continued on without pausing to peer more closely. Glad for the shadows, Cas reached in her pouch for another throwing star. She still had the rifle as well, but if they could slip past the guards without making any noise, they would have more time to escape into the jungle. Then again, if they were forced to engage in a skirmish out there, that might be her opportunity to slip away from her pirate, especially if the guards, considering him more dangerous, focused on him. Once she was on the other side of those bars, she could find her own way home.

"Anything left in your little pouch that can handle locks? Or iron bars?" Cas asked.

"Unfortunately not. We'll have to try another exit. There are others."

Cas shifted from foot to foot. The jungle called to her. Out there, in the night, she could hide. Here, they were simply waiting to be discovered. "I can shoot the lock off."

The lock was shiny and new, but so were her bullets.

"Guns don't solve every problem," Tolemek said, heading for the interior again. "And making noise will tell them where we are."

It would tell them where *he* was. If the guards spotted him, they might forget to worry about her, at least for a few moments. That was all she needed.

Tolemek had no more than stepped past her when Cas lifted the rifle. She fired three rounds at the lock shank from far enough away that the bullets shouldn't hit her if they ricocheted off. But the lock lost the war early on and clanked to the ground. Cas walked up to the gate, gave it a shove, and it squealed open.

"Guns do solve a *lot* of problems." She smiled at Tolemek as he ran back to join her.

"The guards will have heard that."

Cas loaded bullets to replace those she had used. "I expected another fight before getting out of here." With the guards... or with him. One or the other.

She started forward, intending to use the mouth of the tunnel for cover and to shoot anyone who ran their way. But Tolemek gripped her arm, stopping her.

Shouts of, "Over there," and, "The drainage tunnel," accompanied the crashing of foliage.

"What're you doing?" Cas demanded.

"I have one more tool to use." Tolemek opened his palm, revealing a leather-wrapped ball.

"Uh?"

He pulled her back through the gate and into the shadows of the tunnel. She was tempted to yank free and fight her own battle—the jungle foliage wasn't more than a hundred meters away, so if she could subdue the guards in sight, she ought to be able to sprint out there to it... but Tolemek's grip was firm, and he could probably sling her over his shoulder without much trouble. She went along with him. She could shoot from the back of the tunnel if she had to.

"Down," he whispered, crouching again.

A second later, the first guard came into the sight, a dark outline against the jungle. Cas melted to the ground, making herself a small target, and lifted the rifle to aim.

"Wait," Tolemek breathed in her ear.

Two more guards came into view, one holding a lantern, both armed. Cas's finger tightened on the trigger. They might not be able to see her and Tolemek in the deep shadows, but if they started firing into the tunnel, they were bound to hit them.

"They go in? Or run out?"

"They must have come from in there and run out."

A soft rustle of clothing came from behind Cas. The little leather ball flew through the gate, bounced on the ground, and came to rest between the men. Its sides unfurled like flower petals, and some sort of smoke oozed out.

"What is that thing?"

One of the guards shot at the ball, which was inches from another man's foot. Everyone jumped back. The unfurled ball seemed undamaged; if anything it spewed more smoke.

"You boys all right down there?" someone asked from the side.

"I..." The guard who had fired—and doubtlessly caught a big whiff of the smoke—grabbed his forehead and stumbled backward. The next closest man simply pitched to the ground. The third soon followed.

Cas thought she heard a couple of thumps from near the tunnel exit too. How potent was that smoke? She couldn't smell anything in the tunnel, but it had to have a decent range.

"Poison?" she whispered, her stomach queasy at the thought. Yes, she would have shot the guards with the rifle, but somehow this seemed more diabolical.

"Not exactly." Tolemek rose and trotted to the exit. He leaned out and scanned the surroundings to either side before waving for Cas to join him.

She was already on her way, though she held her breath as she drew closer. Just in case.

Tolemek headed straight across the clearing around the base of the fortress toward a vine-draped trail that disappeared into the dark jungle. Cas paused to touch the throat of the first man who had fallen, checking for a pulse. Surprisingly, it was there, beating normally. Aware of the alarm gongs and more shouts in the distance, she ran for the foliage too.

She thought to veer off in a different direction, to find another trail into the jungle, but Tolemek had stopped to wait for her. Was he being thoughtful? Or did he want to make sure he didn't lose her for his own reasons? The latter seemed more likely. But as thick and dense as the vegetation was, she ought to be able to slip away at any point along the trail once they entered the jungle.

"You made them fall asleep?" Cas wondered, noting that he hadn't killed anyone in their entire escape. She couldn't make that same claim.

"They're unconscious. They shouldn't wake up for a half hour to an hour, depending on how much they inhaled." Tolemek looked like he might take her arm, but he stopped himself and simply pointed toward the dark jungle. "More will be coming."

"Right." Cas strode down the path, glancing back before they left the clearing. Dragon Spit leered down from atop its rocky precipice, rock that wasn't as solid as she had assumed when her cage on wheels had been hauled up the winding road to the top earlier that day. That road and the entire above-ground complex were lit by lights now, dozens of yellow dots against the night. There had to be a lot more guards out there searching.

She and Tolemek slipped into the jungle. Though the main road meandered along the rocky coast, that would doubtlessly be watched. Their trail seemed to parallel the coast, but it was difficult to be certain. Even though it seemed to be regularly used, vines and large leaves hung low, and they had to duck often. Branches scraped at Cas's bare shins, and once again, she lamented the shapeless canvas smock she had been forced to don. The shoes—more like moccasins—had soles like paper, and she felt every root and rock on the trail. When she wasn't tripping over something, she was stepping into mud that kicked up, spattering her legs.

The monkeys had fallen silent, but numerous large creatures shifted and rattled the leaves as they passed. A tiger or panther roared in the distance. Even though the jungle didn't sound like a friendly place for a solo traveler, Cas would rather face it than a ship full of pirates.

The trail split, and she saw her chance. Tolemek veered toward the left. Cas would take the right.

She hadn't taken more than a single step in that direction when dark shadows oozed out of the foliage. She barely managed to keep from yelping with surprise when someone appeared right in front of her, blocking her route. She whipped her rifle up, but someone grabbed her from behind. She tried to jerk away, to back into the brush so she would have more space to shoot, but the firearm was torn from her grip. She dipped her hand toward the pouch of throwing stars, but the man behind her caught both of her arms before she could grasp a weapon. She stomped down on his foot, but he was wearing boots, and her pathetic cloth shoes lent nothing to the power of her heel.

Lanterns snapped open, and yellow light filled the pathway. Scarred, bearded faces full of missing or dead, brown teeth leered at her. Tattooed arms were wrapped about her body, restraining her—and squeezing all of the air out of her lungs. All manner of pistols and daggers were being waved about, more than one pointing in her direction. Cas's first ludicrous thought was that these were some savage jungle nomads or bandits who scraped out a living by preying on those who dared walk these paths, but she realized the truth as soon as she spotted Tolemek. He was standing, his hands on his hips, next to a gray-haired man wearing an Iskandian general's gold-braided hat, a spyglass on a thong around his neck, and a breastplate made of human finger bones. There were stories of cannibalism among some of the pirate clans, but they were *just* stories. Weren't they?

"I wasn't expecting you, Captain," Tolemek said as calmly as if everyone had shown up to smoke and play cards together. He looked at Cas and waved to the hulking man holding her. The death grip around her torso loosened slightly, though she still couldn't have slipped a hand down to those throwing stars. At least the pirates had only taken her rifle so far. Maybe she could still find an opportunity to escape.

"We *were* planning to while away the evening in the tavern, conducting a few repairs, and dodging a few lawmen," the gray-haired man said, tapping his spyglass against the breastplate in a soft *clink-thunk* pattern. Was this Captain Slaughter? If so, he was one of the most powerful among the Roaming Curse, and perhaps the most infamous. "But some soldiers came by and were bragging about how they'd so daringly and cunningly captured you and that the commandant was going to torture you ceaselessly. I grew worried about you." He flashed a grin—his teeth weren't quite so poorly cared for as many of the ones in the other pirates' mouths. "And my next batch of projectile naphtha you promised."

"Your concern is touching," Tolemek said drily.

Dry tone or not, when the captain thumped him on the shoulder, Tolemek shared the man's smile. Cas didn't like the easy camaraderie she sensed between the two. With her, Tolemek had seemed normal. Even solicitous. Oh, she was sure he had been using her all along, but, reputation or not, he hadn't seemed like some vile monster. That might change now that he was back among his pirate brethren. Damn, she wished she had veered into the jungle just a few seconds sooner. She might have watched this reunion from some nearby treetop and then sped off before anyone caught her.

"It seems you escaped on your own," the captain said. "Can't say I'm surprised."

Several of the men nodded and chuckled.

"But this isn't quite what I thought you were searching for." The captain extended a hand toward Cas.

"No," Tolemek said.

She caught his eyes—or maybe he was studying her at that moment anyway—and silently implored him to keep quiet about who she was. Or even to let her go. Did he have that kind of sway? Or were all decisions in regard to prisoners left to the captain?

"She someone special?" the captain asked. "Or were you just feeling randy tonight?"

That drew snorts and more chuckles.

"She ain't much to look at," the man standing in front of Cas said. Yeah? Who was he to talk? How could he even chew his dinner with those teeth? "Not with all them bruises. Her whole face looks like someone used it for a punching bag. There's some girls in town who—er..." The pirate's expression grew nervous, almost contrite, when he glanced at Tolemek.

"Wouldn't be afraid to sleep with the Deathmaker?" The captain smirked.

"I don't know," Brown Teeth said. "I mean, I haven't asked. I figure he's purty enough, but I ain't a girl, so I don't know if'n... uhm..." The man clasped his hands behind his back, apparently deciding he had shot enough holes in his flier.

The captain smacked Tolemek on the chest. "Darts just called you pretty. If the girl doesn't entertain you tonight, I think you've got a backup invitation."

"Coming up behind us," someone called softly from ten meters back down the trail.

"Shutter those lanterns, boys," the captain said, pulling a pistol from his belt. "Target practice coming."

Cas caught a grimace on Tolemek's face before the lights disappeared. Her captor—she had yet to see the man's face, but he had the meaty arms of a smith and the breath of a dead fish—dragged her a couple of steps into the foliage. After the light, it took her eyes a moment to adjust, and she wasn't the first to see the figures jogging up the path toward them. Three guards. It was too dark to make out their uniforms, but who else would be searching the jungle at night?

At some unspoken signal, several pistols fired at once.

Two guards crumpled immediately. The rearmost one cried out in pain and tried to run. More pistols fired, hammering him in the back. He toppled into the brush beside the trail.

The lanterns came back up.

"Guess this isn't the best place for a confabulation." The captain grinned and dipped into an ammo pouch to reload his pistol. Cas's gaze snagged on the pouch for a moment. It was probably made from some kind of hide, but that might have been human skin too.

She told herself that as long as she wasn't locked in a Cofah cell, her odds of finding a way back home were still better than they had been before, but it was a struggle to find greater optimism than that.

She wondered what Tolemek thought about the downed guards. After he had worked hard not to kill anyone all night. His face didn't give away much. His ropes of hair hung around his eyes, shadowing them, helping hide his thoughts. Maybe that was why he preferred the style. Or maybe he simply didn't care, and his earlier efforts had been nothing more than experimenting with his various toys. Most of the pirates had the bronze skin and dark hair of the Cofah, though one had black skin and a couple others might have been from Iskandia. Wherever they hailed from originally, they didn't seem to mind killing the Cofah.

"Let's get back to the *Night Hunter*," the captain said. "Too much law down here on land."

"I have an errand to attend to first," Tolemek said. "It shouldn't take long. I'll meet you at the ship."

"And the girl?"

"She helped me escape. Treat her well." Tolemek looked around the circle of men, but he also pinned the captain with his gaze. The command pleased Cas, but she wondered what he risked in trying to give an order to his superior officer. Maybe the Deathmaker had enough of a reputation that Slaughter, too, walked lightly around him?

"You mean, treat her well on the way to town and give her a swat on the rump to say goodbye, or treat her well on the way to our ship where we take her on?" The captain rested a fist against his hip. "If it's the latter, I'll be knowing who you're bringing aboard and why."

Cas held her breath. This was her chance. If Tolemek gave the word, she'd be let go. At the moment, he was the only one who knew who she was, the only one who cared.

He met her eyes and didn't answer the captain right away. She lifted her chin and stared back at him. She wouldn't plead—appearing weak in front of these scavengers was the last thing she dared—but she had to make sure he knew what she would prefer—after all, he had offered her a ride on his ship. She had answered with sarcasm but hadn't given a straight-out no. What if he thought he would be doing her a favor, taking her across the sea, closer to Iskandia?

"I can find my own way home from here," Cas said.

"Wait." A pirate in the back of the group stepped forward, raising his lantern toward her. He had matted blond hair and paler skin than the Cofah men.

Cas's stomach sank lower than the pouch of throwing stars. She didn't recognize the man, but what if he recognized her somehow? She hadn't been flying long enough to be notorious, not like Zirkander and some of the older pilots, but there were pictures of the heroic flier squadrons back home, especially in the capital city, where they had their air base. She had been recognized on the street before.

"That's Gargon Ahnsung's daughter," the pirate said.

Cas didn't move, though her heart threatened to beat its way out of her chest. Was this some colleague—former colleague—of her father's? If her father had ever killed a Roaming Curse member, she might not be any better off than if they knew her as one of Zirkander's squadron, but at least they wouldn't think to use her against the colonel. That would be intolerable.

"The sniper?" the captain asked.

Tolemek's eyebrows rose. "I guess that explains the accuracy with rocks."

"Yeah," Cas managed—her mouth was dry. "We all get together and see if we can knock over empty bean cans at family picnics." In another situation, she would have laughed at the idea of her father hosting some family gathering, not only because she was his only living relative, but because he was as social as a mountain lion.

The pale-skinned pirate was nodding. "Yup, that's her. I been out to Ahnsung's house once to deliver a message, back when I worked for the guild. Seen her then, shooting bows with him out back. Must have been nearly ten years ago, but she was a pretty little thing." The pirate grinned. "Deathmaker, she might be all right once them bruises heal up. You might want to keep her."

Cas bit down her tongue to keep from calling the man a creep for ogling her when she'd been a thirteen-year-old girl. Nobody was cursing or sharing irate whispers about her father—hells, these criminals probably respected a mercenary sniper—so she might still get out of this alive.

"She flies with Zirkander now though," the pirate added.

"*What?*" The captain's head jerked up—no his whole body jerked to attention, the finger bone breastplate rattling with the movement.

A blast of other exclamations, some curses, some streams of anger and disbelief, came from other mouths. The arm around Cas's waist tightened again, putting images of boa constrictors in her mind.

The oh-so-helpful pirate snapped his fingers. "Course, you must have known that, Deathmaker. That's why you brought her out, isn't it? Now that's a fine prize."

"I'll say," the captain whispered, his eyes as hard as steel as they bored into her. One of his hands was balled into a fist, and the other clenched the hilt of his pistol. "That man ruined—" He was so choked with emotion—with *rage*—that he could barely speak. "Were you flying with him last summer, girl?"

Cas doubted he would believe her if she lied—he didn't look like a man ready to believe anything that would interrupt his right to rage—but she kept her mouth shut. Wasn't there a quotation about silence never getting a man in trouble?

The captain slowly pulled out his pistol—every eye there was riveted by it, by him—and stepped toward her. "Answer me, girl. Were you with him last summer?" Between one word and the next, he shifted from a whisper to a yell. "Did you help take down my ship?"

The pirate holding Cas stepped forward, forcing her closer to the captain. She tried to squirm free, to kick him or find an arm she could bite, but the man was no amateur at restraining prisoners.

The captain stalked closer, his face burning as hot and red as a furnace.

Cas didn't notice Tolemek move, but he was suddenly there beside the captain, pressing his forearm—and the pistol—toward the ground. Several of the surrounding pirates drew in startled breaths. The tension was thicker in the air than the humidity.

"She's nothing compared to Zirkander," Tolemek said. "And she's worth even less dead. We can use her to get to him. Set a trap, make her the bait."

Even though Cas had suspected Tolemek had something like that in mind all along, she felt an overpowering urge to shoot him. If only these louts hadn't taken her gun. She had to settle for hurling daggers with her eyes.

The captain looked down at the hand on his arm, then lifted his gaze to Tolemek's. He was hurling a few blades with his eyes, too, but he finally stuffed his pistol back in its holster and muttered, "It must be nice to be able to see everything so logically all the time."

"A boon and a bane," Tolemek said. He glanced at Cas, but must not have liked what he saw on her face, for he soon looked away. "My errand won't take long. Put her in my cabin, and treat her well," he said again, then added, "She'll make poor bait if Zirkander can't recognize her."

The captain walked with him several paces away from the group, and they exchanged a few words. Tolemek must have soothed the older man's anger, for their discussion ended with the captain slapping him on the back and waving. Once again, Cas feared she had made a mistake in not bolting in those first few seconds in the jungle. A big mistake.

Chapter 4

THE AIRSHIP'S HULL WAS PAINTED black, the deck was painted black, and the balloon above was dyed black, so Cas was surprised when the wooden bulkheads and floors below had merely been treated with a clear varnish. Her pirate escort had dwindled to two, but there were guards at the railing next to the sophisticated disembarkation device: a rope leading down to the beach. There were also numerous people walking about on the main deck, all of them armed. It seemed against pirate law to carry less than three weapons about, even when engaged in repairs or polishing cannons. Even if Cas somehow subdued her escort, her odds of getting off the airship weren't good.

The guards pushed her below decks and down a narrow corridor. She could stand up straight, but the bigger men had to duck their heads. They stopped before a side door. They looked at it, then at her, then at each other.

"Deathmaker said to put her in his cabin, right?" one whispered.

"I think so. But maybe we could put her in one of the cells until he gets back."

"He said to put her inside."

"He doesn't usually... I mean nobody goes in his cabin except the captain. If he does girls, he doesn't do them here."

"Maybe she's special."

"Maybe the door's locked."

If Cas's predicament had been less dire, she might have rolled her eyes at this waffling. Why did she get the feeling that neither of them wanted to go through that door?

"Try it."

One of the men grabbed the latch. It turned freely, and he pushed the door open. Neither of them walked right in. The cabin inside stood dark, so Cas couldn't tell much about its occupant, but there was a faint chemical smell. Was this where he made his batches of goo?

"I'll, uh, get a lantern. And shackles. Even if he wants to have some fun, he won't want her touching his stuff." The speaker released Cas's arm and walked farther along the corridor, then disappeared down a ladder, leaving her with one guard.

She eyed the pistol holstered at his belt. A six-shooter, but she didn't see an ammo pouch. It would be risky, but if it was fully loaded, she might have enough rounds to take care of him and clear the deck above, at least for long enough for her to sprint to that rope.

"What's the slimy substance on the floor? Should it be smoking like that?" Cas tilted her chin toward the dark cabin.

"What?" Eyes bulging, the guard took a step back, his grip on her loosening slightly.

Cas grabbed his pistol at the same time as she twisted away. Her canvas prisoner smock ripped, but her captor's hands slipped away. She cocked the hammer, aiming at him. Someone grabbed her from behind before she could shoot. A fist bashed her hand, knocking the pistol out of her grip, and she found herself spun around and slammed into the wall.

The glowering face of the captain closed in, inches from hers, his anger like a wave breaking over her. He had dark brown eyes, but his brow was drawn down so far, the irises were barely visible. He leaned into her ribs so hard, she feared they would bend—or break. Somehow, her feet were dangling off the ground again. Seven gods, she hated being short.

"Do not make trouble, girl," he breathed, the scent of alcohol washing her face.

She wished she could lean away, but the wall didn't help her out. "Sorry," she grumbled as fiercely as she could with her ribs shoved into her organs, "I didn't know you were used to compliant prisoners."

"Just ones not stupid enough to attack their guards." He leaned even closer and grabbed her chin, his fingers hard as they dug into flesh tender with bruises. Her barely healed lip cracked open again and bled. She hoped it would stain his stupid bone vest. Not that he would care. It probably wouldn't be the first blood to splash upon it. "If you think I'm afraid to go against the Deathmaker's wishes," he breathed in her ear, "you're wrong. It wouldn't be the first time."

Cas hadn't thought that at all—wasn't he the captain and therefore in charge?—but she wasn't about to start a conversation with the lunatic. On the other hand, if he brought his ugly snout any closer, she *would* bite it off.

He released her abruptly. She managed to brace herself against the wall and kept from crumpling to the deck, though her ribs did creak with the first full breath she took. She needed to escape from these madmen—Cofah, pirates, they were all the same—just so she could heal.

The captain handed the six-shooter to the guard, who was standing nearby, wearing a sheepish expression.

"Don't lose that again," the captain said.

"No, Cap'n. I won't."

The second man had returned with the lantern. He lifted the shackles in the air. "Sorry, Captain. We'll get her chained up real good."

The captain looked into the dark room. "What is he thinking, putting her in there? Make sure she can't touch anything." He glared at Cas again, and she was certain he would have preferred to tie her in twenty or thirty layers of rope and pin her under a five-hundred-pound anchor.

"Yes, Cap'n."

Grumbling under his breath, the captain pushed past the guards and strode down the narrow corridor.

"You first," the closest guard said. "You've got the lantern."

The man grimaced, but took a deep breath and stepped over the threshold. The second guard pushed Cas ahead of him.

The single lantern wasn't strong enough to illuminate everything—it was a surprisingly big cabin, or maybe a bulkhead had been removed to turn two rooms into one—but it did give the sense of a space packed with built-in tables, counters, and cabinets with glass fronts. Behind that glass lay all manner of books and scrolls, strange tools and quirky gadgets, chemicals in jars, powders in tins, and mysterious substances in clear vials. Bundles of drying grasses, roots, and leaves dangled on twine from the ceiling, and the whole place smelled of chemicals and herbs. All manner of goggles and magnifying devices hung on a pegboard—Cas tried not to find it creepy that hairy tufts that looked suspiciously like scalps were pinned there too. Crates secured to the floor with bolts held metal scrap, and a few mechanical insect-like contraptions rested on the top. Something moved in one of several terrariums along the wall, and she was relieved the lantern wasn't bright enough to show what exactly.

"Put her in the corner?" One guard pointed to the shadowy end of the cabin. The hammock and clothing trunk there appeared out of place in the laboratory.

"Yeah, we'll chain her to that pipe."

Her body too achy to protest further, Cas let them guide her into the corner. Had they been considerate, they might have let her climb into the hammock, but they pushed her to the floor and shackled her to a pipe that ran vertically through the corner.

"Stay out of trouble, girl." One of the guards patted her on the cheek with all the love of a polar bear smacking a fish out of the water, then they both headed for the door.

"You could leave the lantern," she said, then, because they had no reason to want to please her, added, "so I'll have time to look at all this strangeness and grow more and more scared."

The pirate with the lantern snorted. "I reckon that'll happen even more in the dark." He paused in the doorway, and Cas thought some random bit of sympathy might bubble to the surface. But he only glared at her and said, "I lost a friend in that fight last summer. I hope Deathmaker's got a special treat planned for you."

The door slammed shut, leaving her alone in the dark.

No, not entirely alone. Something was slithering around in that terrarium. She hoped it wasn't venomous. And that it couldn't get out.

She shifted around, trying to find a comfortable space on

the floor, but even if there had been one, her throbbing wounds would have precluded relaxation. Lumps and bruises she had been able to forget about while they were running and fighting refused to be ignored any longer. The guards hadn't given her much slack, so she ended up sitting, cross-legged and facing the corner, her forehead leaning against the pipe.

The engine started up somewhere below her, the vibrations humming through the deck. In a few more minutes, they would be off, and there would be nowhere to escape to, even if she could manage it. The Roaming Curse had an aerial outpost out there somewhere over the ocean, and she guessed that was their next destination. Or maybe they were heading straight to Iskandia to set up that trap.

If she were the one to cause Colonel Zirkander's death, she would never forgive herself. He had been one of the few people to trust her, to have faith in her. She owed him every award she had won in her short career—and a lot of laughs too.

Cas blinked, trying to fight back tears. They hadn't threatened when there were witnesses, but here in the dark, it was hard to keep up that shield of toughness.

A doe can stumble and die, a hunter's arrow in its side, without ever having felt sorry for itself. That was one of her father's quotes. He had never been one to accept self-pity or any other sign of weakness, not from himself, and not from his daughter, either. He had hugged her and said nothing about her crying at her mother's funeral, but that had been the last time he had condoned tears. She had been five then.

* * *

Though Port Ariason was several miles from the fortress, Tolemek stuck to the jungle paths rather than venturing into the streets, their corners illuminated with gas lamps. On the way back from his errand, he skirted the town until he reached the southern end where sailing ships and steamers were docked in the harbor. Past them, an oblong shape blotted out the stars over the horizon, though little else suggested a ship was up there.

There wasn't a single lamp burning above decks, nothing to give them away in the distance. With the wooden craft painted black and the envelope made from a similarly dark material, the *Hunter* sailed the skies with impunity on dark nights.

Given the proximity of the fortress and the local garrison, the lightless profile was a wise choice. The Roaming Curse had a reputation grisly enough that most Cofah army commanders looked the other way rather than tangling with them, but if the pirates made a spectacle of themselves, then the military was forced to take action.

Tolemek hoped Captain "Slaughter" Goroth had gone along with his wishes, giving Ahn a spot in his cabin rather than one of the dingy cells near the engine room. It was hot and cramped down there, and there were no portholes. Whatever army she was a part of, she had helped him escape, and he owed her something for that.

He had been on the verge of ordering her released when Malbet had blabbed. Once Goroth knew who he had, there was no way he would let her go. And Tolemek owed him too much to go against his wishes. But if they could, as he had suggested, use her to trap Zirkander, then she need never be harmed. As much as Goroth hated all things Wolf Squadron, he would surely see the benefit of releasing her to gain the greater prize.

Despite these thoughts, Tolemek quickened his step as he approached the airship. Though he trusted Goroth, he couldn't be sure he wouldn't take out some frustrations on Ahn. Tolemek wouldn't have left her, but he had promised that boy his gold coin. He had found the youth, shivering beneath the pilings of one of the long piers that stretched to the harbor's lighthouse. It was the meeting spot they had agreed to. Not only had the boy been forced to take a swim, but he'd been shot in the arm. He had been poor enough that he hadn't protested his injury one bit, merely thanking Tolemek profusely for the coin and running off, but that had only made Tolemek feel guilty. He had risked that boy's life, and for what? His research had been wrong. No, not wrong, but conducted far too late to matter. All he had gotten out of his stay in the fortress was a beating and... a burden he wasn't sure he wanted.

"That you, sir?" a soft voice asked from behind the tree the *Hunter* was anchored to, its dark form floating a few feet away from the top of the stout palm.

"It's me."

One of the cabin boys stepped into view and offered a rope. "You're the last one out, sir."

"Good. Follow me up." Tolemek climbed the knotted rope, his battered body protesting the exertion after the night he'd had. He wondered how Ahn had managed the climb. Judging by the visible bruises, she had received more beatings than he had. He wondered how long she had been a prisoner of war before being deposited at Dragon Spit. He wondered a lot of things about her, foremost among them, whether she would talk to him again.

"That shouldn't matter," he muttered. "You've barely known her a few hours."

"What, sir?" the cabin boy asked.

"Nothing. Just scheming up my next concoction." Though he hadn't used any of his "concoctions" on any of the pirates since Goroth took over three years ago, rumors never stopped flying, and Tolemek found that he could stop all questions pointed in his direction by making such a statement.

Indeed, the boy's gulp was audible, followed by utter silence.

A guard waited at the top, but only nodded when Tolemek climbed aboard. He crossed the dark deck, not needing any lights to navigate the familiar terrain—Goroth had ordered this new ship designed after the same model as the one Wolf Squadron had destroyed the summer before—and headed for the stairs to the officers' deck. He wanted to go straight to his cabin and check on Ahn, but Goroth's door opened as he passed, as if he had been listening for Tolemek. Maybe he had been.

"Come have a drink with me, Mek."

The cabin smelled of brandy; it seemed the captain had already had a few drinks.

"My prisoner being treated well?" Tolemek asked.

"Well enough. This is a pirate ship, not a passenger steamer." Goroth shut the door, waved to one of the benches bolted to the wall, then sat at his own desk. "The boys chained her in there, so she wouldn't bother your work. I'd leave her that way if I were you. Or put her in one of the cells. You'll sleep easier that way. I walked in on her about a half a second away from shooting Bloodnose and escaping, not five minutes after she was brought on board. She may not look like a big cannon, but she'll be trouble."

"Yes, I've seen her shoot."

"Listen, Mek." The captain grabbed a brandy glass from his bar, wiped it clean with his shirt, then poured the amber liquid. "I like the idea of setting a trap with her, but nobody knows where Zirkander is right now. He hasn't been leading his squadron of late. Does she know where he is?" He lifted his brows and handed Tolemek the glass.

"I haven't asked. I will."

"You ask her about the flier power sources at all? Those are worth a fortune, and maybe if you got one, you could figure out how to use it. Then sell the information to the government. Or we could make our *own* fliers and use them for raids. We'd be untouchable. She say anything about them?"

"No." Tolemek sipped from the glass and searched for a political way to tell Goroth that he could be talking to her about these things now, if he would let him go.

"What were you doing down there for hours? Flirting?"

"Escaping."

"Fine, but I want answers now. Before we reach the outpost tomorrow. If you don't question her, *I* will." Goroth's gaze drifted to a cat o' nine tails hanging on the wall. "But you know I'd like that. And have a hard time stopping." His hand tightened around his own brandy glass. "I'd have no trouble shipping her head in a box to Zirkander's office."

"I will speak to her," Tolemek said, keeping his voice calm, though he didn't appreciate the threat.

"I know you won't interrogate her, but speak to her with that truth serum of yours. I want real answers, not lies."

Tolemek set his jaw. It wasn't a bad idea, but he didn't appreciate being told how to handle *his* prisoner. "Yes, Captain," was all he said. He finished his brandy, the liquid burning down his throat, and stood. "I'll begin now, if you need nothing further from me."

"Mek," the captain said, his tone softer, almost apologetic. "Did you find what you were looking for down in that dungeon?"

"No. Whatever scrolls and books were once there had been burned."

"Too bad. It's your project, not mine, but I'd give a lot for the treasures—the power—those sorcerers once wielded."

"I know." Tolemek headed for the door. He didn't want to discuss the topic further. Goroth believed he sought the ancient magic to make his experiments more powerful, and that was something "Captain Slaughter" could support. If he knew the truth, he might become an obstacle rather than an ally. Or even competition. What Tolemek sought was invaluable, especially to one who could use it.

"Mek? Be careful with her. She's Iskandian. She'll know about Tanglewood. She'll shoot you the second she has a chance."

Except she hadn't. Tolemek walked out, closing the door behind him.

Chapter 5

CAS WASN'T SURE HOW MUCH time had passed, but she dozed at some point, weariness finally catching up with her. When the door opened, she woke with a jerk, her shackles clanking against the pipe. Voices sounded in the hallway, a part of some quiet conversation. She turned her head toward the light, hoping one of her captors was bringing food. Her stomach was as empty as her soul.

Tolemek walked in, carrying a lantern. He looked around the room for a moment, then spotted her under the hammock. His lips thinned, then he held up a finger and walked out again. He returned after a moment with a key ring. He stopped only long enough to light a few more lamps from the one in his hand, then knelt in front of her. He unlocked the shackles, but paused before standing up, lifting a finger to her chin.

A gentle gesture, but Cas wasn't sure how she felt about having him touch her—was that the hand he used to pet his snakes? She glanced at the terrarium.

"Someone hit you?" he asked, then backed away so she could stand up. "Someone here?"

She opted for staying on the floor. This corner was less odd than the others, and something about having the clothing trunk on one side and the hammock dangling overhead made her feel protected, like a child in a fort that adults were too big to breach. An illusion, of course, but she leaned her back against the pipe and stayed there anyway.

"Not exactly," she said—he was regarding her steadily, waiting for an answer. "I tried to take advantage of a guard's inattentiveness to arm myself." No need to mention that she would have shot the man and anyone else in her path to the exit if she could have managed it. "There were repercussions."

"Hm."

Tolemek walked over to a counter, unlatched a cupboard below, and pulled out a bowl and a pitcher with a tight lid. Everything in the cabin looked like it was secured, at least somewhat, as things would be on a sailing ship where the pitches of the waves were a constant. The pirates had to be ready for battle at any time, she supposed. Tolemek poured water, dipped a rag in it, then grabbed a small ceramic jar from one of his cabinets.

"Would you like to sit in a chair?" He waved at one at a desk with a lamp on it, then held up the rag. "I'll be able to see what I'm doing."

"Are you a doctor qualified to treat patients?" Cas made a point of looking around the laboratory. "The stories pin you as more of a mad scientist."

"Mad?" Tolemek arched his brows.

"Something has to explain that hair."

He blinked a few times, then surprised her by laughing. It was a pleasant sound that didn't seem to fit with the macabre laboratory surroundings, but she could only stare at him, not finding humor in the situation, or in the entire day. Make that the entire month.

"Sorry," he said. "I didn't think you would talk to me at all, and here you are, as genial as ever."

"If having girls insult you is what you consider genial, then you're spending too much time with the wrong kinds of people."

His lips quirked upward. "Tell me about it." Tolemek pulled the chair out from the desk and brushed off the seat, though she didn't see any crumbs or dust on it. He opened his palm toward it again. "To answer your question, I'm mostly self-taught, with a lot of my education coming through books and experimentation, but I was sent to the field medic course when I was in the army."

Cas struggled not to shudder at what qualified as "experimentation" for him.

"I can get the sawbones if you prefer, but he *does* live up to his name."

"Yeah? Is that where the captain's finger bone chest protector came from?"

"I believe he traded a bottle of brandy to a South Isles cannibal for that a few years ago."

Cas snorted. She bet that story wasn't widely known. "I'm fine." She waved away his offer of help in favor of hunkering in her corner. "I don't need any attention, medical or otherwise." The dried blood on her chin probably said otherwise, but she didn't want to cozy up with the Deathmaker. They'd bonded enough during their escape. More than enough.

Tolemek, the rag and jar in his hands, looked disappointed at her response, but he inclined his head and said, "Very well. Let me know if you change your mind."

Strange. Did he actually care? Back in the jungle, she'd had the sense, just for a moment, that he had planned to let her go, or at least that he had been thinking about it. She had assumed it was her imagination, but maybe it hadn't been. Of course, he might simply be choosing to be nice to make her more amenable to answering questions. Either way, maybe *she* should be nice, or at least not spiteful, so he would see her as more of a human being rather than a recalcitrant prisoner. Maybe she could make him trust her a little, enough to say... leave her unshackled the next time he left the room? Though some of the things in his laboratory made her as uneasy as a flier engine with a suspicious rattle, she wagered there were all sorts of items that might be helpful in an escape. Maybe he had some of those smoking leather balls in a box somewhere. And who knew? Maybe she could get some useful intelligence out of him, something to bring back home with her.

Tolemek had laid the implements on the desk and taken a seat. He was stroking his goatee thoughtfully.

"Sorry," Cas said, "you were trying to help. I get it. I'll ah—" she pointed to the rag, "—take your treatment. Thanks."

Words were one thing, but actions were another. Her body had stiffened while she sat on the floor, and she sucked in a pained breath at her first attempt to roll to her knees and stand.

Tolemek crossed the cabin in three strides and helped her up.

"Didn't think I was old enough to get that stiff," she said. She pretended to stumble—she didn't have to do much pretending—

and gave herself an opportunity to take a quick look at the lower shelves of a bookcase she had noticed earlier, one with a glass cover protecting the contents. All manner of vials hung in racks inside, and a couple looked familiar.

Tolemek slipped an arm around her waist to help her to the chair. She straightened up, not wanting him to notice her spying, and leaned against his side. The support wasn't unwelcome, though she probably should have pushed his arm away. One didn't ask for support from the Deathmaker, right? But she was being nice, wasn't she? To fool him? Just as he was trying to fool her by being a gentleman? She had barely started this new game, and her head already hurt. She was too simple for the intricacies of mind games and spy missions; she just wanted to fly and shoot things.

"I don't think there's any age where beatings feel good." Tolemek guided her into the chair, then pulled up a stool. He pushed the lamp closer to her face, and she could feel its warmth. The pirate ship wasn't cold—they were still in the tropics, after all—but the canvas bag she was wearing left far too much arm and leg bare for her taste.

"Probably not. Would you mind taking those spikes off your wrists before doctoring me?" She nodded toward his wrist braces—the prongs weren't razor sharp, but they certainly had an inimical look to them. "I was a little concerned I'd get perforated during our walk across the room."

Tolemek unfastened them and tossed them on the desk. He had the same bronze skin as the rest of the Cofah, but that didn't mean he didn't tan at all, and she found herself somewhat amused by the paler three-inch bands on his wrists. The Deathmaker had tan lines. Also not mentioned in the stories that circulated.

Cas stayed still as he dabbed her face, wiping her wounds and washing away the dried blood. It stung, but he was probably more gentle than that sawbones would have been. With his face close to hers, she had the conundrum of where to look. It seemed too personal—too intimate—to watch his eyes, but it would have been awkward to lean out to look around him. She settled for staring at the shark tooth necklace, though at some point, her gaze drifted to his collarbone and then down to the pectoral muscles visible beneath his vest. She supposed, if one could get past the I-think-I'm-really-tough pirate clothing, one might consider him attractive. *She* didn't, of course, especially considering his plans for her, so she merely acknowledged that some people would.

Tolemek put down the rag and opened the ceramic jar. The grayish green color of the thick goop inside reminded her of the stuff that had been growing on the walls in those underground ruins. Its dubious scent smelled more medicinal than natural, but she wasn't sure about having it smeared on her face.

"What's that for?" she asked. "And does it have a more confidence-inspiring name than Green Goo Number Three?"

He rotated the jar so she could see the label.

"Healing Salve Number Six," she read.

"It's to assist the body in healing and also to prevent infection. There are antimicrobial compounds."

Anti-what? "Oh, good. And it's stronger than the first five iterations, I'm guessing?"

"More effective, yes."

"It's good to know—" Cas made a face when he touched the first cold, slimy dollop to a swollen cut at her temple. "Good to know some of the things you make are for helping people."

Tolemek had been focused on applying the salve, but he looked into her eyes a moment, his face inscrutable.

"It's not what your reputation is about," she said, explaining by stating the obvious. As if he wasn't aware of his reputation.

"I know," he said softly. Now he avoided her eyes, dabbing goo to her cut lip.

It seemed like there was a hint of regret about him. But maybe this was part of the game too. Pretending to be someone decent, someone who cared.

"I suppose you have to keep your pirate allies healed up, so you have help—" Cas stopped herself from saying raping, pillaging, and slaughtering, but barely. Nice prisoners that could be trusted didn't sling such accusations around. "—on your missions," she finished. There. Wasn't that tactful?

"Most of them prefer the sawbones' sketchy draughts to mine," Tolemek said. "The army too. I tried to send them some of this compound, since it's superior to the crude antiseptic they plied us with when I was a soldier, but knowing it was from me, they wouldn't take it. I even tried to sell it at an exorbitant sum, so they'd be more likely to believe there was something in it for me, but the medical general said no soldier would risk using something I had made."

"So the Cofah hate you as much as the Iskandians, huh?" Oops, so much for tact. That had been rather blunt.

And he winced. "Yes."

"It—what they think—bothers you?"

He had finished with her face and set the jar down. "It... serves me."

Not quite an answer to her question.

"As Gor—the captain has always been quick to point out, enemies aren't eager to pick fights with me. They, too—" he gestured toward the ship as a whole, "—leave me alone to do my work undisturbed. Reputations aren't always founded in truth—the captain's breastplate, for example—but there has to be *enough* truth to make it believable. The instant someone stops believing, he'll try to kill you for your position and for your share of the earnings."

Plunder, Cas's mind replaced the word.

"In addition to worrying about rival clans and armies and lawmen, you have to worry about your own allies. The captain fends off assassination attempts from within every month or two. He owns the ship and a share of the outfit, and anyone who kills him, gets his stuff. That's what passes for law in here. It's like the jungle. Survival of the strongest and the most cunning."

"Why stay in such a place?" Cas thought of the support and camaraderie she got from her unit back home. After the awkward discomfort she had always experienced with her father, it had been a delight to have a different sort of family, one with dozens of brothers and sisters to work with and talk to, people who did dangerous work and formed close relationships through the experience. Just thinking about it, about them, made her chest ache with homesickness.

"There aren't many places available to me," Tolemek said dryly.

"*Now*. You must have made a choice somewhere along the way."

He leaned back, propping his arm on the desk. "You mean after the unit I commanded was decimated in an airship battle with some pesky Iskandian fliers?" He gave her a frank stare. Her first thought was that he was referring to the previous summer's battle again, but this must have been something different. He wasn't commanding anything here, was he?

"I was twenty-four and had just made captain at a ridiculously young age. My father was finally proud of me. I got orders to defend the *Starlight Sailor*, one of our greatest airships, made more so by the fact that it was carrying one of our most legendary admirals and two top diplomats to a treaty negotiation to enlist some of the jungle shamans from the south. Then, out of the clouds—" Tolemek stretched his hand toward the ceiling, fingers spread, "—comes Wolf Squadron. Somehow, they'd gotten intel about our plans and they swept in, strafing our decks with bullets, killing my men left and right. We had artillery weapons and took some of them down, but as you well know, they're good at cat-and-mouse games. The *Starlight Sailor* went down, plummeted into the ocean. The admiral, the diplomats, a decorated airship pilot... all died. There were few survivors."

Of whom, he was obviously one. His sarcastic bitterness was palpable, so she resolved to keep her mouth shut.

"For punishment, I was stripped of all my rights and privileges as an officer and discharged from the army." He lowered his arm and stared down at his hand. "There was nothing to return home to. My father said I was dead to him. I didn't know what to do or where to go. Eventually I got a letter of condolence from another former army officer, a Colonel Goroth who'd been my instructor at the officer proving grounds and who'd had a similar run-in with Wolf Squadron. He'd also been cast out of the army and had his family turn their backs on him. He'd always been a warrior at heart, even when he was teaching, and he couldn't give it up. He was a mercenary for a while but eventually became a pirate. He invited me to join him out here, and feeling like I was practically a criminal already back home, I joined him."

"Captain Slaughter?" Cas asked.

"So he eventually became."

"Look, I don't mean to be unsympathetic, but you—your people—chose this war. *My* people want to be left alone. That's all we've ever wanted. We're doing everything we can to keep our homeland."

His forehead wrinkled. "You're rebels who broke away from the empire, killing all of your rulers in the process."

"We're the native inhabitants of that continent. Your stupid rulers came and set themselves up without being asked. And all of that happened hundreds of years ago anyway. It's idiotic that your people are still wasting resources trying to get us back. If they think we'll ever be content little imperial subjects, they're delusional."

A knock sounded at the door, and Cas nearly jumped out of her seat. For a moment, she had forgotten where she was and that she was surrounded by a ship full of pirates who would happily slay her.

"Come in," Tolemek called.

"Is this all right?" Cas whispered, lifting her un-shackled arms.

Tolemek flicked his hand dismissively as the door opened. A nervous cabin boy stood there, holding a tray with plates and a carafe on it.

"Come in, boy. Set it down." Tolemek pointed to the desk.

The kid couldn't have been more than twelve or thirteen. What calamity had come to *his* life to bring him here? Maybe he was some pirate's son. And here she thought *she* had been born into a disturbing family business.

"Yes, sir." The boy glanced toward the terrariums—hah, Cas wasn't the only one nervous about whatever the Deathmaker kept in there—then scurried to the desk. He set down the tray, looking like he would bolt for the door, but stopped long enough to point at one of the plates. "That one's yours, sir. Cook made you more on account of you being bigger."

"Did he." It wasn't a question.

"Yes, sir." *Now*, the boy bolted.

Slices of bread, fish and sauce, and an orange. There was nothing gourmet about the trays or the presentation, but Cas was hungry enough that she could have wolfed down ten or twenty of the nasty ration bars pilots took on longer missions.

After the door closed, Tolemek set the plate with the larger portion down in front of her. "If you're hungry enough to risk the cooking, I'd try that one." He put the other plate in front of him, though he didn't pick up the fork or knife.

Belatedly, it occurred to Cas to find the boy's words suspicious. "You think that one's poisoned?" She nodded to the smaller portion.

"No, they're not going to kill you. But based on a conversation I had with the captain, I wouldn't be surprised if there might be a dose of a truth serum that would encourage you to answer my questions honestly."

Huh. And he wasn't going to use it on her?

"Truth Serum Number Three?" she asked. She had never heard of such a concoction, unless one counted the honesty-encouraging effects alcohol had, but his scientific interests seemed to be broad.

"More like seventeen. Affecting the human mind in a predictable way isn't as easy as blowing things up."

"How about affecting the human body? Killing people. Is that easy?" And did she truly want to know the details?

Tolemek looked away. "Killing people isn't difficult. There are numerous substances in the world that are poisonous to humans."

"Why seek them out? Why create something that..." Cas prodded a piece of fish with her fork. Hungry as she was, this conversation, and the fact that someone might have been playing with the food, had her worried about sampling.

"If you've ever wondered if the smith regrets forging the sword that ends up taking an innocent man's life, the answer is yes."

Cas had not wondered that, but she did now. With smiths, it would be rare for them to find out how and when their weapons had been used. Though, in making a tool for killing, there could not be much doubt that it *would* be used. A sword, after all, had no other purpose. No one blamed the smiths, she supposed, but what he had done—or, as it sounded like, allowed to be done with his work—was orders of magnitude worse. It *was*, wasn't it?

Tolemek stood up and walked across the cabin to the clothes trunk. He opened the lid and pulled out a couple of tins of sardines and packages of crackers, brought them back, and set them beside Cas's plate. "An alternative if you wish it."

"Thanks," she mumbled. The packages were Cofah, but the Iskandians had similar types of travel rations, so she believed they had come from some general mercantile—or been plunder from some ship's supplies—and were unlikely to have strange serums added to them.

"The wine is probably safe, and there's water in that pitcher. If you don't need anything else, I believe I'll get some rest. Dawn is only a couple of hours off."

He rooted in a cabinet and found a couple of blankets. He tossed one on the hammock, then spread another out on the floor. He blew out the nearest lamp and took the floor position for himself, lying down without a mention of shackles or a suggestion that she stay out of trouble and not wander off. A sign of trust? Or was he going to leave her to her own devices to see if he could trust her in the future? Belatedly, she remembered her mission had been to try and win that trust.

"Tolemek?" she asked.

"Yes?"

"My face feels better. Thanks for the salve. The Cofah army should have tried it before turning it down."

For a moment, he didn't answer, and she wondered if her compliment had seemed out of character, and he knew she was trying to win him over. It was the truth though, even if she wouldn't normally have admitted it. Whatever his salve was exactly, it was doing more than disinfecting wounds. Already, a cool tingling had replaced the pain in her face, and the swelling seemed less extreme.

"You're welcome," he finally said. "You're the first woman who's expressed appreciation for one of my formulas."

"Do women usually show up on your doorstep all bruised and battered and in *need* of one of your formulas?"

"They don't show up here at all," Tolemek said drily. "But when I've sought them out, they've usually been alarmed by my reputation and my work—my *passion*." He said the last in a whisper, an ache in his voice. "Of course, every now and then, one is unsettlingly intrigued. Like she relishes the idea of having her own pet monster." His tone grew dry again when he added, "I already have that relationship with Goroth."

Cas didn't know what to say to that. Monsters weren't supposed to know they were monsters, were they? Her father certainly never saw himself that way, as far as she knew.

Tolemek rolled onto his side, turning his back to her, so he must not expect a response. Or maybe he felt he had shared too much of himself. Cas could understand that. She didn't talk much about her own demons with others. What could be gained from it? Some things were just better kept to oneself.

She peeled open one of the sardine cans and ripped into a package of crackers. Maybe if she were good tonight, Tolemek would be less wary tomorrow. But how long did she have to escape? If she didn't take the first opportunity, would she regret it later, as she had in the jungle?

After she finished eating, she picked up the jar of salve. Tolemek's back was still to her. She swiped out some of the goo, stuck her hand under the baggy prison tunic, and dabbed at her other injuries.

Tonight she would rest, rest and heal. Tomorrow, she would think of escape, or if not escape—for where could she go from here?—sabotage. She eyed that lower bookcase, reminding herself to investigate it as soon as she had a chance. Crashing the airship might be extreme, but there were other ways to cause trouble. She smirked at the idea of bringing the craft into an Iskandian port while all of the pirates were sleeping. Nothing but a fantasy, she supposed, but surely she could come up with *something* to do. Even if she could just find a way to send a warning to Zirkander, that would be helpful. Then he could find a way to turn the trap on pirates.

* * *

Tolemek stood on the deck next to the helmsman, his hands clasped behind his back, the wind whipping his hair around. A dense fog hung over the sea ahead. He couldn't see through it, but he knew it was a man-made phenomenon rather than a natural one. He ought to know. With the help of an engineering friend, he'd invented the machine that made it. To someone in the distance, it appeared more like clouds than fog, and certainly not like anything that could hide a flying pirate outpost with the capacity to hold a thousand men and several docked ships at one time. Only those with the coordinates, coordinates that changed every month, could find the stronghold.

"You get any information out of her?" the captain asked, coming up beside him.

"Good morning to you, also, Captain."

"Morning was four hours ago. Tired after the night's activities, were you?" Goroth smirked at him.

Odd how long they'd known each other and how little Goroth truly knew about him. They had shared more as instructor and student back at the proving grounds than they had in the six years they had been flying together. But that had been a different world, one where trust was the norm rather than the aberration. He considered Goroth a friend and was closer to him than most others here, but not a confidant.

"They were grueling," Tolemek said.

Let Goroth think what he wanted of that. In truth, that conversation with Ahn *had* worn him out. He had wanted to give her enough of himself that she started to believe he was trustworthy, or at least that whatever plans he might have for Zirkander, he would try to keep her safe, but he had shared more than he intended. Oh, his military record was on public file with the Cofah, and there were any number of pirates who knew who he had been before he was the Deathmaker, but her questions about the people who had died because of his toxic inhalant, he wasn't sure why he had answered them. Because she hadn't been afraid of his laboratory and his work and she had talked to him like a human being? Or because he simply hadn't had anyone to speak honestly with for so long? It was a strange world that he'd come to be in, one where one could talk more openly with one's enemies than with one's friends.

"She still sleeping?" Goroth asked.

"Yes."

"Still chained up, right?" Goroth's eyes narrowed. "Most people would be afraid to touch any of your concoctions in there, but she'll be desperate, and I know you have things that could make trouble for us in the wrong hands."

In the wrong hands. Odd how right and wrong had different meanings depending on a man's perceptions and world view.

"She's chained in the corner, yes."

Initially, Tolemek had let her rest without restraint, knowing he would sleep lightly with someone else in the cabin, and trusting that he would hear if she started rummaging around. Besides, he had a few booby traps protecting the truly dangerous mixtures. But that morning, when he had woken to find her slumbering in his hammock, arms and legs flung about in a position that only a monkey could find comfortable, he had checked her hands and found a vial tucked in one. Brown Goo Number Three. He'd been more amused than annoyed—she was a prisoner; what could he expect?—and had plucked it from her grip without waking her. He had also shackled the wrist closest to the pipe again, leaving food, water, and a chamber pot within reach. The ship was already cruising into the fog bank, and he wasn't sure when he would get back to check on her. Goroth usually dragged him to meetings with other captains whenever they docked. In part because Tolemek could contribute, but probably more as a status symbol. Some of the captains had bodyguards; Goroth had the Deathmaker.

"You ask her about the energy sources?" Goroth asked.

"She doesn't know where they come from or how they're

made." And all right, he hadn't asked, but Tolemek doubted a young lieutenant would know about something that had to be top secret over in Iskandia, judging by how little the rest of the world had managed to figure out in the three decades those fliers had been in the sky.

"How about secrets related to Zirkander? Anything we can use against him?"

"She's been close-mouthed anytime I've mentioned him. She won't betray him, I sense."

"Willingly, you mean," Goroth said. "Didn't she eat the food I had Cook send?"

"No, she was suspicious of it."

Goroth slapped a hand down on the black railing, startling the helmsman a few feet away. "No wonder you didn't get anything useful out of her."

"She'll have to eat eventually."

"Your patience is admirable and annoying," Goroth said.

"Thank you."

He pointed a finger at Tolemek's nose. "If the truth serum doesn't work, we'll need to try a more direct method of interrogating her. I know you don't like to torture girls, but she's Iskandian scum, and she doesn't deserve the gentlemanly treatment."

"I wasn't aware being chained in a hammock was gentlemanly treatment."

"You know what I'm talking about. Don't let her sexy little prisoner smock dull your senses, Mek."

Tolemek snorted. That canvas bag she was wearing was about as sexy as a box. If he had any better clothes to offer her, he would have done so. He hoped to find something on the outpost that at least fit her. There were enough female pirates that there ought to be a little shop somewhere.

Goroth clasped his forearm. "If we get Zirkander, you could take his head back to the emperor. Maybe it would earn you the redemption you always wanted."

"I have given up on that dream. Camp Eveningson was to Cofahre what Tanglewood was to Iskandia. Those prison guards and their cudgels were extremely excited to see me." Tolemek rubbed his ribs at the memory. He never had figured out who had leaked his name as the person responsible for all of those deaths, even if someone else had used his aerosol, but there were ears aplenty on a pirate ship, and any man might have wanted to see trouble come to him. Or maybe the governments had simply studied the remains, known of his work, and figured it out on their own.

"Administrations change," Goroth said softly, "and memories fade. Delivering Zirkander would go a long way toward softening their attitudes toward you. And if, before killing him, we could extract information on the energy supplies, that would be an even greater gift that might be offered up. Your lieutenant might not know anything about where they come from, but I can't believe the same would be true for Iskandia's great pilot hero." His lips twisted as he said this last. One man's hero was another's mortal enemy.

"And what will you seek should we successfully kill Zirkander? Your old job back at the proving grounds?"

Goroth released his arm and chuckled. "No, this life suits me. There's nothing left for me back there. This is home—" he extended a hand toward the deck of the ship, now wreathed by the thick fog. "For me... it's just personal. You know that."

Tolemek nodded and repeated, "I'll work on her tonight." Maybe he could extract some information about Zirkander from her, enough to satisfy Goroth, without resorting to potions or anything that would lessen her opinion of him.

He sighed, wondering when that had started to matter. He hadn't even known the girl a full day yet.

"Outpost, ho," the watchman called from the crow's nest near the base of the balloon.

After a few more seconds, Tolemek could see it for himself, the long flying airbase, with six massive envelopes keeping it aloft, five thousand feet over the ocean, along with massive steam-powered propellers that buzzed beneath each corner. Nearby, chimneys wafted smoke into the sky, smoke that blended with the fog, disappearing in the miasma. More propellers lay dormant at the back and the sides of the long platform, those needed only for repositioning.

As the airship glided toward a docking station, Tolemek spotted something unusual among the warehouses, shops, taverns, and hostels: a bronze aircraft with wings. It was sitting on a landing pad near the front of the outpost. At his side, Goroth sucked in a breath.

"Who caught a dragon flier?"

"And does it have a power source intact?" Tolemek mused. He had heard of the Cofah salvaging a few and secreting them away for study, but he would love to have one of his own to examine, or at least access to one.

"We'll have to find out. Looks like an older model." Goroth lifted the collapsible spyglass he always wore around his neck and extended it. "Yes, there's rust on those bolts, and seaweed dangling from the wings. Wonder where they found her?"

"How old of a model? I wonder if it might be Lieutenant Ahn's flier? It sounded like she was a prisoner on a Cofah ship for a couple of weeks before being brought to Dragon Spit. Must have gone down over the sea."

Goroth was already shaking his head. "Haven't seen one that old in the sky for twenty years. That's one of their earlier models. Ah, but is that...?" He took a few steps, leaning to see around some post in his way. "Yes, it is. There's an energy source glowing in the back. There are a couple of hulks guarding the craft, but I'm surprised someone hasn't plucked that out yet to study." He turned a speculative look on Tolemek. "I wonder what you could do with one of those."

Tolemek smiled. "So do I."

Goroth collapsed his spyglass. "Let's go see who found it and if it's available for trade."

A soft jolt ran through the ship. Two men lowered a gangplank. The docking slips were level with the rest of the outpost, so nobody had to climb a rope to get in and out of the craft this time.

A young pirate called out, "We're all secured, Cap'n."

"You calling shore leave, Cap'n?" the helmsman asked.

"We'll see. I—"

"Captain?" a cabin boy called from the gangplank. "Messenger here to see you. Captain Rolostrek sent him."

"Word of our arrival got out fast," Goroth mused. "Or maybe someone's calling a captains' meeting and inviting everyone." He nodded toward the other slips, where six other airships were already docked. The Roaming Curse was one of the biggest outfits in the Targenian Sea, maybe in the world, and Tolemek was reminded of that whenever they returned to the outpost. "Must be some big news."

"Will you share our own news?" Tolemek asked carefully. He didn't want to threaten Goroth on this, but he didn't want hundreds of pirates knowing they had a member of Wolf Squadron on board, either. Not everyone would be swayed the way Goroth had been, to keep her alive in hopes of catching bigger prey. There were other ships in the outfit that had tangled with those dragon fliers, and any crewman would be happy to see an Iskandian pilot dead.

"No, I'm not sharing anything with any of them." Goroth pointed a finger at Tolemek's chest and then at his own. "You and I will handle Zirkander together and keep all the reward that comes with taking that risk."

Not exactly what Tolemek cared about, but he nodded. "Good."

"Now, let's go see what all the fuss is about, eh?"

Chapter 6

When Cas woke up, muted daylight flowed in through a porthole near the hammock. She remembered where she was immediately and opened her hand to check for the vial she had fallen asleep clutching. A chain rattled. She wasn't surprised to see her wrist attached to that pipe again, though it did make her uncomfortable to know Tolemek had done that without waking her. She must have been sleeping hard after being up so late, and after being stuck in such unpleasant accommodations for so long. Odd, all things considered, but she had slept better here than she had in weeks.

The blanket on the floor had been picked up, and Tolemek was gone. So was the vial she had been holding. Somehow she doubted she had simply dropped it on the floor, but she peered beneath the hammock just in case. Nothing there. No, he must have found it and extracted it from her grip. That wasn't surprising, either, though again she felt sheepish at having slept through that. Oh, well. That had been her decoy theft. She tugged up her canvas smock and dug into her underwear, hoping he hadn't presumed to search there. Surely, she would have woken up for *that*.

Her fingers found the hard glass tube, and she grinned.

Now, she had to hope her guess from the night before had been correct. The lamps had been out, with Tolemek's breathing soft and even, when she had crawled out of the hammock to poke around. Earlier in the evening, when she had "stumbled" and peeked inside the display case, she hadn't been able to see the labels of the vials in the rack. It had only been the presence of a little canvas pouch, one identical to the one she had helped knock from the prison roof, that had made her think the brown substance in the vials might be the same brown substance he had used on the hinges and the wall. But now, with light coming in the window, she squinted to read the label's small print. And grinned again. Brown Goo Number Three.

Cas sat up in the hammock, swaying softly and carefully removed the glass cap. She didn't know if the stuff would burn skin, but she didn't want to chance it. Remembering how little it had taken to blow out that wall, she tipped the vial ever so slightly, touching the mouth to the chain securing her to the wall. Unfortunately, the goo was dense enough that gravity didn't do anything to it. She tipped the vial farther. Nothing happened. Tolemek had used a brush, hadn't he? She hadn't thought to pat around for one of those during her nocturnal pillaging.

She eyed the woven strands of the hammock. He had used a special brush, probably something designed to withstand the goo. Well, she could only use what was close to her, which wasn't much. She capped the vial long enough to pick apart a piece of the hammock, a task that involved liberal use of her teeth. She wondered what her father would think of his sniper-trained daughter, chewing apart hammocks to win her freedom. Enh, what did it matter? He hadn't talked to her in years.

Leaning back, Cas plucked a piece of twine from her teeth and dipped it into the goo. It started smoking immediately.

"Uh oh."

She dabbed it against the chain, smearing it all around near the point where it met with her shackle. The rope didn't burst into flame, but it did disintegrate even as she used it as a brush. She let go before the goo, or anything the goo had touched, could reach her fingers. She hoped it wouldn't burn a hole through the floor—now wouldn't *that* be interesting to explain to the downstairs neighbor? Fortunately, the chain was smoking now too. She held her breath, watching smoke rise and crinkling her nose at the burning hair smell that came with it. Or maybe that was burning hammock.

Cas only managed about twenty seconds of patience before tugging at the chain. It snapped as if it were made of the weakest thread instead of solid iron.

"Nice," she purred, climbing out of the hammock.

The rope she had dropped had disintegrated, but the goo

seemed to have used itself up in the effort, for the floor itself wasn't smoking. Good. She had much to do before anyone noticed she had freed herself.

Curious about the diffused light coming through the porthole, Cas padded over to look outside. A dense fog hugged the sky. She pressed her cheek to the hull, peering in both directions. To the right, there was nothing except the bulbous outline of the envelope high overhead, but to the left... she sucked in a breath.

"What is *that?*"

Nothing less than a small city stretched away beneath the fog. A floating city, she realized, seeing the way the end dropped away, like the runway atop the butte back home.

"The Roaming Curse's headquarters." It had to be. She had heard rumors of a floating station out here above the ocean, but as far as she knew, nobody had ever found it, at least nobody who wasn't supposed to find it. "Fascinating." She would have to find a logbook to get the coordinates to take back home. As soon as she figured out how to *get* back home.

She walked around Tolemek's cabin, doing a lot of looking but not much touching. He hadn't warned her about anything, but he had been assuming she would spend the day chained to the pipe. Last night, when she had felt her way into that case in the dark, she had been worried about booby traps, and that fear hadn't disappeared entirely. She would prefer a nice pistol, bow, or even a blowgun to his strange concoctions. But she *did* have a use in mind for the brown goo. She had already stuck the cap on the vial and slipped it back into her underwear. Not the ideal place to store something so caustic, but her prison garb lacked pockets. A Cofah oversight, no doubt.

"Ah ha," she murmured after lifting the lid to the clothing trunk. In addition to more of those black trousers and muscle-displaying vests of his, he had a pistol belt at the bottom, complete with pistols and ammunition. "Tolemek, dear, did you *want* me to escape?"

Telling herself it was a little early to get cocky—even if she got off the ship, she was still on a pirate stronghold—she fastened the belt to her waist, bolstered by the weight of the pistols hanging from either hip. She headed for the door and pressed an ear to the wood, wondering if Tolemek had left a guard. She didn't hear anything, but that didn't mean much.

Cas drummed her fingers on the ivory hilt of one of the six-shooters. She trusted she could open the door and take down a guard before he could get a weapon out to attack her, but a gunshot would be heard all over the ship. Some of the men might have disembarked to visit the outpost, but there was no way the place would be entirely empty.

She eyed the laboratory again, found herself more daunted than inspired by all of the paraphernalia, and settled for a simple idea. She cut down the hammock and, after some fiddling, made it into a net of sorts. She strung it over the door. With some wire, she fashioned a way to pull it down from a few feet away.

"Going to a lot of work if there's nobody out there," she muttered, aware of the time. She wondered how long the ship had been docked before she had awoken. More specifically, she wondered how long she had before Tolemek or someone else returned to check on her. Explaining why she was cutting up his hammock would be difficult.

Once she had her trap placed, Cas grabbed a few of the metal scraps out of one of the crates. She found a spot she liked in a dark corner near the door, then tossed the pieces into the air. They landed with a clatter she trusted would be audible to someone in the hallway.

By this point, she had convinced herself she been wasting her time, so she was almost surprised when the door opened. A pirate strode in, his hand on a pistol.

Cas tugged on her tripwire. The hammock-turned-net fell onto him. It wasn't a particularly insidious trap, but it did its job of confusing him for a second. She slipped in behind him, pressing one of the pistols to the back of his neck.

"Stop moving," she whispered.

He halted.

"Good man." Or boy. He didn't look more than sixteen. "Take a step forward, please." She pressed harder with the pistol's muzzle, in case her words weren't convincing in and of themselves.

When he did so, she kicked the door shut. She wanted to relieve the pirate of his weapons—there was a short sword on his belt in addition to the pistol in his hand—but her net was a barrier for her as well as for him.

"Holster that firearm, and drop your trousers," Cas said.

For the first time, the boy balked. "What? I'm not—"

"Listen," she whispered, rising to her tiptoes and leaning close to speak right behind his ear. "I am an Iskandian soldier, and it's my duty to take down thieves, bandits, pirates, and anyone else who might be a threat to my nation. I will be *more* than happy to shoot you." It was hard to sound steely and menacing at twenty-three years old and five-foot-nothing, but she managed to convince the kid she was serious.

He holstered the pistol and unclasped his belt. His trousers fell to the ground. Cas caught the pistol before it dropped too far, though she was out of hands and had to let the sword clank to the deck.

"What are you going to do?" he asked.

"Me? Nothing, if you cooperate. I just want to get out of this cabin. Look around. This place is creepier than a cave full of bats on All Ghosts Eve, isn't it?"

"You got that right," the kid muttered with a shudder that seemed unfeigned. He was eyeing the terrariums. Everyone did when they came in. Maybe Cas should have taken a closer look at the creatures confined in them. Or... maybe not.

She hadn't been sure how she was going to convince the guard to effectively tie himself up so she could leave him here, but his trepidation gave her an idea.

"Take three steps forward and one to your left." Cas followed him with the gun pressed to his neck as he did so. "See that flask of the red liquid in that case?"

"Yeah."

"Remove it."

The pirate stiffened. "I'm not drinking it or anything like that. I don't care *what* you do."

"No, no, of course not. There's no need for that." Cas waited until the kid, trousers around his ankles, hobbled over to the case, opened the door, and removed the triangular flask before adding, "It's so corrosive that it can sear your flesh to the bone if it merely touches your skin. There's no need for you to ingest it for it to melt you into a pile of goo."

The kid swallowed audibly. "What... should I do with it?" He stared down at his hand as if he held a rattlesnake.

"Put it on your head."

"*What?*"

"Just the flask. I don't want you to pour it out. In fact, I'm trusting you can stand very still so there's no danger to you at all."

"Look, woman." The pirate set the flask on the nearest table. "I don't care who you are. I'm not—"

While he was complaining, Cas plucked up the flask and reached up to plunk it on his head.

He cursed, his hand flying up to hold it there, though with the hammock draped over the top half of his body, he almost knocked it over. He seemed to realize that and froze there, his hand hovering in the air.

"Perfect," Cas said, letting go. "Now, keep facing that corner there, and I'll be back in fifteen minutes to remove it. Of course, you could try on your own, but it's extremely full, and if you spill so much as a drop... well, I understand the Deathmaker's potions are quite potent."

"Yes," the boy whispered, his hand still over his head, draped in netting, "they are."

Cas plucked his short sword out of its scabbard and backed toward the door, the pistol aimed at him. She thought she had convinced him, but one never knew. He might chance yanking it off.

But he didn't move, even when her heel caught on one of the pieces of metal she had dropped earlier, and it skidded across the cabin. Like a statue, he faced the corner.

Cas grabbed one of the bits of metal that had a hook-like protuberance and took it with her. She was already carrying a small pile of weapons, but one more thing shouldn't matter. She eased the door open, checked in both directions, then stepped out. She fished the vial out and, using her mouth, tugged off the cap. Better not be too careless with this stuff, she warned herself, then dabbed the hook into the jar. It started smoldering, but she only needed it for a moment. She dabbed some of the goo into the lock on the door, hoping the mechanism would melt, and the pirate wouldn't be able to simply walk out once he grew brave enough to risk touching that flask. Her trap wouldn't hold him forever, but she didn't plan to be onboard that long. When she had looked out the porthole, she had spotted three other airships docked, and one of them had been little more than a personal yacht. If its owners were off enjoying the taverns and brothels, she might be able to slip aboard without being spotted.

"One step at a time," she murmured and headed for the ladder leading to the main deck. She still needed to get off *this* ship without being spotted.

* * *

Tolemek leaned against the wall while Goroth and several other captains and first mates settled at the big oaken table in the center of the room. A few bodyguards stood against the wall, too, but nobody came close or spoke to him.

Wenches in low-cut dresses carried trays of food and rum out of a larger common room where raucous laughs alternated with angry shouts and the sounds of smacking flesh. Gunshots had already fired once out there in the five minutes Tolemek and Goroth had been inside. A few of the captains spoke, while others shifted and sighed. One had a girl in his lap and was fondling her and suggesting that he might find something else to do if the meeting didn't start. Two seats at the head of the table remained empty.

A plump black-haired woman in an apron came in, clapped her hands, and said, "Out, ladies. The last two people have arrived."

As the servers strolled out, sashaying their hips and smiling at the men wearing more gold than others, Stone Heart, the captain of the *Burning Dragon*, walked in, accompanied by a man in a dirty, ragged Cofah military uniform. His sword was missing, and a couple weeks' worth of hair sprouted from a head that should have been shaven.

Tolemek had assumed this meeting would have something to do with the salvaged flier, but perhaps not.

"Gentlemen," Stone Heart said, walking to the head of the table. "Allow me to introduce Corporal Tyrson. He wishes to desert from the Cofah army and seeks refuge with us."

Several of the captains gave each other so-what looks. Tolemek waited for more information—Stone Heart was wearing an I-know-something-you-don't-know smirk as he massaged his shaven head. Or maybe he was scratching an itch. He had added a couple of daggers to his collection of scalp tattoos since Tolemek had seen him last.

"It seems," Stone Heart continued, after pausing long enough for dramatic effect—and to annoy people—, "our friend here is the sole survivor of an epic battle that took place high in the Iskandian Ice Blades. Given that he didn't die when his airship crashed or during the ground skirmishes, as the rest of his comrades did, he's elected not to return home."

Goroth gave Tolemek a long look over his shoulder. Yes, Tolemek had no trouble understanding the corporal's reasoning. Even if he hadn't been in command, there would be assumptions of cowardice, and he wouldn't be looked upon favorably by his superiors.

"He was part of a secret mission," Stone Heart said, "to spy on the mines where the Iskandians are extracting the crystals that power their dragon fliers."

A number of heads lifted at that announcement, including Tolemek's. *Mines?* He had yet to see one of the energy sources up close, but he had assumed they were man-made, rather than being some natural resource.

"Guess who the Cofah airship smacked into while he was there?" Stone Heart asked.

"Who?"

"Colonel Zirkander," the soldier said, speaking for the

first time. "Nobody expected him there. Turns out he was commanding the mining outpost."

Goroth gave Tolemek another look. Odd how often the man's name was coming up this week. Had Tolemek been remiss in not questioning Ahn more seriously? Was it possible she knew something about this?

"He didn't have his squadron or his fliers there though," the soldier went on, "and we had a mercenary shaman aboard, so we all figured we had the advantage. But he pulled a rusty old flier out of some forgotten crevice, and then..." The man licked his lips, and his voice lowered to a whisper. "There was a witch working with him. Or maybe even a sorcerer, like the ones from the old days. I heard the shaman talking to the captain. He seemed confident he could deal with her, until the end. They fought down in the fortress, and it was crazy. All flying sparks and lightning and blasts of power and I don't know what. You see, she had this sword. A glowing sword."

"A *soulblade*?" Tolemek asked before he could think better of showing his interest. He couldn't help himself. So much of his research had pointed to Iskandia as one of strongholds of the ancient sorcerers, but he had assumed that there would be little left but buried ruins. He hadn't dreamed there might be soulblades floating around the continent.

The soldier's brow crinkled at the term. "I don't know what it's called, but when she was holding it, it glowed and kept bullets from hitting her and, and, and she cleaved our shaman down like he was nothing. I saw it with my own eyes."

"Fantastic," one of the older captains said, his tone drier than a mouthful of sand. "Zirkander didn't have enough of an advantage. Now he's got a witch in his back pocket."

The corporal nodded fiercely. "*That's* why we failed. If it had been just him..." He smacked a fist into his palm.

"*Why* was it just him?" Goroth asked. "Why would he have been sent to a mountain mine without his squadron?"

"Must be a secret location," one of the captains said. "And only the top, most trusted people get sent there."

"But why a pilot to command a fortress? A pilot without his

squadron, at that. Surely they have other lickspittles they trust."

"Something to do with the energy sources?" Tolemek suggested. "Maybe his experience with them makes him a good candidate for locating them or interacting with them or whatever is done at this mine."

"Huh." Goroth scratched his jaw and looked at him. "If only we knew someone who might know more about Zirkander and this whole incident."

Tolemek shut his mouth and stared back. The last thing he wanted to mention in a room full of captains was that they had a Wolf Squadron pilot. His reputation might protect her on the ship, but there were people here who would risk much to do exactly what he and Goroth planned: using her to trap Zirkander. Then there were the more shortsighted people, those who would simply kill her for revenge. If his memory served, there were even bounty posters around the outpost offering rewards for the heads of particularly vexing Iskandian pilots. Ahn might not have been flying long enough to have one, but he couldn't be certain, not with that aim of hers.

Tolemek pointed at the soldier. "Would you be able to lead an airship back to those mines?"

"Yes, good question," Scarred Brea, one of the two female captains in the outfit, said. "It sounds like the Cofah ship didn't survive to report home, but their government would pay a fortune to know where the source of the energy crystals is." Brea tapped her fingers together as she gazed at the soldier. Maybe thinking of making sure he didn't change his mind and report home before some entrepreneurial pirate could sell his information first? "I'll offer you a spot on my ship."

"Wait, wait," another captain said. "I've got a spot open too. Fighter sergeant. Comes with a two percent booty share."

"Why don't you idiots see what his answer is first?" Goroth grumbled.

The corporal wore a hopeful expression, but it wilted at this pragmatism. "I *might* be able to find it. But I wasn't looking over the railing much when we were flying out there. And on the way back, I stowed away on one of their supply ships, and I was hiding in the cargo hold for the whole trip. I don't think you can get there on foot at all. It's real high up in the mountains, and it's winter there now. Whole place is buried under snow. Also..." He shrugged. "Someone in my government already knows about the mines, too, and was pretty sure on the location. That's why they sent us. I do remember us flying around for some weeks before we found them though."

"He talks a lot, doesn't he?" Captain Brea said. "To basically say no, he can't find the place."

"Rethinking your offer?" someone asked.

Tolemek ignored the rest of the meeting, his thoughts turned inward. If Zirkander knew someone who had a soulblade, Ahn became even more valuable to him. Goroth might want to kill Zirkander, but Tolemek wanted to question him first. Or even snoop around in his home, see what information he might have on the sorcerers of old. Sorcerers who were supposed to be long dead, not fighting alongside the Iskandian military again. Even more, he wanted to question the woman with the sword. Maybe she would know where another one was. But sorcerers could read minds, so being in the room with one would be dangerous. Maybe he could get her sword somehow when she was elsewhere. Was it truly bonded to her, as the soulblades had been in ancient times? Or would it accept another handler?

He had far more questions than answers, and all he knew was he needed to find Zirkander more than ever. And he needed to talk to Ahn.

Chapter 7

Much to her chagrin, Cas hadn't been able to simply sneak off the ship. Judging by the few people below decks and the quietness of the overall craft, much of the crew had left to enjoy the outpost's facilities, but there had been too many pirates and cabin boys wandering up above for her to make it from the ship's ladder to the gangplank. For a moment, she had fantasized about a mad sprint where she shot wildly, knocking down anyone who thought to stand in her way, but that wasn't some mecca of freedom down there. If she charged off the ship, guns roaring, she'd probably be shot before she reached the end of the gangplank. Maybe sooner if Tolemek or his captain had told the other pirates in the outpost about her.

So, backup plan. She'd gone down instead of up.

From the shadows near the door, Cas eyed the engine room. There were a few portholes, but whatever fog or clouds lingered outside kept much light from seeping inside. She didn't see anyone, but there were shadows everywhere, and the engine, furnace, boilers, and bins of coal took up a lot of space. Some diligent pirate or cabin boy might be working in a nook not visible from the door. She didn't know what they would be doing though. The flywheels and pistons of the engine stood dormant, the fire in the furnace allowed to burn low. Since a lighter-than-air gas mixture kept the balloon full and the ship in the sky, the boilers only had to be heated when the propellers were needed. With the craft docked, she shouldn't have to worry about that for a while.

Cas thumbed the vial of goo as she listened for signs of life in the room. The glass was warm from being held in her hand. At some point, she needed to find some decent clothing, something with pockets perhaps.

"Later," she murmured and walked over to the engine,

considering places where a little sabotage would go a long way. A fire should draw the crew down here—fires on wooden ships were never a good thing, so all hands ought to report promptly to help. That would be the time to escape.

She thought about sabotaging the boiler—she wasn't an expert on engines but mused that she might be able to create a delayed explosion that would irrevocably damage the whole ship.

"They would really hate me then." She was a long ways from safe, and, though she hated to admit it, there was always the possibility that she would be recaptured. Better not to do something that would anger them to the extent that she became a shoot-on-sight foe instead of a capture-for-later-use one.

She paused next to a coal bin. If all she wanted was a fire...

Yes, that might do. But as long as she had the goo, she might as well do a small bit of sabotage. Something that would delay them if she managed to escape in some other ship, so that they couldn't come after her right away. She brushed some of Tolemek's concoction onto the metal bar of one of the pistons. In the shadows, she couldn't see the smoke rising, but she smelled the acrid stuff working.

She grabbed one of the lanterns by the door and set a fire in one of the metal bins. Before leaving the room, she opened a couple of portholes to let in fresh oxygen to fuel her flames. And it might prove useful to her escape attempts if some ominous black smoke poured out through the portholes as well. At the least, it should alert the men on deck to the problem sooner rather than later.

As soon as she was certain her blaze would burn without further help from her, Cas returned to the corridor. She had the problem of where to hide while people from the deck above ran down to the engine room. Tolemek's cabin would have been a logical place if she hadn't left a guard inside and melted the lock. She settled for the shadows behind the narrow metal steps leading above decks, hoping the pirates would be too busy racing to put out the fire to look closely at the spot beneath their feet.

She had barely slid into the tight space when the door banged open overhead. Heavy boots thumped on the metal steps, the heels scant inches from her nose.

"Hurry, hurry."

"Get water."

"Here, hold the door. Get a hose through here. Hurry!"

Cas pushed her back against the bulkhead, trying to blend in with it, as the boots raced toward the engine room. The pirates ran down the corridor without looking back, their eyes riveted to the door at the end. When one threw it open, an impressive amount of smoke flowed out, wreathing the closest men in gray plumes.

Two ran in, and one ran right out again, racing for the steps. Cas held her breath. With the man running this way and facing her, her hiding place didn't seem that clever.

He raced up without glancing through the steps and soon reappeared with other men and with a hose. It was busier in the corridor than Cas had anticipated, with people running in and out of the room, some operating the hose and others fetching buckets of sand. She had to wait longer than she would have wished for the way out to be empty. When she got her moment, however brief, she left her hiding place and charged up the steps.

She ran out, hoping everyone would be below decks now—or at least extremely distracted—but she ran into a man striding toward the hatchway as soon as she sprinted out.

His eyes were shadowed by a giant-brimmed hat, but there was no mistaking his hand reaching for one of the pistols at his belt. Cas had her purloined pistols ready. She shot the weapon out of his hand before he had lifted it more than two inches from his holster, and sent a second shot *through* his hand. She could have sent it through his chest, but, again, she was concerned with doing too much damage—leaving too many bodies behind—when her escape might be unsuccessful. And, later, if she thought about it more, she might accept that she didn't particularly want to do so much that Tolemek would be furious with her. As it was, he would probably get in trouble for not restraining her in such a manner that she couldn't escape.

The pirate howled and grabbed his hand. Cas ran around

him, checking the rest of the deck as she did so. Uh oh, there was one more trying to take a shot at her. She fired, lancing him through the knee. He dropped his weapon and crumpled to the deck, clutching the injury and howling as he rolled around. He was out of it for the moment, but the first man was glaring at her as much as he was gasping in pain. And those shots might have been heard by those below.

She jerked the pistol toward the hatchway. "Drop your sword and get down there. Help your friends put out the fire."

"I'm not—"

"*Now*," Cas snarled, pointing the pistol at his face.

He pulled out the sword with his good hand and dropped it, then backed toward the steps she had just left.

"In," Cas ordered.

He turned and jogged onto the steps, though he didn't start down right away. It didn't matter. Cas slammed the door shut behind him. She grabbed the sword and rammed it through the wheel that opened and closed the door, hoping that would jam it shut, at least for a time.

After once more scouring the deck with her eyes, checking for pirates and spotting none, Cas sprinted for the gangplank. She intended to charge down and to quickly disappear into the large floating outpost, but she nearly tripped over her own feet as something unexpected came into sight. She flailed to catch her balance, though a surge of vertigo hit her when she found herself leaning over the side of the gangplank, the brilliant blue of the ocean visible through the fog. Thousands of feet below. That was one fall that she did *not* want to make.

She lurched back to a vertical position and waited until she had crossed the gangplank and her feet were on solid… pavement, if not ground, then stared to the right again. She was lower now, and buildings blocked much of her view, but she could still make out the bronze hull of a dragon flier parked on a landing pad at the end of the outpost.

"Forget the yacht," she whispered. "We're seeing if that thing flies."

Muffled gunshots came from the ship behind her. Someone

trying to shoot his way through that hatch? She wasn't going to stick around to find out. She sprinted across a street that probably went all the way around the outpost and between two buildings with wood and corrugated metal sides. The floating platform itself might be a miracle of engineering, but the construction that had sprung up on it made it look like a shanty town, at least the part she was in now. She passed sturdier structures as she wove deeper into the maze, trying to parallel that main street and make her way to the flier, but she started passing more people too.

One man paused to eye her canvas prisoner's outfit. She wondered if he recognized the style. She smiled, waved, then ducked into an alley. She hid behind a pile of boxes that doubtlessly passed as a trash collection area, dropped her hands to her knees to catch her breath, and peered back the way she had come through a crack between the boxes. The man was staring down the alley in her direction. He scratched his jaw. Cas checked the ammunition in her pistols and loaded rounds to replace the ones she had spent. She had stolen enough bullets for a quick skirmish but not an all-out gunfight. The man returned to his walk. She couldn't help but wonder if her presence would be reported. She hadn't seen a mirror and wasn't sure how crazy she looked, but she doubted she looked anything like a pirate.

"Something to remedy."

Enough running around like a blind fool. She needed to slow down and figure out how to reach the flier without getting caught. And she had to assume she would need to spend time to learn if it was operational too. Even in the distance, she had been able to tell it was an older model.

"One thing at a time."

* * *

"I want answers," Goroth said as he and Tolemek walked back from the meeting. "I want that truth serum in her gullet, and I want to have a long chat with her."

Tolemek kept his sigh to himself. He doubted Ahn had the

knowledge Goroth sought. Depending on how long she had been in the prison and how long she had been in Cofah clutches before arriving there, she might not know anything about Zirkander's secret assignment. From that soldier's words, it sounded like this had all occurred recently. "You know where I keep it," he said.

"You're not going to help question her?"

Tolemek would prefer to be there to keep Goroth from growing overly irritated—and violent—if he didn't get the answers he wanted. "I'll help. I didn't want you to think I was impeding you." Or that more brutal methods would be required.

"I don't think that. I just think you're forgetting who she is because she's young and cute. Don't—what in all of the hells? The ship is smoking!" Goroth sprinted ahead.

Tolemek stared at the black plumes wafting from the portholes on the starboard side toward the stern—where the engine room was. His stomach went for a swim in his boots. Maybe Goroth was right. He had been too lenient, and now she had escaped and done something to the ship.

"You don't know it's her," he muttered and ran after Goroth, though he couldn't imagine what else might have happened. The Roaming Curse captains were all allies, and no other pirate outfits were allowed to dock here.

By the time he reached the end of the gangplank, no less than four men had rushed up to Goroth and were explaining the situation—or maybe making excuses—speaking a thousand words a minute. Hoses ran through the hatchway leading below decks, and a sword was randomly lying beside them.

A moan of pain came from beside Tolemek. He ran over to Grimsaw, who was sitting on the deck against the railing and struggling to tie a makeshift bandage around his knee.

"What happened?"

"That bitch shot me," he groaned.

"My—the prisoner?"

"Who else?" It was a testament to Grimsaw's distress—or pain or anger or both—that he glowered at Tolemek and answered sarcastically, forgetting his usual wariness toward the Deathmaker.

"I'll get something for your knee and find the sawbones as soon as the fire is out."

Tolemek ran for the hatchway, intending to help the men below decks, but Goroth lunged out of the group and clasped his arm.

"Your prisoner did this," he said.

"I know."

"And she's gone."

Tolemek frowned, though he could hardly claim to be surprised. She had probably set the fire as a distraction. But how had she escaped from his cabin to start with? He had taken that vial from her hand and left her locked up.

"Didn't you shackle her?" Goroth demanded.

"I did, actually, and I searched her before leaving this morning."

Goroth grumbled some choice curses under his breath, his fists clenched so hard his knuckles stood out as much as the bones on his breastplate.

"I'll find her," Tolemek said.

"You better. Go do it now. We'll handle the fire."

Tolemek hesitated, not wanting to abandon the ship if it was in danger—this was the only home he had, and all of the mixtures he had made and the ingredients he had gathered were in that cabin. He would hate to lose everything again. Not to mention his collection of pets. "Will you get my spiders and snakes out if my cabin proves to be in danger?"

"Spiders! What a thing to care about now." Goroth looked like he wanted to punch Tolemek. Perhaps it hadn't been the right thing to mention, but in addition to keeping them as pets, he extracted venoms for some of his work.

"Snakes too."

"Just get the girl."

"Very well."

"And put her in a devils-cursed cell when you get her, not your cabin where she has access to who knows what." Goroth flung his arm toward the smoking portholes.

A throat cleared behind them. Most of the men who had

reported to the captain had run back to help with the fire. This was someone Tolemek hadn't seen before. Clad in browns and blacks, he wore nothing resembling a uniform—and his left sleeve was tied in a knot at his elbow, showing his arm to be cut off at the joint—but there was a badge pinned to his jacket. The Roaming Curse outpost had patrol officers? Tolemek had never seen such a thing.

"Who are you?" Goroth demanded.

"Post Administrator and Port Inspector Dancun. Keeping the outpost safe for all." The man spoke in a deadpan voice, his lips barely moving. He pointed at the smoke wafting up from the craft's stern. "That's a problem."

"We're working on it."

"You'll have to move away from this berth until your fire has been out for at least two hours. We can't risk it spreading."

The captain looked like he wanted to gnaw off a few of his own teeth and start spitting them at the man like gunfire. "We need access to the outpost."

"You can access it again two hours after your fire's out."

Goroth glanced at Tolemek, made a shooing motion, and mouthed, "Go."

Tolemek was about to when a cabin boy strode out of the smoking corridor, walking quickly, though his eyes were riveted to something he was holding. It was the young fellow he had left outside his cabin to guard Ahn. A strange net was tangled around his shoulders. With one hand, he was holding up his trousers, and with the other he held... Odd, Tolemek recognized that flask.

"Sir," he blurted, charging straight toward Tolemek. "I wanted to make sure you had this, and that the fire didn't—that everything was safe."

Feeling rather confused, Tolemek held out his hand mutely. The boy sagged in relief as soon as the flask left his fingers, then launched into an explanation. Tolemek's silence continued as he listened and digested the information.

"Lieutenant Ahn?" the administrator asked, joining them.

Tolemek hadn't realized the man had been listening. He

frowned. The cabin boy had blurted Ahn's name during his explanation. He hoped it wouldn't mean anything to the port inspector. A vain hope, apparently, for the man was pulling a small notebook out of his pocket. He laid it on the railing so he could flip through the pages one-handed. Tolemek glimpsed names, dates, and notations in extremely neat printing.

"Go help with the fire, boy," Goroth ordered. He too was frowning at the administrator and his notebook.

The page flipping stopped, and the man pointed to a name. "Ah, yes. I thought that sounded familiar. Lieutenant Caslin Ahn. Flight name: Raptor. Member: Wolf Squadron. Active since the third of Maynok, 937." His tone never changed as he spoke.

"Who is this hedgehog?" Goroth, standing behind the administrator's back, mouthed.

Tolemek could only shake his head. A pirate outpost ought to be the last place one could find someone so organized. He might admire such meticulous note-taking in other circumstances, but not now.

The administrator lifted his brows. "You did not think it important to report that your vessel contained a wanted pirate enemy, Captain Slaughter?"

"I've been busy."

"This is a bounty," the administrator said, "though I'm more concerned about maintaining peace on the station. She will need to be located." The inflection in his deadpan voice never changed, but his eyes had a slight gleam as he said, "This can be accomplished easily with enough people searching."

"I'll find her," Tolemek said and headed for the gangplank. He had to make sure he found Ahn—Caslin—before this overzealous port attendant put the word out to everyone. It would be nice to use her first name, now that he knew it.

Goroth caught up with him at the gangplank, lifting a hand to make him pause. "I'll take care of the fire. And you're welcome." His squint said he placed the blame for the mess straight on Tolemek's shoulders. Rightfully so. "It might be a while before I can bring the ship back over though—" he waved to the smoke, "—so you'll be on your own over there. Stay out of trouble. Meet back here—no, let's meet at the Squatting Crow, midnight. Just in case we're under scrutiny." He frowned at the administrator who was making notes in his book.

"I'll have her," Tolemek said.

CHAPTER 8

THERE WERE TWO GUARDS WANDERING around the dragon flier, occasionally answering questions but mostly turning away curious pirates who ambled close. Cables stretched across the bronze wings and ran to eyelets on the landing pad, as if force were required to keep the craft from taking off. Fliers did look vaguely like crouching dragons, wings spread, ready to leap into the air and take off, but they were ultimately just machines and wouldn't go anywhere without a pilot. This particular craft looked like it had been pulled out of the depths of the ocean, with brown sludge dulling the hull and crusty grime caking the wings. Some kind of banner or sign hung from the cockpit. Cas thought it might declare the craft's owner—whoever had salvaged it—but she was too far away to read the lettering.

She crouched on the roof of one of the sturdier buildings, keeping her back to a vent spewing bacon-scented smoke. It wasn't much in the way of cover, and she felt exposed, since many of the airships docked to either side of the floating outpost had decks as high as her position. She wished night would fall, but she had no concept of how soon that might be. The strange fog that hugged the whole place hadn't abated.

Shouts came from a nearby street, and a squad of men ran into view. Their eccentric clothing, most of it doubtlessly plundered from ships all around the world, kept them from looking like an organized military unit, but they were sticking together and peering into alleys. They were also armed.

Cas flattened to her belly. She didn't recognize them as men from Captain Slaughter's ship, but she hadn't met everyone there either, having been busy starting fires in their engine room.

What if Slaughter had told everyone on the station about her and had them hunting for her? She craned her neck to look at his ship—she couldn't see the deck, but its big black balloon was distinctive and visible. Though, oddly, it seemed farther away than before. She risked rising into a crouch again. Yes, it had moved away from its berth and floated perhaps a hundred meters away from the outpost. Something to do with her fire?

A faint rumble reached her ears, and Cas forgot about the searchers and Slaughter's ship. The noise sounded familiar, very familiar. Propellers.

She checked to make sure the search party had moved off the nearby street and that nobody was creeping up on her before focusing on the nearest of the giant propellers that helped hold the outpost aloft. Their hum was a constant here, and it continued on as it had before. This was a new noise, and it seemed to be coming from the fog beyond the outpost rather than some machinery on it. And there was more than one propeller making the noise, she was sure of it. She couldn't guess why they were coming—they couldn't know she was here... how could they?—but the rumbling grew louder and filled her with hope.

An eardrum-piercing wail erupted from horns mounted on poles at the corners of the outpost. Someone else had noticed the noise and knew what it meant.

The first dragon flier came into view, yellow eyes and a gray snout painted on the nose of the craft. Cas grinned so hard her mouth ached. Wolf Squadron.

Several more craft followed the first out of the fog. She couldn't make out the numbers on the sides of the fliers yet, but she recognized an attack formation when she saw one. She caught herself standing and waving, but forced herself back into a crouch, not wanting to draw the attention of enemies in the streets below. Pirates were flooding out of buildings, shouting over the sirens and racing to artillery weapons stationed along the edges of the outpost and also on some roofs.

Before the twelfth flier came into sight, the first was already firing, strafing the side of the outpost and spraying bullets. No, it wasn't aiming at the outpost but at the airships docked along its edge. Pirates were out on the decks and running toward weapons, the same as the people on the station were doing, but everyone had clearly been caught off guard.

The fliers streaked toward Cas's end of the outpost, and she shrank back, bumping into the vent. They couldn't possibly know she was alive, and they might kill her without knowing she was there. She ought to run for one of the few brick or stone buildings—they would be the most likely to survive gunfire—but if the pilots started lobbing explosives, it wouldn't matter how thick the walls were. Besides, she wanted to know what they were after.

The answer to her question came almost immediately as the three lead fliers swerved in, under the giant balloons that marked the ceiling of the outpost, and veered toward the flier. Her first thought was that they might have some crazy plan to throw cables around it and take it with them, but that would be dangerous even without the pirates firing at them. A gray cylinder shot from the teeth of one of those fliers, exploding when it struck the landing pad near the salvaged craft.

"They want to destroy it?" Cas slumped. She wasn't surprised—there were standing orders not to let the power crystals fall into enemy hands—but that had been her ride home. If they blew it up, she wouldn't have a way to escape.

A bomb landed on the building next to hers. It exploded on impact, and rubble flew in a thousand directions. Cas dropped to her belly, throwing her hands over her head. As the squadron swooped across the outpost, bullets and explosives laying waste to the structures and docked ships, she stopped worrying about escape and started worrying about surviving. To the fast-moving fliers, she had to appear as nothing more than one more pirate to be exterminated.

The locals had found their posts, and the booms of cannons and explosives roared above the buzz of the propellers. Guns fired from the decks of the individual airships too. The fliers weaved, making hard targets, but their maneuverability was limited between the envelopes and the building-filled outpost itself.

More shrapnel clattered down on Cas's rooftop. She didn't know where it was coming from this time, but staying up there wasn't safe.

When another wolf-nosed craft streaked in her direction, she rolled to the edge and scrambled down into the street. It didn't fire near her though; it was aiming toward the salvaged flier. The seaweed- and grime-covered craft had already been damaged with that first explosive, and its cockpit lay torn open like a flower shredded by the wind. Yet a glow came from its engine compartment. The crystal powering it must have survived even after years in the ocean. Cas grimaced again, knowing she might have been able to get the craft working and flown home. It was too late now.

In an impressive feat of piloting, the flier weaved between the gunfire of two deck-mounted artillery weapons, dropping a pair of hooks on cables as it flew. The pilot was going to pluck out the energy source—or try anyway. Those crystals were securely mounted into their slots.

Cas leaned to the side, squinted, and was finally able to read the numbers stenciled on the side.

"W-83?" she blurted. That was Colonel Zirkander's flier.

Was he back? Or was someone flying it for him? The pilot wore a helmet and goggles—it was impossible to tell from a distance, but that craft *was* weaving and dipping in his style of semi-controlled recklessness.

The hooks missed on the craft's first pass, scraping the surface of the crystal but not finding purchase. By now, the gunners were aiming at it almost exclusively, despite two wingmen flying nearby, trying to take out the nearest artillery weapons. A cannon fired, the black ball blasting past W-14—Captain Crash Haksor—and heading straight for 83. It skimmed across the cockpit.

"It's getting too hot," Cas whispered. "Get out of there."

The squadron might have taken the outpost by surprise, but that was wearing off now. More than that, the pirates seemed to have recognized what the 83 meant too. All of the cannons and guns on that side of the outpost were locking in on Zirkander's craft. Two of the launched airships were moving away from their berths and veering in that direction too. A pair of large doors, or perhaps sliding panels, had opened at one corner of the outpost. A thunk-clank sounded and a bulky machine rose from the compartment, some giant cup-shaped apparatus holding netting. It almost looked like an old-fashioned catapult. Whatever it was, that netting was more sophisticated than the hammock Cas had tossed over that kid's head. A big enough net hurled at a flier could be trouble.

The streets were deserted around her now, with all of the pirates manning a station or back on their ships. With her pistol in hand, Cas ran toward the catapult. She had some vague idea of helping by disabling it. More than that, she wanted Zirkander, or whoever was flying his rig, to *notice* her helping. There wasn't room in a flier for a second person, but she would jump on the back and cling to the top of the cockpit if it would get her home.

She hadn't run more than two blocks before a gang of pirates stalked out of an alley with bags and chests balanced over their shoulders. They all carried swords or pistols too. She tried to veer around them to continue past, hoping that in the chaos they wouldn't notice her, or at least wouldn't identify her as anything other than a fellow pirate.

But one pointed at her and yelled, "Witness. Get her!"

Witness, what?

Several guns were aimed in her direction. Her instincts took over, and she threw herself into a roll, angling toward the closest cover: a street lamp. Guns fired, and bullets skipped off the pavement around her. She lunged to her feet, firing as she ducked behind the post. It wasn't that thick, but she wasn't that thick, either. Besides, there were no other options nearby. Aiming by instinct, and years of experience, she leaned out slightly and fired three times in rapid succession. They fired back. One of their bullets clipped the lamp fixture, and glass exploded over her head. All she did was lean closer to the post and shoot around it twice more.

"Cover," one of the men yelled, "find cover."

She thought this was a reflection of her marksmanship—three men were writhing on the ground, after all—but the buzz of propellers hammered her ears as a flier roared over the nearest building. The pirates stopped firing at her, dropped their burdens, and ran for an alley.

As much as Cas would have liked to jump on and get a ride, she doubted the pilot would recognize her. Who was that? Lieutenant Sparks? Smoke combined with the fog to turn the air a soupy gray that made it hard to see more than fifteen meters. She waved anyway, glancing over her shoulder, as she ran. The craft laid down bullets, obliterating the bags and boxes the pirates had abandoned—and obliterating some of the men she had injured as well.

Cas gulped and lunged into the alley—on the opposite side of the street from the pirates—and raced for the next block. Only when she glanced back to check for pursuers, did she notice the gold coins and small treasures that had spilled out of the dumped cargo. Those men must have been taking advantage of the chaos to loot. From their own people. What heroes.

Cas reloaded her pistol and started toward the catapult again. The side of the landing pad and the railing marking the end of the outpost platform were visible at the end of her street. The net-weapon, if it hadn't already fired its load, would be off to the right. A couple more blocks, and she could reach it. And help her comrades—and maybe be noticed by her comrades. She wasn't ready to give up on the idea of rescue.

Before she reached the end of the street, a great explosion thundered not fifty meters away from her. The ground—a floating platform thousands of feet above the ocean, she was reminded—heaved like a wave, nearly hurling Cas into the nearest building. Shrapnel pummeled the pavement, some pieces so large they could have killed a man. She ducked into a doorway for protection. A head-sized piece of black pavement slammed down two feet away, its ragged edges smoldering. More chunks hammered the street. The whole platform seemed to tilt downward now. What had they blown up? More than a building that time.

Cas poked her head out of the doorway long enough to look toward the landing pad.

"Oh." The landing pad was gone. The whole open area she

had been aiming toward was gone, too, including at least one of the giant propellers that helped the outpost remain aloft. For the first time, she worried that the squadron might succeed in utterly destroying the floating city. "Not a goal I'd normally object to, but now..." She eyed the six giant balloons above. *They* at least seemed stable still, some coating doubtlessly protecting them from the bullets. She was surprised any of the fliers had carried explosives powerful enough to destroy the landing pad and the surrounding platform. Then another, "Oh," slipped out of her mouth. The power crystal. If the colonel hadn't been able to extract it, he might have blown it up. Yes, she had seen one destroyed before. That had been in the air rather than on the ground, but the explosion had sent a shockwave that she had felt, flying far behind the lead craft.

After the debris quit hammering the street, Cas slipped out of hiding, changing her plan. In case the platform *was* on its way into the ocean far below, she needed to get to one of the ships. As much as she loathed the idea, that might mean returning to Captain Slaughter. He wouldn't be tickled to see her after she had started that fire, but where else could she go? She wouldn't be able to sneak onto anything now; all of the pirates would be aboard and fighting. She didn't even know if any of the ships were left in dock. She halted, groaning as she remembered that Slaughter's ship had left to deal with the fire.

"Nice job, L.T.," she grumbled to herself. "Sabotage the ship you need to get away in."

She jogged in the direction she had last seen it anyway. Or started to. Another explosion came from that side of the outpost. It wasn't as violent as the last one, but it filled the sky with more black smoke. It was one of the smaller airships, one that was— she snorted—flying a yellow-and-blue Iskandian flag. Or at least it had been. That flag, its pole shattered, was fluttering to the pavement where what remained of the craft was berthed. What remained wasn't much. Little more than a charred, smoking husk. No less than six fliers sailed away from the destroyed craft, their mission apparently accomplished.

Strange. What had been on that ship that had demanded

such attention? Cas had assumed the salvaged flier was the main mission—keeping it and its crystal from being sold to the highest bidder for study—but perhaps that had been a side mission, or even a diversion?

The pirates had marshaled their forces now, and four airships, cannons and guns blazing, chased after the six Wolf Squadron pilots. Smoke drifted from the wing of one flier and from the engine area of another. Cas clenched a fist, silently willing them to get out of there. She couldn't tell whose craft those were through the smoke and the distance, but she didn't want to hear of any of her comrades going down.

They seemed to be done with their mission, though, and were forming up to fly away. Smoke notwithstanding, all twelve fliers were accounted for. The pirate ships sailed after them in pursuit, but couldn't match their speed. One after another, the fliers disappeared into the fog.

A lump formed in her throat. They were going home... and she wasn't. Had anyone even noticed she was here?

Someone grabbed Cas from behind, pulling her off her feet and toting her toward an alley. She tried to wrench herself free even as she lifted her pistol to aim over her shoulder. A hand clamped down, pinning hers in an awkward position, her finger off the trigger.

A shot fired, but it wasn't hers. A bullet smashed into the corrugated metal corner of a building, a building she had been standing next to seconds before. Standing and staring, without paying attention to her surroundings.

"It's me," spoke a familiar voice in her ear. "You're about to be the most wanted person on this station. What remains of it."

Cas stopped her struggles, though she wasn't sure Tolemek was an ally after what she had done to his ship. Hells, she hadn't been sure he was an ally before, either. Someone she was using in the same manner as he intended to use her, perhaps. Still, he had just pulled her out of the line of fire.

"I don't suppose you have a suggestion on how to deal with this new problem?" she asked.

For the first time in she didn't know how many minutes,

the noise was fading around them—the cannons had stopped booming and the guns still firing were on the ships flying after the squadron, their noise muffled by distance and the fog.

"Yeah," Tolemek said. "Hide."

"Hide?" Fleeing had figured more prominently in her mind.

"The captain will need time to repair the ship, which was damaged even *before* the attack." His face was next to hers, since his arm was still holding her against his torso, so he couldn't glare at her, but he was probably trying to anyway.

At least he didn't seem furious about the fact. But then, he could be hiding it. Cas had seen him vent frustration, however briefly, in that empty library, but when it came to dealing with people, she had a feeling he was the type who could be utterly furious with a person yet never show it... until it was too late for his target to respond.

"I won't be able to protect you, either," Tolemek went on, "not after your squadron just laid waste to half the ships in dock. Hells, they'll want to lynch me when they find out I brought you here. Unfortunately, we can't leave until the captain does some repairs. So, yes. Hide."

"On the station, or off? I only ask because I'm questioning the air worthiness of this outpost right now."

"It's not going to drop out of the sky. I've seen the blueprints; there's a lot of redundancy built in."

"Did you by chance have a hand in designing it?" Cas asked.

"Just some of the defenses. Like the fog. Which didn't fool your people one iota today. If I thought you had any dragon blood, I'd suspect you of calling out to them somehow."

Cas shuddered at the idea of having witch blood, or even being accused of having it, but she forced a sarcastic indifference into her tone. "If I could do that, I would have called out for them to take me with them, don't you think?"

"Yes."

"Now that we've settled that, would you mind putting me down? And letting go of my pistol hand?" She had another pistol and could reach it with her left hand, but wasn't inclined toward shooting him at the moment.

Tolemek let go of her weapon, and the arm around her waist loosened. She slid down him, her toes touching the debris-littered pavement.

A pirate jumped around the corner, pointing a pistol into the alley. Cas cursed—of *course* the man who had shot at her would try again. She reacted on instinct again, firing a split second before Tolemek dragged her toward refuse bins against the wall.

"Damn," he whispered, stopping in the middle of his lunge. Cas's shot had taken the pirate in the forehead. "That's uncanny."

No, that was having a dad who had been training her to follow in the family business since she had been old enough to toddle. She wished he hadn't taught her so much indifference when it came to drilling people with bullets, but perhaps it served her in this situation.

"I'm ready for that hiding spot now." Cas waved the pistol. "I'm getting low on the ammo I purloined from your trunk."

Tolemek nodded toward the far end of the alley. "This way."

Since all she had managed was to get herself shot at when she had been choosing a route, she was content to let him lead. She would be even more content if darkness would fall. With pirates streaming about on high alert, it was going to be hard to sneak anywhere. She reloaded her guns and strode after Tolemek, though she couldn't help but gaze toward the sky in the direction the squadron had flown off and wish she were with them.

* * *

Tolemek saw the longing looks Ahn sent in the direction the fliers had gone. He chose not to tell her how relieved he was that the squadron had departed without destroying the outpost, his ship, or *her*. He wasn't sure when he had started to feel responsible for her safety, and ferocious toward things that threatened it, but when he had been charging around the station, dodging shrapnel and searching for her, he'd had men take one look at his face and then flee the other way. If he'd had a weapon capable of shooting down those fliers, he would have.

The attack squadron had annihilated Stone Heart's *Burning*

Dragon. Though he had wondered briefly at the notion that Ahn might have somehow summoned them, he had a feeling the Iskandian military had been tracking that Cofah corporal all along. They must have realized someone had survived the battle at their secret mines and wanted to ensure that he didn't report back to his people.

Tolemek stuck to the alleys, picking a route that would lead to the opposite end of the outpost, though at the shouts he started hearing in the streets, he wondered if a closer hiding spot would have been better.

A cry of, "Ten gold coins to the man who finds her," from a nearby street did not sound promising at all. Tolemek had hoped the attack would have delayed that administrator from relaying the information on Ahn's presence, but it seemed not.

"I don't suppose he's lost his grandmother and is looking for help finding her," Ahn said.

"Grandmothers aren't much of a fixture here." Tolemek ducked into an alley behind one of the few brick buildings, stopping by a series of metal boxes on its back wall. He spun a lock on the biggest one and entered a combination. "Unless you count that lady who runs the laundry service and keeps all the cats. She calls them her children. And her children are prolific."

Ahn pointed to the box he was opening. "If that's access to the control panel that will allow us to blow up the entire station, I think we should make sure we have a way off first."

Apparently she had escape on her mind, not cat-granny jokes. Appropriate, he supposed.

"Nothing so sinister." Tolemek opened the door and slid a few levers from a neutral position to the maximum setting, then closed the panel. "It'll thicken the fog more."

He led Ahn toward another alley entrance. "I can't believe Stone Heart had a flier squadron tailing him all the way from the mainland and didn't notice it. He's an experienced captain. It's unthinkable." He looked at her, in case she might want to posit an alternative theory, but she kept her mouth shut. Her expression was particularly grim this evening.

Tolemek supposed it wouldn't mean anything to her if he said that he was starting to find even her grim expressions attractive. Maybe it was just the fact that her bruises were healing nicely, and her face had taken on a more normal shape, but he doubted it. He almost grinned at the memory of that cabin boy explaining how she had tricked him into dropping his trousers and holding an innocuous flask of liquid over his head until he had figured out a way to escape, something he might not have been inspired to do if not for the smoke wafting past the porthole.

Ah, but what was he to do about these inconvenient feelings? Nothing. Whether or not he had stopped considering her the enemy, he knew she still considered him one. And rightfully so. Attraction or not, he wasn't going to pass up the opportunity of using her to get to Zirkander, *especially* if Zirkander had a witch ally who knew something about soulblades. To finally have a real lead on a quest that had occupied all of his free time for the last three years... he couldn't pass up that opportunity.

"Am I looking inscrutable?" Ahn asked. "Or is that the look you wear when you've forgotten the way to your secret hiding spot, and you're trying to remember it?"

"I was—" Tolemek stopped and listened as no fewer than ten men strode down the nearby street, their weapon-laden belts jangling. He drew Ahn into the deep shadows of an alcove. "I was merely waiting for the fog to deepen so we could move on with less risk of discovery."

"Huh, that's interesting." She peered into his eyes.

"What?"

"Seems like I've been around you for long enough now that I can tell when you're lying."

Tolemek avoided her eyes, looking at the cheap veneer on the wall on the other side of the alley instead. "All right, I *was* scrutinizing you."

"So long as you weren't contemplating unique and effective torments as revenge for me stealing some of your goo and making a mess with it."

"No." He gave her a curious look. "I didn't get a chance to see much of the damage, but from the report I heard, you could have done much more."

This time, she avoided his eyes. "I just wanted to escape, not annoy your captain so much that he'd devote the rest of his life to hunting me down."

It was silly, but he wished she'd said *he* was the one she didn't want to annoy. Tolemek thunked his head against the wall and reminded himself that feelings would only distract him here.

"I'm not sure he'll appreciate your solicitude," he said, "but I do. Come, the fog has thickened. We ought to be able to reach the spot I have in mind without being noticed."

"What is this stuff made from anyway?" Ahn waved at the soupy air as she followed him into a space between two buildings that was too narrow to be considered an alley.

"My special proprietary blend."

"In other words, you're not sharing your secret?"

"Not until you renounce your Iskandian citizenship and agree to become my loyal lab assistant."

Ahn snorted. "Sure. I'll send in the paperwork tomorrow."

Tolemek stepped out from between the two buildings, only to halt and squeeze back into the crack. Pirates carrying guns and lanterns were striding down the street that he and Ahn needed to run down to reach the next alley. It was only twenty meters away, but a party was coming from the opposite direction as well.

"Check between those buildings," someone called, not from either of the groups in the street but from the block they had left.

"These search parties are getting a little too organized for my tastes," Tolemek muttered.

"We can handle it." The click of a gun being cocked reached his ear.

"Let me take care of it. These are... Ahn, I can't be seen with you if you're going to run around shooting everyone on the station. These are my people, my allies."

"Yeah? I saw some of them looting one of the shops earlier. Loyalty seems fleeting here."

"Some of them are closer allies than others." Tolemek lifted a hand to forestall further arguments—or derisive commentary on the pirates—since the parties had made their way closer.

They were going to cross paths right in front of his position. He lowered his voice to a murmur and added, "Don't shoot unless it's an emergency. And watch the route behind you."

"Understood."

Tolemek remained still, hoping the fog and the shadows might hide him. Maybe the men would simply walk past without noticing.

"Who's that there?" One of the pirates lifted a lantern in Tolemek's direction.

He leaned his shoulder against the corner to block the view of Ahn. "Deathmaker." He made his voice as chill and forbidding as he could manage. Meanwhile, he slipped a hand into a pouch at his belt. Though he hadn't stopped by his cabin since the meeting, he always kept a few vials and contraptions with him. The pirates might be the only people in the world he could claim as allies, but that didn't mean he trusted all of them.

The men exchanged glances with each other.

"You seen the Wolf Squadron girl?"

"They say she came in on your ship," someone in the back of the group added. "With you."

"She escaped our ship, yes. I don't know anything about it. I was called out here to fix the fog. It's thicker than porridge." Indeed, it wafted down the streets, curling about the legs of the pirates. Tolemek might be able to roll something out there without them noticing. The other group was approaching, so he decided to wait. Maybe he could hit both parties at once.

"Yeah, getting worse by the minute. What happened?"

"One of the fliers hit the control panel and damaged it," Tolemek said.

A tap came at his shoulder. "The ones behind us are looking up the alleys," Ahn whispered.

"Strange that the Iskandians found us through it," one of the men said.

Tolemek slid a leather-wrapped sphere out of his pouch.

"They say there's a witch working for Zirkander now," the man went on. "Maybe she helped him find us."

Huh. Word from that meeting had gotten out quickly.

"*What?*" Ahn whispered.

One of the pirates squinted at Tolemek. "There's not someone behind you in that crack, is there?"

"No." Tolemek pointed toward the roof of the building across the street. "Think I saw someone move up there though. Anyone got a reason to spy on you boys?"

Not all of them looked—more than one man squinted at Tolemek—but he didn't care. He armed his sphere and bent slightly, to roll it toward the center of the groups without letting it make noise.

He slipped a hand behind him to push at Ahn. They would need to back out of the range of the odor that would soon be disseminated. But she had already moved. He glanced back, afraid she had left for some reason. She was in the center of the narrow alley, down on one knee, fog whispering past her shoulders as she aimed a pistol toward the opposite end.

"What is that smell?" one of the men in front demanded.

"The fog," Tolemek said. "I'd best see to the repairs." He backed into the alley, wrinkling his nose as he caught a whiff of his concoction, a faint rose-petal scent not quite masking the more sinister chemical odor beneath it. He would have to work on that, so long as he didn't pass out from inhaling his own knock-out gas first.

He squeezed through the alley toward Ahn, his shoulders brushing the walls, and knelt behind her.

"You shouldn't need to fire," he whispered. "The search parties I was talking to will be unconscious shortly, and we can go that way."

In the deepening gloom, he could barely see her, but he thought she nodded. Another half hour and night would fall, making it easier to move about, but he hoped they had reached the spot he sought before then. Every moment they were out in the open, they risked being caught—or shot.

Soft thumps came from the street behind him.

"That should be it," he whispered and started to back in that direction.

A clank-clunk-thump sounded, something bouncing off

the wall and into their alley. Tolemek grabbed Ahn's shoulder, images of grenades bursting in his mind, but not before she got two shots off. One of them seemed to strike the item, for the clanks sounded, going in the other direction. Tolemek had scarcely seen anything. He pulled Ahn toward the street.

A flash of light and a boom came from the object—it was farther away than he would have expected. Shouts of surprise—and pain—arose from that direction. Ahn must have shot the grenade itself, knocking it back toward the men who had thrown it. Tolemek could barely see in the shadows and fog and couldn't imagine how she had made the shot.

Ahn, less constricted by the narrow walls, spun and pushed at him—as if he hadn't been trying to pull her in that direction all along. "Time to go. That won't stop them for long."

Tolemek jogged into the street where he had rolled out the sphere. Even more fog had gathered, but not enough to hide the lanterns lying on the pavement, lanterns that had been in men's hands before. He ran past the slumbering figures, leading Ahn up the street, across it, and into a new alley.

"You should have stored those leather balls somewhere obvious, so I could find them in your cabin," Ahn said. "I wouldn't have had to burn holes in the engine. Could have just knocked out everyone on the deck to escape."

"Yes... In the future, I'll make sure to organize and label my lab for the convenience of prisoners."

"Maybe add a map and some diagrams too."

Tolemek found himself grinning despite the circumstances—and the fact that he was going to have a difficult time walking about on the Roaming Curse outpost again without getting shot, assuming he made it off this time without getting shot. He took a final turn, then stopped before a brick wall at the end of an alley. Shouts echoed in the streets behind them, calls for reinforcements. So much for sneaking over to this end of the outpost without being noticed.

"You'd think they would have repairs to worry about," he muttered.

Ahn tapped the brick wall. "Dead end?"

"No." The fog obscured the ground, so Tolemek tapped around with his boot until he located a spot that clanged instead of thudding. He knelt and found a grate.

"Sewers? I wouldn't have thought this place had anything intricate beneath the platform."

"It doesn't. These grates just funnel rainwater off the streets and into the sea below. But they also lead somewhere else." Not surprisingly, the grate was locked.

"Want me to open that?" Ahn asked.

"Your opening method leaves a lot of destroyed evidence behind to mark a person's passing."

Shouts came from a nearby street.

"Is that a no?" Ahn bounced on her toes, one of the six-shooters in hand again as she watched the path behind them.

"Correct." Tolemek pulled out a vial, uncapped it, and carefully poured a couple of drops of gray liquid into the lock hole. "We're not going far once we crawl down here, so I don't want anyone noticing that someone passed through."

"With all this fog, you can't even see the grate itself."

"True, but it's possible someone will turn that down at some point. I'm not the only one on the station who knows how to push a lever."

"You should have booby-trapped it then," Ahn said.

"That would have been needlessly destructive."

She glanced back at him, giving a pointed look toward the grate. He didn't think she could see the hint of smoke rising from the lock, but she might be able to smell the melting mechanism.

"And possibly a good idea," he admitted. "Suggest it earlier next time."

"Next time? Are you planning on escaping from a lot more angry mobs with me?"

"Judging by what I've come to know about you in the last twenty-four hours, it seems inevitable. If we continue to spend time together, that is." Tolemek tried the grate. The locking mechanism had disintegrated, and he opened it with ease. "My lady. Your duct awaits."

Chapter 9

Cas peered into the dark vertical drop below the open grate. From what she could make out, the walls were dark and slimy, and the lighter gray at the bottom suggested an opening about fifteen feet down. An opening that couldn't lead to anything except a drop of thousands of feet, followed by a plunge into the ocean filled with sharks. Not that the sharks would truly matter. At the speed one would hit the water, it would be like landing on cement. "I think you should go first."

"I need to close the grate behind us."

"I can do that."

"You're too short. The shaft leading to the side is nearly seven feet down."

"What shaft?" Ahn asked. "All I see is a well with a long drop at the bottom of it."

"There's another grate across the bottom, but I can lower you down, so you can crawl into the access shaft before landing on that grate."

"You've done this before?"

"I've studied the blueprint."

"Oh, that's all manner of comforting."

Weapons jangled in the street closest to their dead-end alley. Tolemek threw an exasperated look in that direction, then whispered, "Fine, you'll have to crawl down me then."

Without hesitation, he slipped into the hole, lowering his body until only his hands remained, gripping the sides of the rectangular opening. For a moment, they didn't move. Was he patting around with his feet for that side passage?

Cas crouched in the fog beside the opening, ready to shoot whoever came into their alley. She heard scuffling. At least two men. They paused to have a whispered conversation. She caught snatches of it.

"...they go this way?"

"Don't know... don't really want to find them. You see all those men down? The Deathmaker is with her."

"Solid gold coins on her head though."

"It's *his* head I'm worried about."

A pat at Cas's foot nearly made her jump up.

"Now," Tolemek whispered. "Climb down me."

Though Cas wasn't convinced relying on vague memories of blueprints was a good idea, she put the pistol in her mouth and lowered herself into the hole. It was a tight fit with Tolemek there, standing on some ledge, and he hadn't been joking: she had to use him for handholds. The slick, algae-coated wall on the other side didn't offer much to grip. Questioning whether there truly was a protective grate below, she grabbed him harder than he might have had in mind, wrapping her legs around his, as if she was sliding down a tree.

"Interesting place to store a gun," he remarked as their heads drew level. He probably couldn't *see* it in the dark shaft, but when she clunked him in the eye with the handgrip, he must have figured it out.

"I like the taste of metal," she grumbled, the words probably not intelligible with the barrel in her mouth.

"I didn't understand that," Tolemek verified, reaching up to pull the grate closed behind them. "I'll do you a favor and not imagine it was something lewd or innuendo-filled."

"Thanks. You're a gentleman." She lowered herself, hands gripping his shoulders, and reached down with a leg, patting around to try and find the ledge. Ah, there.

The horizontal shaft was larger than she had imagined, perhaps three and a half feet high. Once her boots were planted on the bottom, she swung in, landing in a crouch. It was another rectangular space, the sides still slimed with algae, a nice dense growth. It reminded her of the gunk in the ruins below Dragon Spit. She wondered if that meant the transportable pirate outpost spent a lot of time hiding in tropical climates. Once she was done picking the gunk out from beneath her fingernails, she would write down the intel for her commanders.

On hands and knees, she crawled in a few feet so Tolemek would have room to climb in behind her. An oddly strong draft skimmed past her cheeks, and the rumble of machinery came from somewhere ahead, the *whum-whum-whums* reminding her of the propellers on a flier. She stuck her pistol into her holster and decided to wait for him before crawling farther. For all she knew, this was some underground labyrinth with plenty of spots where one could fall into the ocean below.

A light touch on her shoulder told her Tolemek had joined her. She couldn't see much. She scooted to the side to let him pass. This space wasn't much wider than the last, and it took some maneuvering and much brushing of shoulders and hips before he could crawl into the lead.

"You sure this hiding spot of yours is a good idea?" Cas whispered. "If we end up trapped, and they figure out where we are..." She frowned at the image of being stuck in a dead-end duct with pirates at the entrance, peppering them with bullets.

"It's a maze down here, and there are other ways out. If they figure out we're down here, there are only a couple of people on the station who will know it well enough to find their way around, and they're techs, not fighters."

"Hm." Cas's new mental imagery involved her and Tolemek getting lost in said maze, running out of food and water, and dying without the need for any shooting.

He reached back and patted her on the shoulder. "I have a good memory. It's all in my mind. We won't go far, either. Just ahead, there's a spot where we can stand up and climb onto a ledge. Then our legs won't be visible if someone does figure out we went through that grate and decides to come down for a look."

He was moving off as he spoke, and Cas had little choice but to follow him. The lush carpet of algae squished beneath her fingers. "How long did you say we have to stay down here?"

"A few hours. We're meeting the captain at midnight."

"Oh, good. I'm sure he'll be excited to see me again." Nothing like rejoining the ship one had sabotaged.

"Perhaps not exactly the word I'd use, but he *was* distraught to learn you had left us."

"I'll bet."

She caught up with Tolemek, or rather his legs. Another shaft opened up from their crawl space, this one heading upward at an angle. His legs soon rose out of reach. She crawled after him, running into him again shortly, as soon as the bottom of the duct leveled out. He seemed to be standing. When she tried to do the same, she clunked her head on some edge or corner above her.

"What *is* this place?" she grumbled.

"Access ducts to all of the propellers on this end of the platform and to the holding tanks for the hydrogen for the balloons." His voice was hollow, echoing oddly from several feet above. He was definitely standing up.

Cas patted overhead, finding the outline of the hole, then maneuvered into a standing position too. She was facing Tolemek, squeezed close by the narrowness of the walls, her smock brushing his chest. Feeling overly intimate in the position, she shifted her hip toward him, though that involved some bumping of body parts too. She was glad he hadn't made those innuendo-filled comments about the gun earlier.

"Is this our final destination?" she asked. "Maybe I'll just sit." Except then her butt would be in that squishy algae. Ugh, didn't pirates clean their maintenance ducts?

"Your choice. And, yes, I think this is a good place to stay until it's time to meet the captain."

Cas didn't sit. She sighed and leaned her shoulder against the wall, something that didn't keep her other shoulder from touching his chest. Oh, well. So long as he didn't prong her with those spiked wrist guards of his, she could survive the closeness. Besides, as far as chests went, it wasn't a bad one to be pressed up against, as long as she didn't think overmuch about his past.

"My apologies," Tolemek said. "This spot looked bigger on the blueprint."

"A closet would have worked if all you wanted was to get me alone in the dark."

He snorted softly. "Oh? Would you have agreed to spend time

in a dark closet with me?"

"If it was between all of those gun-slinging pirates and you, yes."

He seemed to consider that—or perhaps something else—a moment before saying, "What if it was between me and some handsome Iskandian lad?"

"I don't know," Cas said, caught off-guard by the question. "Does he wash his hair?"

Tolemek chuckled softly but didn't otherwise respond, willing to let the topic drop, it seemed. That was good. He would be a wholly inappropriate choice when it came to romantic dalliances. To sleep with him, or do *anything* with him, wouldn't just be a betrayal to herself. It would be a betrayal to her people, to all those who had died horribly at Tanglewood, and to countless others who had been killed, raped, plundered, and gods knew what else at the hands of these pirates.

Still, she found herself asking, "When did that... become a concern for you?"

She wanted to know if he was genuinely interested in something physical—which would mean she should be on guard more than ever around him—or if he was simply making jokes to pass the time. They *were* going to be stuck in here for hours, after all.

"Sometime between you helping me escape," Tolemek said, "and me getting the story from the young man in my cabin, who was apparently quivering and holding a flask of Fen Tree Oil above his head, while wearing his trousers around his ankles." There was a fondness in his voice that should have made her wary, but she found herself smiling in the darkness. Not all men appreciated her... determined approach to dealing with problems.

Tolemek shifted his weight to lean his own shoulder against the wall and ended up behind her back. He was probably just searching for a more comfortable position. It wasn't as if there was room in the shaft for any physical activities even if he had such in mind. Cas leaned forward, but that resulted in her forehead pressing against the algae-covered wall. Grimacing, she drew back, wriggling an arm up to wipe away the moistness. She tried to find a comfortable position that didn't involve touching, but it didn't work. Sighing, and telling herself it didn't mean anything, she finally let her back lean against his chest. For a moment, he didn't move, almost as if she had caught him by surprise, but then he slipped his arm loosely around her torso and rested his chin against the top of her head.

She waited very stilly, afraid she had inadvertently given him some invitation. Her heart beat faster as she wondered if he would presume to do more—and what would she do if he did?—but he didn't. She could feel the rise and fall of his chest against her back. He seemed relaxed. Contented?

Cas licked her lips. "Is Fen Tree Oil dangerous, by chance?"

"No, medicinal. It's one of the ingredients in my salve."

Cas touched her cheek, the effects of that salve vivid in her memory. It hadn't yet been a full day since he had applied it, but all of the swelling had gone down, and she had to press on the spots she had been struck to find a hint of lingering soreness. "Your army was foolish for not buying that from you. I'm amazed how much better I feel today, despite having just spent the afternoon dodging bullets and shrapnel."

"Could be the healing power of being wrapped in my arms."

"Please. Your awful bracers are an inch from eviscerating me." They weren't, but she was pleased that her response elicited another chuckle from him. He had a pleasant laugh.

For a murderer, she reminded herself and swallowed. Even if she could somehow forgive him for his choices, his history, there was still the matter of Colonel Zirkander and the fact that he wanted to use her to get to him.

"So," Cas said, "where to after we meet with your captain?"

"Iskandia."

"To drop me off and then leave without hurting anyone? Especially squadron leaders of mine?"

Tolemek lifted his head from hers and sighed, his breath stirring her hair. His arm fell away from her, leaving a cold chill behind.

"I thought so." Cas didn't pull away from him—as if there was somewhere to pull *to*—but she did fold her arms over her chest and glower at the wall. It was what she had expected, but for some reason she had thought... what? That if he was developing some feelings for her, he might abandon his pirate ways? Sure, Cas. Sure.

"Did you see the ship that was destroyed?" Tolemek asked. "The one that seemed to be either the secondary or primary target for your squadron?"

"I saw it."

"Did it have any significance to you?"

"No..." Cas wondered if he was deliberately trying to change the subject so she would forget about his ulterior motives or if he truly wanted to discuss this. "I didn't see the name before they pounded it full of explosives. I might have seen it before, but pirate ships all look the same after a while. You'd be amazed at how many of them think it's charming to paint the hull black."

"It was the *Burning Dragon*, commanded by Captain Stone Heart."

Cas wondered why he was volunteering the information. As they had just established, they weren't exactly on the same side, cozy moments in dark ducts notwithstanding. "I've heard of it, but I don't know why it would be targeted above all the others, if that's what you're asking."

"It's not. I already know."

Cas waited curiously. It had been almost three weeks since her flier had gone down and she'd been captured. That was an eternity in war time, and a lot could happen. She longed for information on what her squadron was up to, even if she couldn't be there with them and a part of the action.

"Oh?" she prompted when Tolemek didn't go on. Surely he wouldn't have brought it up if he didn't mean to explain it to her.

"I would like to trade this information to you, in exchange for you answering a few questions of mine."

Cas stiffened. And just what questions might *those* be? "I'm vaguely curious about what the squadron is up to, but I'm not betraying any of my people, and certainly not my commander, for the information."

"I know. What I would like to ask should not be a betrayal. I simply wish to know where you stand on some matters, so as to decide if there is a way we can work together instead of in opposition to each other."

Cas chewed on that a little, trying to decide if he meant to try and trick her into cooperating or at least leaking sensitive information, or if he genuinely might want to figure out a way to go ahead as... something other than enemies. And if there was some of the latter in his words, was that what *she* wanted? If nothing else, should she not try to lure him into some trap, even as he and his captain tried to use her to lay one for Zirkander? She had to be careful thinking like that though. He might not stroll around with books clutched to his chest and quotations of mathematical formulas on his lips, but the very existence of all of his potions and inventions suggested he was a very smart pirate.

"Go on," she finally said.

"Was that an agreement to answer some questions for me?"

"You give me your information, and I'll consider answering some questions."

"Consider, huh?"

"That's more than you were getting before."

His soft grunt wasn't quite a laugh, not like the chuckles from before, but he sounded more amused than irritated. Good.

"All right," Tolemek said. "I don't know whether he was back on the ship when your people attacked, but Stone Heart had brought an interesting passenger with him to the station. He showed up to talk at a meeting of all the captains currently docked here. He is—or was—a Cofah soldier who was part of an attack on a secret mining installation in the mountains of your homeland. According to him, it's where your flier power crystals come from."

He paused, and Cas expected a question. Such as did she know anything about this? The answer was no—her flier had simply come with a crystal installed in the engine. She knew their origins were a secret of the kingdom, and she had never asked about them. What did she care, so long as the power crystals worked reliably and got her into the air?

"It seems your Colonel Zirkander was there, in charge of this secret installation," Tolemek said.

That made Cas pull her head back in surprise. *That's* where the higher ups had sent him? A mine in the mountains? *Why?*

"It seems there was also some witch or sorceress with a soulblade there working with him," he said.

"Uh, *what?*"

"That's what the Cofah corporal said."

"Maybe the Cofah corporal got walloped hard on the side of the head while he was serving."

"He said he saw the battle with his own eyes and that the sorceress was the only reason they were defeated, because they had a mercenary shaman of their own."

Cas shook her head all through his explanations. "There's no way my military, my government, or anyone on my continent would have anything to do with a witch. Sorcerer. Whatever." She had no idea what the difference was; hells, she hadn't even thought they existed anymore. She'd always thought accusing people of witchcraft was something the superstitious hill folk did to get rid of annoying in-laws and neighbors. It certainly never seemed to happen in the big city, where she had grown up. At least not that she had heard about. "I don't know how it is in Cofahre or on floating pirate outposts, but people get drowned over accusations of witchcraft in Iskandia."

His voice grew noticeably grim when he said, "Cofah traditions are not dissimilar."

"Even if someone in my country did have some sort of power, if she was even vaguely smart, she would hide it. She wouldn't be out in the middle of some fortress, throwing magic around with a—what did you call it?"

"Soulblade."

"A magic sword?"

"Essentially. But it's more than a simple tool. These ancient swords contain the souls of powerful sorcerers who once walked the world as mortals but then, when learning that disease or old age was creeping up on them, undertook a special ceremony to transfer their essences—all they knew and all they were aside from their physical bodies—into a sword. The weapon could then be handed to another sorcerer, often some youth coming up through the Referatu training system. They would be bonded somehow, and the sword would become a mentor and an ally. The swords themselves possessed some of the power that the owner had wielded during life, so a sorcerer with a bonded soulblade could be extremely powerful, more so than one sorcerer alone."

"This all sounds like goat droppings," Cas said. She couldn't believe he knew so much about it. Surely he didn't *believe* any of this? "This soldier told you all this? How could you know he was telling the truth? It sounds like a fanciful tale to me."

"He told us of the battle and of seeing the sword-wielding woman defeat their shaman and use the blade to deflect bullets and magical attacks. Based on his description, I deduced that he had seen a soulblade. And a powerful sorceress."

So all that knowledge about souls and dead sorcerers was Tolemek's from some past research? Cas remembered his words in the ruins beneath the prison, that he had sought some ancient magic to help... it had been a little sister, hadn't it? Or had that been some lie meant to win her over to his side? Maybe he had spent time researching these swords because he wanted one.

"So, would a normal non-witchy person gain anything from wielding one of these swords?" she asked, wondering what he had *truly* sought down in those ruins.

Tolemek shifted his weight behind her. "Hm, possibly? From my research, I got the impression that it was unlikely a soulblade would deign to be handled by someone who didn't have dragon blood. They're supposed to be sentient still, and they might harm you to keep you from even picking them up."

"Huh," Cas said. It was about all she could think of to say. All of this sounded like fantasy to her. "I still think your Cofah soldier might have been hit on the head, or that he was telling your captains a tale he thought might get him accepted into the outfit. If he truly saw those mines..." Cas shut her mouth. She didn't want to speculate about top-secret mines with him. She didn't know where they were, so she was certain *he* shouldn't know where they were either.

"Any chance your Colonel Zirkander is being controlled by this sorceress?"

"Please, the king can't even control him. Or the commandant. Or anyone in his chain of command."

"Yes, but they're not pretty women, presumably."

"He's not the type to—" Well, Zirkander liked pretty women just fine, and she had seen him go home with some of the ones from the taverns before, but, no, he wouldn't let one sway him like that. "He wouldn't let a woman control him, and certainly not some witch. It's true he's a little on the superstitious side, but not hugely so. He wouldn't let that blind him or scare him." She decided not to mention that dragon carving he flew with. "He certainly wouldn't get into bed with a woman who had ulterior motives." Much like Cas wouldn't get into bed with a pirate who had ulterior motives. "He's got a lot of flatterers. He's good at sussing that stuff out."

"You seem to know a lot about him, outside of his professional persona." Tolemek's voice was neutral, carefully so, she thought. Was he suggesting something untoward?

She scowled over her shoulder, though he probably couldn't see it in the dark. She couldn't see much of him except for a vague darkness against the wall. "We all know a lot about each other. We spend all day together then go out at night because..." She shrugged. "It's like a family. A family where everyone has something in common and understands what the others are going through. Sometimes the men who are married don't even get that kind of understanding at home."

"I see. Well, I wasn't suggesting that Zirkander was in this woman's bed necessarily, but that she might be controlling him, possibly without his even knowing it. Most of the sorcerers of old were telepaths. Some specialized in beast control, and some of the ones who went rogue, who made everyone hate and fear sorcerers and want to get rid of them, could control people."

"I still think that if someone showed up at his fortress with a glowing sword, the colonel would figure out something fishy was going on pretty quick. I don't think your Cofah was a reliable witness, and I refuse to believe anything about magic until I see it for myself."

"Hm. Do you know why Zirkander was sent to that fortress to start with? A ground-based fortress high in the mountains? Seems a strange place to send a pilot."

Punishment, Cas thought with a guilty twinge. Because of that incident with the diplomat. Because of *her*. "He didn't tell us."

"Top-secret government movements, eh?" Something about Tolemek's voice said he knew she hadn't told the whole truth there. Too bad. She'd told him she would *consider* answering his questions; that was it.

"I guess. Lieutenants don't get included in many meetings."

"That much I believe." He grunted, as if at some memory of his own.

"Are we done with the question and answer session yet?"

"I've answered far more questions of yours than you have of mine."

"Yes, but you've given me fluffy fairy-tale answers about magic swords and sorceresses, neither of which has been seen in Iskandia for hundreds of years."

"Three hundred," Tolemek murmured.

Cas didn't ask him for clarification. She didn't want to admit that he might know more about her continent's history than she did. That subject hadn't been a passion of hers in school.

"One more question," he said. "Zirkander."

She tensed, not wanting to say anything more about him, fearing the little she'd said already constituted disloyalty.

"From what you've said so far, I'm gathering he's not an ass to work for," Tolemek said. "Is there any scenario in which you would..."

"Betray him? No."

"Help me get to him to ask him some questions," he said.

"Questions. Right. That's what you and your captain have wanted all along. To use me to get to him to *question* him."

"It's true that I originally saw you as a way to get to him to kill him, something that would... if not win me a spot in Cofah society again, at least make them think a little more kindly toward me. And it's true that Goroth wants him dead. With the vengeful fire of a thousand suns. But I... I don't know, Ahn. Or can I call you Caslin, now that I know your name?"

She hadn't given it to him and wondered when he had gotten it. It hardly mattered when she was leaning against him—damn, she didn't even remember doing that, but somehow the back of her head was resting against his chest again. Maybe she was just tired. And afraid of the moist, bumpy growth on the wall.

"Cas," she said.

"Ah, thank you. Cas, then. I have always considered Zirkander an enemy—as I told you, he's the reason I was cast out of the Cofah army—but time has worn away my bitterness, and I no longer imagine that his death would fill a great emptiness in my soul. I've had enough of death, to be frank. I also find myself reluctant to lose your... well, I don't know if I have anything of yours, but I should not like to earn your utter hatred. Nor, given your accuracy with everything from pistols to rocks to hammocks turned into nets, would I want you gunning for me for the rest of my life."

She thought about telling him the net had been a trap, not anything she had shot or thrown, but waited to see what else he had to say instead.

"After hearing that soldier's story—and I saw the fear in his eyes when he relayed it, so I don't think it's as tall a tale as you believe—I'd like very much to find a way to speak to Zirkander and find out more about this woman."

"You want the sword," Cas guessed.

"If she *is* a sorceress, trying to take the sword could be suicidal. I might not be above trying to find some clever way to do so, I suppose. But if the weapon came out of those mines, not unlike your power crystals, maybe it's possible I can find one for myself. For my sister, actually. I mentioned her, I believe."

"Yes," Cas said, though she didn't know if she believed this sister was truly who he wanted the sword for. If there *were* such things as magic swords, and they were as powerful as he suggested, they would be worth a fortune. Or maybe he thought he could channel the sword's power for himself, for some new invention of his. Just because he had treated her fairly so far didn't mean she had seen the *real* man. "Here's the problem: I can't imagine the colonel wanting to sit down and have a chat with you, about sorceresses, swords, or even his latest toenail fungus. You and your pirate buddies are loathed where I come from. You especially."

"I know. I suppose that's where I see you coming in."

"Arranging a meeting?"

"Yes. Preferably without weapons."

"Uh huh." Cas turned around to face him. "Listen, Tolemek. I appreciate that you've been decent to me, and I believe that maybe you were thinking of letting me go back in that jungle, but on the other hand, I figure you're a bright fellow, and you could be telling me all the things you think will make me want to help you. Either way, what you want probably doesn't matter all that much when your captain is the man we're meeting at midnight and who is presumably taking us to Iskandia. And who is, as far as I've seen, the person you answer to."

A long moment passed, during which Cas hoped Tolemek would proclaim that he wasn't utterly loyal to the captain, but he eventually said, "Yes. He is."

"I won't ask why, because you didn't ask why I wouldn't think of betraying my colonel, but just in case you didn't know about it, I will say, he told *me* that he's not afraid of you. That he's crossed you before and would do so again."

"I would not expect him to be afraid of me. He was my instructor at the proving grounds more than ten years ago. And when we both ended up cast out of the military, he was the one to offer me a position here. To allow me to do my research and explore my interests with minimal interference."

Cas thought he might go on to explain how and why the captain had crossed him before, but he either knew about it and was dismissing it or he didn't believe her statement. Uttering it a few more times wouldn't make him more likely to do so, so she didn't mention it again. Maybe she had planted a seed and she would get lucky. But she doubted it. Tolemek and the captain had seemed close from the beginning, and nothing in this conversation suggested otherwise.

"As long as you're following his orders..." Cas stopped herself before declaring that she wouldn't arrange anything between Tolemek and the colonel. She ought not be so honest with him if she was entertaining the idea of trapping him somehow. "That's a problem," she finished, since he could guess that much anyway. "Unless you'll consider leaving him."

"There is... nowhere else for me to go." His hand came up, brushing the side of her head, making her shiver a little, or maybe it was the poignant sense of regret that had entered his voice.

"I can understand wanting camaraderie, of a sort, and someone to watch your back, but don't you think it would be better to live alone than to live with villains?" Cas winced, because that sounded so condemning. But these pirates *were* villains; they weren't soldiers fighting for their country and couldn't simply be considered men on the other side of the war. Despite whatever circumstance or choice or fate that had brought them to this lifestyle, there was no denying that they were here, and they were committing crimes.

Tolemek lowered his hand and spoke so softly she almost missed the words. "Where else would a villain live but among other villains?"

She didn't know what to say to that.

Chapter 10

A FEW MINUTES BEFORE MIDNIGHT, TOLEMEK led Cas out of the maze of ductwork and into the streets above. The fog had not only diminished; it had been turned off. Stars glittered overhead, and the horizon stretched for miles without a cloud in the sky. He supposed the administrators saw little point in expending energy to create the fog when the Iskandians knew exactly where they were. Presumably the outpost would move soon, but for now, repairs were underway. Lights burned on the ships in dock, and the sounds of hammers and rasping saws drifted on the breeze.

Tolemek hoped the industriousness meant that the bounty hunters had been called off Cas's trail, but he stuck to the alleys anyway, walking with caution toward the tavern the captain had named as a meeting point. Cas walked at his side, or slightly behind, not saying much. She hadn't since she had made the suggestion that he leave the pirates—and he had rejected it.

It was something he had considered in the past, after Tanglewood and Camp Eveningson in particular. He had gone off on his own for a month that time, but he had been hunted relentlessly by Iskandian and Cofah spies. And more than that, he had learned he hadn't the stomach for a life of solitude. When he had started to grow excited at the appearance of bounty hunters, realizing that they and their pursuit represented an odd sort of company, he had known he had to return. What was the point of creating and inventing if there was no one to share the results with? When Goroth had sent that note, saying he hadn't given away his cabin yet, Tolemek had been back within three days.

A part of him wondered if he should have been less honest with Cas, maybe playing along with the notion of leaving Goroth in the hope that she would consider arranging the meeting he sought. Or maybe in the hope that she would go back to leaning against him and letting him nuzzle her hair. That had been... pleasant. And she hadn't pushed him away. Of course, she hadn't exactly given the impression that she was enjoying his touch either.

Even so, when she had mentioned the idea of him leaving the pirates, he had found himself wondering what he would do if she offered him a home in Iskandia. Not that she could. A lowly lieutenant would have no sway with her superior officers and certainly not with her government. She couldn't offer him refuge. To even defend him to her people would get her in trouble. Did the Iskandians have courts-martial? Probably.

"There's the Crow," Tolemek said, drawing her into the shadows of a dark storefront a couple of buildings down. "It's still standing, even if it doesn't look very busy. That's our meeting spot." He didn't head for it immediately. He had a feeling he shouldn't stroll in, not after he had been running around the station, knocking out pirates and helping a pirate enemy evade capture.

"There's someone in the shadows over there." Cas pointed toward the alley beside the Crow.

"Ah, good eyes."

But was that someone Goroth? Tolemek circled around the back of the store, so he would come out in the alley across the street from where the man was standing. He didn't have to guess as to the person's identity, for the figure met them halfway down the passage.

"Amazing how much trouble you can get into in a few hours," Goroth said.

"Is he talking to you or me?" Cas asked.

"*You* seem to only need a few minutes," he snarled, thrusting a finger toward her nose.

"Should that make me feel suboptimal?" Tolemek asked, hoping to lighten Goroth's mood. He didn't sound happy.

Goroth merely snarled. He had a couple of bulky bags slung over his shoulders, in addition to wearing all of his gear and weapons. "Neither of you better be seen on the outpost for a while. Come on. We've got a new ship."

"A new ship? I thought you were making repairs to the old one."

"We did. It's operational now." Goroth glowered over his shoulder at Cas. Fortunately, it was the most threatening thing he had done. His desire to strangle her must have waned somewhat in the intervening hours. "But we can't take the *Night Hunter* to the Iskandian capital."

"Sure you can," Cas said. "I'll even direct it past some nice wall-mounted cannons in the harbor that you might like to visit."

"You'll be on it with us, girl," Goroth growled. "I shouldn't think you'd want it shot down."

"It's a good thing she's not our pilot," Tolemek said. "She's not, is she?"

"No, I'm bringing Moonface and some other good men. Leaving Drakath in charge of the *Night Hunter*. Told him if he didn't take good care of the ship and turn it back over to me, he'd die horribly, due to a booby-trap you've set to go off if anyone except me is commanding the ship for more than a week."

"Nice way to inspire your troops," Cas muttered, too softly for Goroth, in the lead, to hear. A good thing.

Tolemek merely said, "And here I've always wondered where these stories about my dastardliness started."

"They've served you well enough over the years."

Until recently. Ah, well.

"Speaking of dastardliness, I packed some of your supplies." Goroth unslung one of the bags on his shoulder and handed it to Tolemek.

Glass clinked inside. No vials with volatile contents, Tolemek hoped.

"I figure we'll need some of your tricks when we get there, so that we can accomplish—" Goroth glanced at Cas, "—what we need to accomplish."

Cas glared at him, but said nothing. As if she didn't know exactly what he had in mind.

"Yes," Tolemek murmured, thinking of his conversation with Cas, his proclamation that it wouldn't bother him if Zirkander went on living and her rebuttal that what he thought mattered little as long as he was going along with his captain. He had spoken the truth to her, but he secretly admitted that he would still prefer to see Zirkander dead rather than alive. It was cowardly, but the thought had crossed his mind that if he simply stepped back and let Goroth do the deed, Cas might not blame him. Or might at least forgive him some day.

They paused at the mouth of an alley, waiting for a repair crew to go by. Tolemek wondered if Cas thought it strange, seeing pirates marching about with toolboxes in hand and lumber balanced over their shoulders. After all the damage the outpost had endured that day, someone would have to take a supply-gathering trip if the station was to be repaired to its former glory. Not his problem at the moment.

When the route was clear, Goroth trotted across the street to a craft that was more dirigible than airship, with an enclosed cabin snugged below its massive gray balloon. Lanterns burned to either side of the extended gangplank, and Tolemek could just make out the Iskandian flag painted on the side of the envelope.

"You stole one of our freighters?" Cas asked.

"Actually I bought one of your freighters," Goroth said.

"From someone who stole it?"

Tolemek smirked, despite the exasperated look Goroth gave her. What did he expect? Love and respect from a prisoner?

"Will the *Night Hunter* be following along in the distance?" Tolemek asked as they walked up the gangplank—it was a wider and fancier version of the simple board their own ship employed, one that looked like it folded and extended from the large double doors of the cabin itself. "In case we get into trouble? I imagine that even freighters flying Iskandian flags are boarded for inspection when they arrive in port. Especially if we're angling for the capital." He looked at Cas, wondering if she would offer a helpful answer, but she gave him nothing. No, she wasn't going to help them infiltrate her homeland.

"Oh, they'll be around." Goroth's grin had a wolfish aspect to it.

"What do you have planned?"

"Nothing that needs to be discussed in front of our prisoner." Goroth pointed at Cas's nose before unlocking the cabin door. "And I expect you to lock her up. Somewhere without any handy goop nearby for melting locks."

Tolemek hated the idea of chaining Cas after all they had been through, but he understood Goroth's wariness. Gods knew, she would escape and make trouble if she could. Right now, she was trotting along nicely, still wearing his six-shooters in her holsters, but where else did she have to go? Once they neared her homeland, there would be nothing keeping her from trying to flee.

"I will," Tolemek said. He tried to give Cas an apologetic look, but didn't know if it would be decipherable in the low lighting from the lanterns.

Goroth disappeared into the dirigible, and Tolemek extended a hand for Cas to follow. He brought up the rear. Judging from the clanking and thumping coming from the back of the cabin, someone was already inside. Lanterns were lit in the wood-paneled corridor and more light came from the navigation area up front. Goroth would have brought an engineer as well as a pilot, and perhaps a couple of other men as well. Tolemek itched to take him aside and find out what he had planned as far as backup went for this little invasion of theirs. Leading a small, secretive team into the city didn't sound like a bad idea, but that wasn't Goroth's standard operating procedure. He liked to make a show of his attacks.

He had already stomped up to the navigation cabin and was talking to the pilot, so their chat would have to wait.

"Let's find a room for you, shall we?" Tolemek asked.

Cas was standing at his shoulder.

"Room or cell?" she asked.

"I'm not entirely sure what to expect on an Iskandian freighter. Would they have cells for restraining prisoners?"

"Not likely. You might find a wine cellar for restraining the captain's favorite vintages."

A wine cellar? On a freighter vessel? Either she was joking or, "The centuries of war haven't deprived your people as much as I would have guessed."

She snorted and headed down the corridor, but not before taking a long peek toward the navigation cabin. As a pilot, she probably had an interest in anything resembling a cockpit.

"Can you fly a dirigible?" he asked.

"Yes, they taught us how to pilot everything at the academy. Not everyone gets picked for a flier squadron. There's actually quite a long waiting list. I was lucky to get selected for my first assignment right out of school."

"Because of your marksmanship skills?" At some point he would have to ask her about her father.

"Something like that."

Tolemek stopped in front of a cabin with the door open. Unlike some of the others, there weren't any bags or clothes tossed on the bunks. "Does this look acceptable?"

Cas peered through the doorway. "I don't know. I don't see any pipes running along the walls. Where will you chain me?"

"I thought I'd just lock the door. And..." He found himself reluctant to go on, but he had little choice. "And take your guns. Which are actually my guns, so you shouldn't miss them overmuch."

Wordlessly, Cas unfastened the belt and handed it to him. She didn't meet his eyes. She didn't looked any more irked than usual—in fact, she was going along with the situation without much objection—but her stance and the lack of heart in her quips made him feel like something had changed. Or gone back to the way it had been. Instead of sharing the adventure of escaping together, they were prisoner and master again, a role that suited him less and less with each passing hour.

"Cas..." He licked his lips, not sure what to say.

"Tolemek, you got that girl locked up yet?" came Goroth's voice from the navigation cabin. "We're taking off soon. And having a meeting."

Tolemek gazed at Cas, wishing...

She arched her brows. "Don't worry about me. This is the most comfortable prison I've been in for weeks." She walked over to the bottom of two bunks and flopped down on her back.

"Yell for me if you need anything."

"Some food would be nice. I haven't eaten since... I don't know when."

"I'll see what I can do."

She gave him a vague salute. He had the feeling that she wasn't sorry to see him go—she probably wanted to start plotting an escape. He glanced around the room, but aside from the bunks and an armoire bolted to the wall, its doors open to reveal it empty of clothing and anything else, there wasn't much to use to facilitate an escape. Tolemek closed the door and was about to call to Goroth, asking about a key, when the captain appeared at his shoulder. He jangled a key ring.

"Allow me."

After locking Cas in, he headed for navigation again, tossing the ring on a hook near the exit as he passed. There were two seats up front, and Moonface, a graying man with big cheeks and a round face, already sat in one. An engineer and two fighters from the *Night Hunter* leaned against the wall. Goroth took the second seat. It was bolted to the floor but had the ability to swivel, and he spun around to face Tolemek.

"We've been cleared to depart," Moonface said, his hands tapping controls on a panel that stretched across the width of the cabin with all manner of gauges, levers, and buttons on it.

"Let's get going then." Goroth waved to him, though he never looked away from Tolemek. "While you were doing the gods know what with your prisoner, I was in a meeting, talking a number of the other captains into helping us. And helping themselves, of course." His wolfish smile returned. "The *Night Hunter* will follow us. And so will—" the smile broadened, "—the entire outpost. As soon as the majority of its repairs have been completed."

"The outpost?" Tolemek asked. "It's following us? To Iskandia?"

"Yes, as well as seven other heavily armed ships. As you might imagine, all of the Roaming Curse was riled after today's attack. Angry and hungry for blood. If not Zirkander's blood, then the blood of his people. With the help of your fog technology, they're going to attack the city."

"The capital city? There's nearly a million people there. And who knows how many troops? Their airbase and an army fortress are right there in the harbor."

The engineer was scratching his head at this revelation too. Moonface didn't look that surprised—he was guiding the dirigible away from the docking station, and his hands never stopped moving across the controls. The lights beyond the big glass viewing window were drifting off to one side, and the stars and the black night horizon stretched before them.

"Hence the need for the fog," Goroth said. "Which I promised you could deliver."

"I don't understand. Even if the outpost is shrouded by clouds, the soldiers in that city are going to catch on right away when bombs are being dropped from the sky. Their fliers will simply breach the fog the way they did this afternoon."

"Ah, but we're not going to put the fog around the outpost." Goroth smiled. "We're going to smother the city in it. Their fliers will have trouble taking off and landing. None of the ground troops will be able to see our ships, so they won't be able to aim their weapons. Their defenses should be rendered far less effective than usual. The outpost and some of our ships will attack. Others will land and raid their museums, universities, shops, anything with valuables. It'll be a risky raid for them, but worth it if they can bring home a lot of loot." Goroth leaned back in the chair, his hands clasped behind his head. "And while the rest of the pirates are busy doing that—effectively distracting the entire city—we, my friend, will locate Zirkander and kill him. Though not before we find out everything about that sorceress and figure out how to get that sword. And any other invaluable magical items we can get our hands on."

Despite the ludicrousness of this plan, Tolemek found himself intrigued by the idea of fogging in the city. Could it be done?

"Some techs dismantled the fog unit on the outpost, and I had it loaded on here. It's back in the engineering section."

Tolemek rubbed the back of his neck and stared thoughtfully at the deck. "I designed it to cover the outpost and the surrounding ships, but that's a much smaller footprint than an entire city. This will take some time and thought."

"Which I intend to give you," Goroth said. "But you'd better get to work. It's not that long of a flight to Iskandia."

Already mulling over potential modifications, Tolemek nodded and headed for engineering.

* * *

Cas poked into the armoire, checked under the bed, and tapped the walls, hoping for secret compartments full of tools, weapons, or something else she could use to escape. Oh, it wasn't as if she had somewhere to go, but she had a notion of sabotaging the engine, or perhaps the docking hooks—something that would cause a bumpy descent into the capital. If they crashed, the small crew would be scrambling, and she might be able to slip out at that moment. All she would need was ten minutes to run and tell the dock master that there were pirates in the city. Tolemek and his captain would be caught and executed for their crimes against the nation. The idea of a bullet shot into Tolemek's forehead disturbed her, but what choice did she have?

"He shouldn't have locked me in here if he wanted to live," she grumbled. More, he should have volunteered to leave his crusty captain and come over to her side. "Unrealistic expectations, L.T.," she sighed. "Unrealistic expectations."

She had to arrange her own escape before worrying about such things, anyway.

The doorknob rattled.

Surprised, Cas faced the exit. She hadn't expected someone to facilitate her escape. Ah, but maybe it was Tolemek bringing her something to eat. Except why would he turn the knob without first applying the key? He had been the one to lock the door; he had to know it would still be locked.

The knob rattled again, then someone knocked softly.

Hope swelled in her chest. It wasn't possible that someone was here, trying to rescue her, was it? But who? All of the Wolf Squadron fliers had departed, and since the cockpits only had room for one, it wasn't as if someone could have been dropped off.

No, whoever this was... she doubted it was a rescuer.

Cas cut out the lantern hanging by the door and climbed onto the top bunk. She might not know who was coming through the door, but it represented an opportunity, regardless.

Metal scraped against metal, a key being inserted in the lock this time. It turned, then clicked. The door was thrown open so hard it banged against the wall. An unfamiliar man lunged inside, pointing a pistol. Someone else lurked behind him in the corridor, glancing both ways. They both had the mismatched garb, scars, and tacky bone-and-teeth jewelry that she associated with the pirates. Enemies.

If Cas hadn't doused the lantern and climbed out of the line of sight, she might have been shot right away. She had a split second before the man's searching eyes located her, and she lashed out from her spot on the top bunk, kicking him in the face so hard that he staggered backward, dropping the pistol.

She jumped off the bed, pouncing on the weapon.

The first man had stumbled back into his comrade, who was trying to right him, or maybe push him aside to fire. Cas was faster. She snatched up the pistol and shot twice. She didn't know who these two hedgehogs were, but they clearly wanted her dead. She made sure they wouldn't want that—or anything else—again, then checked the pistol. Four more rounds.

She gnawed on her lip. She could get to the engineering room now, but Tolemek and the captain would charge out of navigation any second, having heard the gunfire. If she was going to sabotage something to set a trap, she wanted to do it stealthily, so they wouldn't be expecting the trap to be sprung later on.

More gunshots rang out, this time from the front of the ship. Someone screamed in pain, then a ringing thud sounded, followed by something heavy crashing to the ground. Maybe this hadn't been about her after all. Maybe someone was trying to take over the ship. To what ends, she didn't know, and she wasn't sure she cared, though a thread of worry wormed through her belly at the thought of Tolemek in trouble. He had been heading up to navigation for some meeting, hadn't he?

More shots were fired, two from navigation, and then three more in rapid succession from the engineering room. Cas knelt and patted down the pair of dead attackers. She might need more than four bullets to handle whatever came at her next.

She found an ammo pouch and another pistol in a holster. Since she didn't have any pockets, she took the moment to unfasten one of the men's weapons belts and claimed it for her own. More sounds of fighting reached her ears, both from up front and from the engineering area. She thought about staying where she was and seeing what happened, but an image of Tolemek bleeding on the floor flashed into her mind.

"Hope I don't regret this," she whispered.

Stepping over the dead men, Cas headed for navigation first, thinking he was most likely to be up there. Another shout came from that direction, followed by a gunshot. She didn't hear any noises in the side corridor that led to the ship's exit, and it was dark in that direction, so she only glanced that way and continued toward the navigation door—unlike when she first entered, it was shut.

She caught movement out of the corner of her eye and realized her mistake immediately. She ducked and fired at the same time.

Something leaped out of the darkness and slammed into her, taking her to the ground. Metal glinted, reflecting the orange of the nearest lantern. A knife? She fired again, her barrel pressed into someone's abdomen.

A hand like a claw gripped her shoulder. She pushed and kicked at the man—she'd already shot him once, if not twice. He couldn't possibly want more of her. But her opponent was huge, protected by layers of blubber. His hand tightened, and his other arm raised, a dagger clenched in his fist.

On her back and jammed against the wall, Cas kicked out again, aiming for the blade this time. Her foot connected, and the weapon flew out of the man's hand.

She expected to hear it clunk off the wood paneling or clatter to the floor, but someone gasped instead. Not daring to glance away, Cas fired into her assailant's gut one more time. Finally, the claw-like grip on her shoulder slackened. Even though he had stopped fighting, pushing him off was like moving a log. She squirmed out, nearly losing her prison tunic in the process. Blood coated her hands and her body.

"Got him, Moon," came the captain's voice from the navigation room.

Someone had opened the door.

Cas scrambled to her feet, but didn't take more than a step before halting in stunned silence. The dagger. It had flown from her attacker's hands and cut into the throat of someone walking—or maybe fleeing—out of navigation. The man—she thought she recognized him from passing by him on the *Night Hunter*—was leaning against the wall, clutching at his neck with both hands. Blood poured between his fingers.

She stared in horror, less because he was dying—there were men dying all around her—but more at the freakishness of the accident. She couldn't have known the knife would strike someone; she'd only been defending herself.

The captain charged out of the navigation room, his temple bleeding and more blood spattering his garish bone breastplate. He had a pistol clutched in his hand, and when his gaze landed on Cas, she lowered into a tense crouch. She was still armed. If he aimed his pistol at her...

Hells, why wait? This man was a criminal. She didn't know who these intruders were, but if she could fire first, she could eliminate the biggest obstacle in her path to freedom. He stared at her, his hand tightening on his own pistol, as if he read every thought in her mind.

A gurgle came from the man with the cut throat. He stretched out a blood-drenched hand, then collapsed.

At the same moment, footsteps sounded behind Cas. Fearing some new enemy, she backed into the cross corridor, the narrow stub that led to the dirigible's exit doors. She never took her eyes off the captain. He glanced toward the dying man, his empty hand twitching in that direction, as if he wanted to help.

Now. This was her chance.

But Tolemek charged into view, with a burly man on his heels. He too was armed, and blood smeared one of his arms. His own? Or someone else's? She didn't see any wounds on him, but couldn't tell for sure.

Whether intentionally or not, she didn't know, Tolemek stepped between her and the captain. "What happened?"

Reluctantly, Cas lowered her weapon.

"Moonface is dead," the captain said. "Torin too. *That's* what happened."

"One of these intruders almost cleaved my skull in half with an axe," Tolemek said. "Who are these people?" He looked at Cas.

"I have no idea, but two of them charged into my room," she said. "After trying the door, finding it locked, then going off to locate a key. It seemed rather deliberate."

"All this to get at you?" Tolemek stretched a hand toward the dead pirates. "The bounty they placed on your head isn't *that* big."

"Maybe someone didn't like my idea." The captain touched his temple and scowled up and down the corridor. "I thought I had everyone going along with it, sold them on the notion of looting—" he glanced at Cas. "Nobody openly objected."

Cas glowered at him. Looting *what*? Going after the colonel wasn't enough? Now, these cretins had another scheme they were planning? Why hadn't she shot the captain when she had the chance? Her hand flexed around the pistol's grip. Tolemek was still standing between the two of them. She turned her glower onto him, but he was looking at the dead men in the corridor instead of her.

"Even if they didn't agree with your idea," he mused, "what would killing us do? Didn't you already set things in motion?"

"Yes. Yes, I did. And we're not discussing it further here." The captain pushed past Tolemek and lunged toward Cas.

She lifted the gun, stepping back to put more space between them so she could shoot, but her shoulder rammed against the corner of the intersection. The captain moved more quickly than she had anticipated, too, smacking the pistol out of her hand. He grabbed her before she could decide if she should duck and try to dart after the weapon. As soon as his hand wrapped around her forearm, she knew it was too late. She had missed her chance. Fool, why had she hesitated? For Tolemek's sake? That was ludicrous.

"Congratulations." The captain sneered at her. "You're our pilot now."

Chapter 11

Dawn was bleeding pink into the sky beyond the portholes when Tolemek, yawning so hard his jaw cracked, made his way up to the navigation cabin. One of Goroth's fighters had dragged the bodies of the dead into an empty cabin, but smears of blood painted the walls and the floor. That was going to be hard to explain to an inspection team. As was the big fog-making machine sitting on the deck in engineering. Tolemek had finished his modifications, but he needed to tell Goroth that there wasn't enough of the murk-making materials to last long, especially not if they planned to blanket the whole city. Or maybe he didn't need to tell Goroth. Maybe he ought not to help this scheme along too much. Hadn't he caused Iskandia enough grief already?

Sighing, he pushed his hair back over his shoulders and opened the navigation door. He was relieved to find Goroth and Cas sitting in the chairs, if not in amiable silence then at least with neither sporting any new bruises. He had been reluctant to leave them alone when Goroth sent him back to finish his work in engineering, especially after catching them in the corridor with guns almost aimed at each other instead of at the injured foes on the floor.

Goroth waved him in, a sandwich in his hand. "You're just in time, Mek." He smiled, oddly chipper, considering he hadn't slept all night, either, unless he had dozed up here, but he doubted he would dare leave Cas unattended. A pilot could do all manner of sabotage.

"Oh?" Tolemek asked.

Cas smiled over her shoulder at him, a surprisingly cheerful and agreeable smile. In other words, one Tolemek had yet to see from her. A queasy feeling came over him that had nothing to do with the grayish colored meat dangling from between

Goroth's pieces of bread. There was a crumb-decorated plate on the control panel beside Cas too. In all the chaos, Tolemek had forgotten to bring her a meal. Had she found a chance to eat the day before? She hadn't in the hours she had been with him. She must have been ravenous. Ravenous enough to accept food from her mortal enemy? Goroth was clearly eating from the same plate, but he was tricky enough that he could have inserted something into one sandwich unseen.

"Yes," Goroth said, "we're about to have a chat, me and your pilot friend here."

"About?"

"Zirkander. Where he lives. Who he knows of the magical-sword wielding persuasion."

Instead of tightening her lips and glaring the way she usually did when someone tried to extract information on Zirkander, Cas nodded and smiled again.

Tolemek closed his eyes, feeling sick. Goroth had been in his laboratory, had even packed a bag for him. Slipping a few vials of the truth serum into a pocket would have been easy. After all the years they had worked together, Goroth knew about most of Tolemek's formulas and where he kept them. Applying the liquid serum to something like bread or meat would be difficult, but... he eyed a smudge of mustard on Goroth's upper lip and fought the urge to think bull's-eye and punch him.

"Don't look so irritated, my old friend," Goroth said. "You want this information too. I know it. Zirkander for me. Sword for you, yes?" He held out a fist, inviting the clashing of knuckles pirates sometimes did to seal deals.

Though his hackles were up at the idea of tricking Cas into betraying herself, he couldn't bring himself to walk back out and leave the questioning to Goroth. Tolemek *did* want the information. She might hold the answers, however inadvertent her knowledge, that could lead him to the prize at the end of his years-long quest. And this was a better way to get those answers than through brutal means, wasn't it? That was why he had invented the serum after all.

Wordlessly, Tolemek bumped knuckles with Goroth, then

leaned against the wall beside the door. He opened his palm toward Cas, inviting his friend to do the questioning. Tolemek knew everything about the serum, so he knew Cas would remember this later. He couldn't bring himself to be the one who asked her to betray herself, though he supposed all that made him was a coward. She wouldn't likely think any more highly of him for standing in the background and listening, for not doing anything to stop this.

Goroth finished his sandwich and rotated in his chair to face Cas, his hands on his knees, his face intent. "So, Lieutenant, is there anything you'd like to share about your commanding officer? Colonel Zirkander?"

"I don't think so. Why?" Cas smiled.

Tolemek grunted, amused by the scowl that flashed across Goroth's face. Maybe she would find a way to fight the effects of the serum. He doubted it though. He had made it well and tested it often.

"Where does he live?" Goroth asked.

"On the army base behind the pilots' barracks, Griffon Street. He and the other senior officers have little cottages there. His is the third house after the fountain, south side."

Goroth plucked a notepad off the control panel and scribbled down the information. He had come in prepared, it seemed. Beyond the window, the sun was coming up, and the sea below gleamed beneath its warm rays. There wasn't a cloud in the sky, though a red hue to the horizon made Tolemek suspect a storm might be coming. Too bad it wasn't there now. Goroth wouldn't have dared question his only pilot if she had been busy keeping them from being struck by lightning or blown off course.

"He also has a cabin on a lake," Cas volunteered. "That's his, not military quarters. I haven't been there, though, so I'm not sure exactly how to find it. I think it's a couple of hours out of the city by horse."

"Guess that answers one of my questions," Goroth told Tolemek.

Tolemek lifted his brows—he hadn't gotten anything out of that addendum, except that Cas wasn't holding back information anymore.

"Whether or not she'd slept with him," Goroth explained. "I can't imagine how someone so young would get onto Wolf Squadron otherwise."

He couldn't *imagine* another explanation? Hadn't he seen her shoot? Tolemek glowered.

"I was actually hoping that would be the case," Goroth went on. "Then Zirkander would be more attached to her, and she would work even better as bait for a trap. You know how stupid men get when they come to care about women."

Tolemek would have had to have been stupid and deaf to miss Goroth's censure for him in that comment. He folded his arms across his chest and said nothing.

"No," Cas sighed. "He never asked. I used to wish he would. A lot."

The admission struck Tolemek like a dagger to the heart, and he forgot all about Goroth. For whatever reason—the age difference, maybe, or the fact that she never got dreamy-eyed mentioning the man—Tolemek hadn't suspected she might have romantic feelings for Zirkander. His head thunked back against the wall. Apparently, instead of asking her if she would pick Iskandian lads with nice hair over him, he should have been asking about infamous pilots.

"After I got out of flight school and joined the squadron, it didn't take long to see he thinks of us all like little brothers and sisters." Her disappointed face... erg, she was twisting the knife and didn't even know it.

Goroth was stroking his chin. Doubtlessly mulling over whether a "little sister" would be effective bait for a trap.

"How *did* you get selected for the squadron?" Goroth asked.

"Me? Zirkander picked me. It wasn't... an obvious choice." She waved to Tolemek, her face gone wry. "Nobody else wanted me. I thought I'd be lucky to get a job swabbing the hangar deck. I never even would have gotten accepted to flight school, if the colonel hadn't stepped in on my behalf."

"Why?" Tolemek found himself asking, despite his resolution to leave the questioning to Goroth.

Cas shrugged. "Because of my father. On the official city records, he's just a bodyguard who specializes in security services—" she rolled her eyes, "—but everyone knows he's killed some important people, some criminals, yes, but some who weren't. Anyone in the government who had a problem with his career, or with *him*... well, they had a tendency to disappear. Apparently people decided it was best to leave him alone and pretend he didn't exist." Another shrug. "It wasn't any secret that he was raising me to follow in his footsteps—good money, he always said, job security. Someone always wants someone else dead. I'm not sure that was always his plan, but after the fire— after my mother was killed by a vengeful relative of someone he'd killed—he wanted to make sure I could take care of myself. It suited me fine as a kid—he spent time with me, in the city and out in the woods, and we practiced hitting any and every kind of target. It was fun. It wasn't until I was older that I learned it was a little strange to teach a little daughter to use guns instead of to play with dolls. But I didn't care, not until the targets shifted from bales of hay to living, breathing things." For the first time in the interview—for the first time since she had consumed the truth serum—her expression grew pained. She looked away from Tolemek and out the window. "I didn't want to be a sniper after that. Growing up, he'd taught me to distance myself from emotion somewhat, to not dwell that much on the pain and feelings of others, thinking that was a wonderful thing. I suppose it is if you want to kill people for a living. And I have to admit, he did a good enough job that it wasn't empathy that made the job unacceptable to me. I just didn't want to do it for money. And I didn't want to kill people who were targets just because someone *had* money. If I was going to do it, I wanted it to matter. When the Cofah started coming more often, and our reprieve from the war seemed to be over, I realized I wanted to use my skills to protect people. I wanted to protect our country. What was the point of money if the world was in ruins?" She turned her eyes back on Tolemek, her expression beseeching. Her voice dropped, and she whispered, "I tried to explain my feelings to him, but he said I was being foolish. That if things got too bad, we could leave the country and find another place for our business. He didn't understand. I ran away from home. I was sixteen at the time. He didn't come after me; guess he figured I'd be back, or that I would figure out that I didn't have many other skills to rely upon, so I wouldn't be able to make it without him and his money and his job contacts."

Tolemek found himself listening to the story in fascination as the words flew out of her, in part because he cared—whether she ever would reciprocate that feeling or not—but also because his own father had been such a problematic figure in his life. He thought Goroth might be scoffing or cleaning his fingernails throughout this tale, but he was hard to read at the moment. He was listening and watching her though.

"In a way, he was right," Cas said. "I didn't have a lot of friends—our house was on the outskirts of the city, and I don't think it ever occurred to him that a child should have peers to play with when growing up—so I really had no one to turn to. Not many friends of the family either, oddly." Her lip quirked. "I ended up living on the street down near the harbor—it's not the best area for a girl—and stealing to eat. I saw an army officer walking after dark, wearing a leather cap with goggles up on his forehead and looking lost in his thoughts. I wasn't dumb enough to try and steal from someone with military training, but some ten-year-old boy was—and got caught. I figured the officer would either knock the wings off the kid's flier or turn him over to the law. Instead, they ended up in this in-depth conversation about some air battle or another, and the officer and boy were soon using dented cans and other street litter to represent airships and fliers. All this in the middle of one of the worst neighborhoods in the city. I later learned that the man had grown up there and didn't see it the way others did. At the time, I crept closer, curious about him, and I got caught up in the story of this air battle too. He was a good storyteller. Near the end of it, this pack of street toughs walked up, brothers or cousins or some relation to the boy, and one of them told the officer to give him those fancy goggles and how they would take them if he didn't. They all had pitted knives and homemade clubs. They figured they were what passed for fierce in that area."

Cas glanced at Tolemek's bracers and Goroth's breastplate before quirking her lips again and continuing on. "The officer said he'd prefer to keep his goggles, so they'd have to take them if they wanted them. I'm not sure what I was thinking, but I grabbed a fistful of rocks and started pelting those thugs. My aim's decent."

Tolemek grunted, imagining these kids taking rocks in the eyes.

"They decided they didn't want to deal with me *and* the officer, so they ran off. The boy ran off too. The officer—I later learned this was Zirkander, of course—turned around, at which point I caught a glimpse of a gun holstered under his jacket. I felt silly, but he tipped his cap, gave me his name, and thanked me for my help. He also suggested that I ought to sign up for the military. I lied about my age and did so the next day. Under an abbreviated version of my father's name. I served two years, and nobody figured out who I was—and my father never bothered me, though he must have known where I was—until someone recommended I take the officer candidacy exams and apply to flight school so I could take my marksmanship skills into the air. At that point, there were background checks. I arranged to cross Zirkander's path again, explained my situation and that I didn't want anything to do with the family business, and that I'd be a good officer. He remembered me—I wasn't sure if he would—and vouched for me. Four years later, when I graduated, I heard that my father had made a threat or two, and that nobody wanted me assigned to his unit. I guess he hadn't minded when I was soldiering and studying—he probably still thought I'd end up working with him and that the military training couldn't hurt—but he thought only fools volunteered to throw themselves into the sky. And it's true that there aren't a lot of pilots who live long enough to retire, not when we've been a target for the Cofah for as long as anyone can remember." She gave Tolemek a dirty look. He wondered why Goroth didn't receive a similar look, but she had been telling most of this story to Tolemek with only a few glances to the side. "Anyway, in the end, the colonel was the one who took me. I have no idea what kind of conversations he may or may not have had with my father over the last year and a half, but he's definitely not someone to back down to bullies. Or superior officers he doesn't respect, either." She grinned. "I don't think my father would go after him, anyway. That's one assassination the government wouldn't look the other way for. There are a lot of people who would avenge his death." Her grin disappeared, and she glared at Tolemek and Goroth again.

Goroth didn't appear fazed by this threat. In fact, he leaned back in his chair and smiled at Tolemek. "You know what this means, don't you?"

"What?"

Goroth jerked a thumb at Cas. "She's *better* than some lay. The little sister whose career Zirkander has shaped. He'll risk his life to protect her. I'll bet my left arm on it."

Little sister. Tolemek had never spoken of his own little sister to anyone in the Roaming Curse; Goroth couldn't know what such words—such a relationship—meant to him.

"Then that is good for your plans," Tolemek said softly.

"For *our* plans. Don't worry, I'll let you question him about the sword and the witch before I kill him."

"Good."

If the bluntness of Goroth's words bothered Cas, she didn't show it. Still under the serum's influence, she would still be feeling mellow and amenable—what glares and glowers she had given them hadn't been heartfelt, not like her usual expressions of scathing loathing. No, she was busy gazing out the window. And dreaming about unrequited love?

Tolemek left the navigation room. He had much to think about.

* * *

Cas woke from a nap, still sitting in the pilot's chair. The dirigible moved with the elegance and swiftness of a turtle, so she doubted she had missed anything, but she checked all the gauges and took a reading nonetheless. A stolid guard leaned against the wall by the door. For some reason, she had expected Tolemek there, and she paused in her check, trying to reconcile fuzzy thoughts. She had dreamed that she was telling the story of her life—and of meeting Zirkander—to him and his captain. But it had only been a dream, hadn't it? She wouldn't share her past with those two, especially not Captain Slaughter.

Then her gaze swept across the empty chair beside her... and the plate full of crumbs sitting in it.

"It wasn't a dream," she whispered, something between horror and terror snarling into a knot in her stomach. What had she told them? About meeting Zirkander, yes. More? Anything about the unit, their strategies? Her thoughts were so fuzzy. Tolemek's truth drug, that's what it had been. Had he been the one to put it in her food? She hadn't thought bread and meat could be tainted so, and the captain had eaten from that plate, too, letting her select a sandwich first. Had he doused all of the food, not caring if he ended up telling some truth? Probably. That bastard. Seven gods, she'd given them the colonel's address, hadn't she? She scraped through her thoughts, trying to remember what else she had given Slaughter. And *Tolemek*. He had stood right there and watched the captain interrogate her. Even though she knew they had been captor and prisoner from the beginning, and their goals were at odds with each other, she couldn't help but feel betrayed. Why had he treated her decently, with *respect*, all along when he was just going to step aside and allow something like this to happen?

"You're to keep on course for the Iskandian capital," her guard said.

"Yeah, yeah." Cas glanced down her form. As suspected, no pistols graced her waist, nor was she carrying so much as a knife on her belt. She slid her hand across the control panel, mulling over what sabotage she might manage from here, sabotage that she might walk away from and which they wouldn't.

Or...

Was it her duty to make sure they didn't reach the harbor and threaten Zirkander, even if it meant her own life? By crashing the dirigible into the ocean? The captain was up to something that went beyond whatever he planned for the colonel. Would it end with the loss of his life? Those people who had stowed away and jumped them, she didn't think they had been there for her. Slaughter had suggested as much himself. She needed to find out what they had been trying to stop, then find a way to escape her captors and get to the colonel first. Or she had to crash the dirigible and make sure none of these pirates ever made it to her homeland. And she only had... she glanced at the chronometer and her location calculators. She had lost the entire morning to that truth serum idiocy. It was an hour past noon, and she had less than six hours until they reached Iskandia. This time of year, it should be dark by then. She eyed controls for landing lights. She might be able to flash out a message, using the Korason Alphabet. Assuming someone was paying attention. If she landed at the military air base, they would be, but freighters came in farther up the harbor, over the civilian docking area.

Flashing a message in the sky wouldn't be enough to guarantee the captain's plan failed. A crash. That could be enough. Even if she didn't walk away from it. Wasn't she on borrowed time anyway? Hadn't she almost died three weeks ago? Maybe it was meant to be.

The door opened, and Tolemek walked inside.

Cas gave him a single icy glare, then avoided looking at him. His face was unreadable, regardless. He probably didn't care about her feelings toward him.

"Take a break, Orfictus," Tolemek told the guard. "Grab some lunch. I'll keep an eye on her."

"Yes, sir."

The guard walked out, and Tolemek kicked the door shut. He moved the plate, sat in the other seat, and faced Cas. She continued to study the controls, though they weren't all that engaging. Piloting a dirigible took considerably less skill and concentration than handling a flier.

"I doubt you're of a mind to accept it," Tolemek said, "but I would like to offer an apology."

He was right. She wasn't of a mind to accept it. And she wasn't of a mind to acknowledge his presence, either.

"Goroth doctored your food without my knowledge. When I realized what had happened... I shouldn't have stayed and had anything to do with the questioning, but I wanted to stay to make sure he didn't go too far."

Cas gave him a scathing look. Making her betray her commander, that wasn't going too far? Or having her make a fool of herself by talking about silly infatuations? What was? She didn't ask. She didn't want to hear anything he had to say right now. She refocused on the instrument panel.

"Listen, Cas, please." Tolemek leaned his elbows on his thighs, interlaced his fingers, and gazed intently at her. "I need your help."

She glanced at him, despite her determination not to. That wasn't what she had expected him to say. "After you let your captain drug me and question me, you want my help?"

"I believe you might want a chance to get him back, and I can use that."

"How?"

Tolemek held up a small vial, his tidy writing on the label: Truth Serum. It was empty.

"That's what was used on me?" Cas asked.

"It's another vial. The contents are in the wine he's drinking right now."

Cas kept her face neutral, kept herself from smiling or doing anything that would reveal the hope in her breast. Maybe this was just some new trick. Either way, it didn't mean he was thinking of coming over to her side. It just meant... what? That he wanted some information.

"I expect he'll be back up here after he has his lunch. I want you to question him about something for me. You'll have about a one-hour window while he's under the influence of the serum."

"Question him about what?" Cas asked. "And why can't you do it?"

"I've questioned him about this before. He'll be wary of talking about this subject with me, to the point where he might be able to guard the truth, even under the influence of the serum."

"You think he'll tell the truth to *me*? Why?"

"Your opinion doesn't matter to him. And because," — Tolemek looked hard into her eyes, as if he could read her thoughts through them, "—according to you, he already told you he betrayed me once."

"Oh." Cas hadn't been sure he had heard those words or, in hearing them, hadn't dismissed them immediately. She couldn't read him at all at the moment. Was this to be some test? To see if she had been lying? Trying to turn him against the captain? She licked her lips, nervous even though she *hadn't* been lying. But she *had* been hoping he might choose her over his commanding officer of countless years. "So you want me to ask what that betrayal was?"

"Yes."

He kept staring into her eyes. It made her feel like squirming, but she didn't look away. She was the honorable person here, not his conniving captain.

"Anything else?" she asked when several seconds had whispered past.

"Yes." Tolemek stared down at the empty vial, rotating it a few times between his fingers. "If he mentions Tanglewood or Camp Eveningson, get the details."

He stood to leave, but Cas stopped him with a raised hand. "What's Camp Eveningson?"

"The Cofah equivalent of Tanglewood. And the reason I can never go home again." Tolemek took two steps, then paused with his hand on the door latch. "I'll be listening."

After he left, Cas faced the control panel again. Dampness slicked her palms. Why? This wasn't her trial. Unless the captain figured out what she was up to and shot her. She grimaced. How had she gotten herself stuck in the middle of this? And what line of questions could she ask to get Slaughter to incriminate himself? Would the truth be enough by itself? If she could make Tolemek her ally, everything changed.

The guard returned, wordlessly taking up his spot beside the door. Maybe Tolemek's plotting would be for naught. Maybe the captain hadn't drunk his afternoon wine. Or maybe he had taken a nap afterward and didn't care what was going on in navigation.

Maybe—

The door opened.

The captain walked in, ambled to the open chair, and sat down, kicking his heels onto the control panel. Relaxed now, was he? "How's our progress, pilot?"

"Six hours to the capital."

"So we'll arrive at night? Good, good."

Cas chewed on her lip and thought about how to bring up Tolemek's concerns. Did she need to wait first, to make sure the serum had taken effect? Did she need to ease into the questioning? *He* hadn't, she recalled. He had bluntly asked about the colonel and she had burbled out... far more than she wanted them to know. Far more than she wanted anyone to know, damn them. She could kill the captain for the mere fact that he possessed her secrets.

The guard walked out. Odd. He hadn't asked for permission. Even odder, the captain hadn't seemed to notice. His hands were folded across his stomach, and he continued to gaze out the viewport, a contented expression on his face.

Time to start.

"So," Cas said, "you want Zirkander, and Tolemek wants the sword. What happens if those two mission goals end up being mutually exclusive?" She looked at Slaughter, but only so she could see the door out of the corner of her eye. Tolemek had said he would be listening. But if he wasn't in the room, how could he? Ah, the door was cracked open a hair.

"They won't be," Slaughter said.

Cas looked forward again, not wanting to risk drawing the captain's attention toward the door. "But what if they are? What if Zirkander is the only one with information on the sword, and in killing him, Tolemek loses all chance of learning about it?"

The captain shook his head. "Not going to happen."

"But if it did... you said you'd betrayed him before." Cas held her breath. Was that enough of a leading line? Or would he be able to ignore it?

He gave her an annoyed look, though it lacked the fire of the expressions he had launched at her previously. "For his own good."

"For his own good? Or for yours?" She was guessing, having no idea about their past.

"Both."

"What happened? That time you betrayed him."

"I recruited him, you know. Heard about his disgrace in the Cofah army—it wasn't unlike my own—and offered him a position with the pirates. I was actually a first mate then, and my own position was tenuous, but I praised him to my captain, explained what skills he could bring to the ship. I'd known him when he was a student at the proving grounds, seen that infantry was a long way from his passion and that he had only gone into the military because of his father." Slaughter looked at her, his eyes bleary as if he wasn't sure who she was.

Cas gave him an encouraging grunt. This wasn't what she had asked, but she remembered how the serum had made her ramble as well and how she had—unfortunately—gotten around to sharing what they wanted. Besides, she admitted a certain curiosity in regard to Tolemek's past.

"He *should* have been a research scientist," Slaughter said. "I had a hunch that if I could bring him on board, we could team up, work together, and take the ship from the captain. I'd lost everything when I was forced out of the army, the same as him. Even more so than him. He had been discharged, and I... well, that doesn't matter now. My plan worked. With his potions, we were able to take down the captain without much of a fight, and we made the ship ours. Mine, I should say. He didn't care about commanding anyone again. He just wanted to be left alone to do his research. Although he did have this odd notion of being accepted back by the Cofah. Or maybe by his father. You'll have to get him to tell you that story. I don't know it in full. I just know he became the emperor card I kept up my sleeve. He was dangerous, and I made sure everyone knew it. People left us alone that way."

"You were always intent on helping him then?" Cas asked, though she hoped the answer was no. "You never truly betrayed him? Were you lying to me?"

"I was always helping him, yes."

Disappointed, Cas fiddled with a control lever.

"Even when he didn't think I was," Slaughter added.

"Such as... at Camp Eveningson?" She didn't know why she picked that name instead of Tanglewood. Maybe because it meant nothing to her and the details, one way or another, wouldn't make her gut writhe.

"Yes. He had concocted this... weapon, I suppose you would call it." Slaughter closed his eyes, his head back in the chair. "A weapon in a metal canister, a little rocket really. It was designed to shoot up into the air over a populated area and distribute some kind of gas that people would inhale and that would kill them. He said... and I still remember this vividly, because it was a real sign of how out of touch with reality people like him can be... he said, if there were an incredibly deadly weapon in the world, something capable of destroying millions of lives, less people would die."

"How so?" Cas whispered, chilled but wanting—needing—to understand too.

"Because if something so horrible existed, there would be no need to use it. People would give up. You don't fight something like that. He was going to give it to the Cofah, and then they could finally bring the Iskandians back under their sway. Forever." Slaughter gave her a big, unfriendly smile.

Cas rubbed her face. *This* was the truth Tolemek had wanted her to hear?

"He was still a little irked with the Iskandians for destroying his career at the time. And he wanted his life back, access to his homeland, a hero's return to his city. He thought he'd get that if he handed them the ultimate weapon. But I knew him. Better than he knew himself. He was just a kid then. Twenty-five, I think."

Cas debated whether to point out that she was twenty-three. She decided to keep her mouth shut. He was rambling his way toward the end of the story, from the point of view Tolemek wanted.

"He was going to arrange some test for an administrator

using—I don't know. Monkeys, something like that. He'd never tried this toxin on humans, but he thought monkeys would be close enough. We happened to have two spies in the Roaming Curse. One Iskandian. One Cofah. We're a big outfit. Spies are common. Sometimes we even know who they are and play them against each other." He opened an eye and grinned at her.

He didn't know she wanted to wrap her hands around his throat and direct him back to the point.

"I told our spies about Mek's concoction. Or rather, I told other people about it where the spies could hear."

"Had he sworn you to secrecy?"

"Oh, yes. But I was always going around, driving terror into people on his behalf, so they would leave him alone."

"And leave you alone too?" Cas asked.

"Yes, there was some of that. I won't lie. I've benefited tremendously from having the Deathmaker at my back. This is when he got that nickname, you know. Each of the spies stole canisters from him, and each of them went out to test it on the enemy nation. I couldn't have designed things better myself if I'd been giving them orders. This way, both governments would know exactly how effective his concoction was. Dead monkeys wouldn't drive fear into men's hearts."

"I don't understand," Cas said. "Why would you tell both sides? Didn't you have any loyalties?"

"Not even remotely. That's what a pirate is. Someone too jaded for loyalties, someone who isn't going to let some government lead him around with a bit in his mouth. You're only out for yourself out here, and the sooner you're honest about that, the sooner you'll make a life you like." Slaughter shrugged. "Looking back, I wouldn't have done it again. It was horrible. From hearing him talk about it, I didn't truly grasp how awful of a weapon he'd created. I don't think he did, either, honestly. We flew to your Tanglewood—when he learned that the spies had stolen his vials, he wanted to chase after them and retrieve them. We didn't make it in time. We saw the aftermath. And that scared me pissless. I was sure when we got down there that we'd be affected by the toxin, too, and be dead before we got back to the ship. It had dissipated by that point though. Still, it was a long time before I went into his cabin—into that laboratory of his—after that."

Cas wondered if this was the same version of the story that Tolemek had heard. Or had he only known about the spies and not how his captain had deliberately fed them information?

"Camp Eveningson was the same," Slaughter said. "Disturbingly horrible. Mek disappeared for a while after that. I didn't know if he would come back—or if he would do something drastic to himself. While he was gone, I made sure the governments knew who was responsible."

"Er, why?"

"So they would know not to bother the Roaming Curse."

"I don't get it," Cas said. "Weren't you afraid they would hunt him down for his crimes?"

"I thought they'd be too afraid to bother him. And it was mostly true. There were some bounty hunters, but the big threats, men like your pa, were too smart to go after him. That's what I heard anyway. That someone offered Ahnsung the job, and he refused. Might just be a rumor though. All I know was that after Mek came back, nobody bothered him. And after he got over his funk, he stuck with me. He didn't have anywhere else to go."

Cas considered him, wondering how long she had until the serum wore off. "Are you sure that wasn't part of your plan all along? To make sure his invention didn't turn him into some government's hero, or savior, or dark little secret kept in the basement? To make sure both parties were too upset to consider working with him? So that he wouldn't stray from your side? He's *your* secret weapon, after all. You need him to ensure your continued power amongst a fleet of bloodthirsty men."

Slaughter's eyes were closed again. He yawned and said, "You talk too much, woman."

Please, he had been the one babbling.

"But I'm not wrong, am I?" Cas glanced toward that cracked door. She had heard enough to form her own opinion on the matter, but she wanted the captain to make a beyond-question, self-condemning statement.

"He's my secret weapon," Slaughter agreed softly.

Cas wondered if that had been enough of a confession. Tolemek, if he was indeed standing out there, didn't barge in. In fact, when the door opened a few minutes later, it was the guard who returned. Cas didn't catch a glimpse of anyone else in the corridor. Had she accomplished anything at all with her probing?

"One last question," she whispered, hoping the guard wouldn't hear or wouldn't think anything of it. "What are you planning to do to my city? Besides find Colonel Zirkander?"

Boots still up, Slaughter laced his hands behind his neck and smiled. "Invade it, of course. And destroy it. With Tolemek's help."

Cas stared at the control panel in horror. If she didn't do something to stop them, there would be pirates assaulting the city by midnight. She had to crash the ship before it reached the harbor. No choice.

Chapter 12

THE LIGHTS OF THE CAPITAL came into view on the dark horizon, the bright pinpoints close and dense in the miles around the harbor, then growing more sparse as they traveled into the hills beyond. Heavy clouds had gathered in the sky overhead, but the rain—or maybe it would be snow here in Iskandia—hadn't started yet. Winds already batted at the dirigible, and Cas had to keep a hand on the controls to stay on course.

At the northern end of the harbor, atop Pinnacle Rock, the lighthouse sent its beam seaward. The craft had already passed the lookout towers miles out in the surf, where men were stationed to give advance warning if enemy steamers or airships appeared on the horizon. No alarms had gone up, not at the approach of an Iskandian freighter.

On the butte at the southern end of the harbor, gas lamps burned along the runway and all around the hangars of the airbase. For weeks, Cas had dreamed of seeing home again, but approaching it in a stolen vessel, with Captain Slaughter rubbing his hands and smiling as they grew nearer... that hadn't been part of the dream.

Her stomach twisted with anxiety as she eyed the controls beneath her fingers, contemplating a crash for the five hundredth time. She hadn't seen Tolemek since the captain relayed the story of their past. She had hoped he might do something and that she wouldn't feel compelled to crash the dirigible, but he hadn't sent so much as a note all afternoon. Of course, Slaughter hadn't left the navigation area for more than a minute, either. He was watching her carefully, his gun in his lap. It had been there since the truth serum had worn off, a moment she had sensed by the hard, cold stare he turned upon her. As if she were the one to have fed him the stuff. Maybe he thought she had.

She tried not to watch that gun. She would die if she crashed the ship, anyway, she told herself. What did it matter if he was thinking of shooting her? That would simply ensure the vessel's plummet into the ocean, unless these log-heads could dock a dirigible on their own. Granted, she hoped to survive a crash, inflicting most of the damage to the captain's side of the ship. Surviving a bullet to the head was a trickier matter.

"Take us to Air Pier Two," Slaughter said. "It looks quiet there."

Though she had other things on her mind, it bothered Cas that he was familiar with the harbor.

She adjusted their course slightly. She had already lowered their altitude, and the roar of the waves was audible over the soft rumble of the propellers in the back. By design, their route would take them in past Pinnacle Rock and the lighthouse. It was visible to the left side of their viewing window. She didn't angle them too close to it, not yet.

An irritating bleep sounded on a panel to Slaughter's left. Technically, he was in the co-pilot's seat, even if he had yet to touch a control.

He frowned at the noise. "What's that?"

More bleeps followed the first.

"I'm not sure," Cas said. "What's that label say? Something to do with the hydrogen mix in the envelope, isn't it?"

The hydrogen was fine—she was running a routine test of the alarm systems and hoping Slaughter wouldn't recognize it as such. He was no stranger to airships, but maybe his unfamiliarity with an Iskandian model would confuse him. She only needed him distracted for a moment. As he frowned at the display, she nudged the control lever. Ever so slightly, the dirigible's course shifted. More of the lighthouse—and the massive rock it was perched upon—came into view.

"The levels look fine," the captain said.

"Can you stop that beeping?"

He pushed a couple of buttons. "I don't know. Aren't the controls over by you?"

"Not for the balloon gases. There's just a display up here. I think you have to adjust things in engineering." Cas urged him to go back there for a moment to do so, or at least to talk to the engineer.

Instead, Slaughter squinted suspiciously at her. He happened to glance through the viewport too. His eyes widened, and she sighed. They were lower than the lighthouse now, skimming along a couple dozen feet above the waves, but that rock was visible, thanks to the city lights behind it, so he would see that more of it occupied their horizon now.

"You're off course," the captain said. "The pier is over there."

Cas did her best to pretend she was trying to adjust the course without actually touching anything. "Strange. It's not responding."

The captain's pistol came up to her head so fast she barely had time to lift her hands from the controls. The cold metal muzzle pressed against her temple.

"Adjust the course, girl."

Hands hovering over the controls, her rapid heartbeat echoing in her ears, Cas tried to make what might very well be the last decision of her life. If she took them to the dock, there was still a chance she could escape somehow once they were in town, report to her superiors, and warn them of the impending pirate attack. But if she crashed and killed Slaughter, the leader of this whole invasion scheme, this attack might never happen.

Cas set her jaw and dropped her hands to the controls. She made an abrupt turn, and Pinnacle Rock filled the air ahead.

Slaughter's finger flexed on the trigger. "Wrong choice."

Something cracked, and Cas ducked, nearly pitching out of her seat. She caught herself on the control panel. She touched her temple, even though her mind had caught up with her reflexes, and she realized that crack hadn't been a pistol being fired. Nor had she been hurt. Slaughter, on the other hand, was crumpled on the floor beside his chair, grabbing his head and writhing.

Tolemek stood behind him, wearing a heavy cloak and carrying his bag slung over one shoulder. He lowered a truncheon clutched in one hand; he held a syringe with a big needle attached in the other.

"Yes," he told the man at his feet. "It was."

When Slaughter tried to get to his knees, Tolemek dropped the truncheon, grabbed him, and jabbed the needle into his neck. He thumbed the plunger down, and the red-brown liquid—it reminded Cas of blood—was pumped into the captain's vein.

Cas could only stare, relieved by his intervention but also horrified by his method. "Will that kill him?" she asked.

"No." Tolemek pulled out the needle and tossed the syringe onto the control panel. "Uh, Cas?" He pointed at Pinnacle Rock, which was now taking up their entire view. "Please don't crash us."

Though Cas wasn't sure about all of the ramifications of Tolemek's appearance—Did this mean he was on her side now? Did he control the engineer and the guards? Could he stop the invasion of his colleagues?—she grabbed the controls and pulled them hard to the side.

The dirigible had the maneuverability of a boulder. Afraid it would be too late, she watched with wide eyes as they flew closer and closer to that rock. Too late. She had been too late.

A jolt coursed through the dirigible.

"Balloon hitting?" Tolemek asked.

"Yes."

"Will it, ah...?"

"Rip? They're pretty sturdy, but this is a freighter, not a military-grade vessel."

Another jolt went through the craft. Cas imagined a child's balloon being scraped along a brick wall until it popped. She also imagined the gas flowing out and being ignited by the flame of the lighthouse. No, it was too high above them for that. She hoped. The worst that would happen is that they would drop into the harbor, and probably not until they were close to the docks anyway. If they had to, they could swim. There weren't *usually* sharks in the harbor.

"You look concerned," Tolemek observed.

"At this very moment or just in general?" Cas asked, her humor bleak.

"At this moment. Your usual look is more determined."

She wasn't surprised when a bleeping started up on the alarm panel. This wasn't a systems test; not this time. The envelope had been breached. "That may be a small leak," she said, though she didn't feel very optimistic. "We're not that far from the waterfront at least. But, ah..." She tapped the altimeter at the same time as another alarm started bleeping. "We've dropped below the level of the air piers."

"If this were a Cofah airship, we would be able to land in the water safely, balloon notwithstanding. Am I correct in guessing that this gray metal box won't float?"

Cas decided it wasn't the time to go into aerodynamics and explain why the Cofah wooden-sailing-ship-in-the-sky designs were idiotic. "We'll be fine," she said, maneuvering the controls. "I'm going to take us to one of the sea docks. We'll land right on top."

"Those docks all have a lot of ships tied to them."

"I see that." Cas licked her lips. The docks weren't particularly wide either. They were meant for people to walk along, not for dirigibles to use as landing pads.

She guided them closer, aiming for the center of one of the wider ones. The alarms bleeping in her ears didn't help her concentration, but she had flown a lot faster before, while being shot at, so this wasn't *that* big of a challenge. She just had to accept that those merchant and fishing vessels on either side of the dock were going to get smothered if the balloon's frame had been damaged, and the envelope fully deflated.

As they drifted lower, Cas watched the street beyond the head of the dock. It was only an hour past sunset. Though the waterfront wasn't traditionally busy at night, there might be people about, witnesses for this. A couple of horse-drawn carriages and a steam wagon passed on the street. It was too dark and too far to make out details, so it was doubtlessly only in her imagination that the passengers gaped and pointed at her.

Cas turned off the propellers as they reached her target landing spot. In another moment, the bottom of the dirigible cabin settled on the dock. The creaking and groaning of boards drifted through the hull. She hoped the pilings were solid.

"I'm surprised the engineer hasn't come up to check on us," she said, turning off the controls and searching for the mechanism that opened the side doors and extended the gangplank. "Or yell at me."

Tolemek pointed at the syringe. "Neither the engineer, nor the guards are awake. The fog machine has also been disabled."

"What does that mean?" Cas whispered. She was thinking of the attack on her city—would the other pirates call it off when they found the harbor untouched by those thick, obfuscating mists?

"That I can never go back."

Cas caught his reflection in the dark glass. His face was grimmer than a crematory, and his eyes were haunted, the eyes of a man wondering if he had made a mistake. Or condemned himself to death. She wished she could tell him he hadn't—in her eyes, he had certainly made the right choice, or at least the choice that helped her the most—but she wouldn't be able to protect him from her people. As soon as the law or the army identified him as a notorious pirate, he *would* be dead.

She blinked her eyes, turning to look at him. Seven gods, how was he going to get off the continent without being shot? And if he *did* get off, how would she ever see him again?

Tolemek handed her a parka, let his hand drop, then lifted it again. He touched the side of her head, a single soft stroke of her hair, then lowered his arm for a final time. "Let's get out of here before they wake up."

"Are you sure it wouldn't be wiser to... ah..." Cas waved vaguely at the inert captain. It wasn't in her stomach to shoot an unconscious man, but if Tolemek let them live, wouldn't he have to worry about them coming after him to seek revenge for the rest of his life?

"I'm sure it would." Tolemek walked out the door, and she barely heard his addition. "And I'm sure I can't."

* * *

The air smelled of damp and snow, and the cold breeze scraped at Tolemek's bare arms, another reminder to keep his hood over his head and his cloak wrapped around him. As if he needed reminders. He knew he couldn't let himself be recognized here. He needed to finish his quest, then find a way off the continent. Forever.

Following Cas, who was practically bouncing as she strode down the waterfront street, made those thoughts hard to come by. If it hadn't been for her, he didn't know if he would have ever bothered to defy Goroth. He had long suspected what the captain had admitted under the effects of the truth serum, so the information hadn't been a shock. Realizing how much he cared that Cas knew the truth, that had been the shock. Goroth's words hadn't exactly exonerated him, but he hoped...

What? That she would forget his crimes and promise him her love?

Nice thought, but she was in love with her commander.

Cas stopped in front of a two-story building with lamps burning behind the shutters. "I'll be right back."

Port Authority, a sign by the door read. Tolemek didn't stop her from going in. He couldn't bring himself to kill Goroth, but if the man ended up arrested, was that any worse than what he had done to Tolemek all those years ago? Except, if the Iskandian port authorities found him, he would be arrested, then *killed*. Well, maybe not. He was a crafty sod; he might find a way to escape. Tolemek decided to hope he did. He snorted at himself, wondering if other pirates who turned on their allies felt as conflicted afterward.

The first snowflakes fell as Cas came back outside. Two men in dark uniforms and armed with rifles jogged out of the building after her, heading toward the dock with the dirigible cabin balanced on it, its balloon sagging against the frame as gas escaped.

"I need to report in." Cas took his arm and led him up a street. The butte with the air hangars on it loomed in the distance. "Let them know where I've been and warn everyone that there might still be pirates coming. Where, ah, do you have plans still?"

"Griffon Street."

She halted, her hand tightening on his arm.

"Just to question him," Tolemek said. "I don't know how I'll get back home to see my sister, even if I find what I seek, but my quest hasn't changed. Odd as it may sound to you, if that Cofah soldier spoke the truth, Zirkander is the most likely one here to know about soulblades." He expected an objection, if not an accusation. To her, this all might be part of some lie. She might believe killing Zirkander was what he had wanted all along.

"I'll go with you then. I can report in to him as easily as the night duty officer, and things will probably happen faster that way, anyway." Cas smiled, leading him up the street again.

Tolemek wished that smile were for him and not for the commander she would shortly see again. He strode through the snow at her side, keeping his hood low as they passed horsemen and vehicles. Fortunately, the impending snow was keeping many people off the streets. Unfortunately, that snow might make for poor enough weather that the armada of pirates might attack the city anyway, especially if they believed the fog was on its way.

"There's one thing about your quest that I don't understand," Cas said, as they walked between pools of light cast by the gas lamps on the corners, the airbase butte looming larger with every block.

"Just one? I haven't spoken of the details to anyone."

"What can one of these swords do for her? Cure her of some malady? You've never said what's wrong with her."

No, he hadn't. He didn't speak of her to anyone. But what secrets did he truly have left from Cas now? For good or ill, she knew a lot about him. Maybe it was foolish, but he had come to trust her. He doubted she would relay this information to anyone who might use it against him. Besides, he might need her to help convince Zirkander to talk to him. Tolemek would be shocked if the infamous pilot greeted him with anything except guns.

"It's not a disease," Tolemek said. "If it were, I would have... I'm sure I could have done something for her. She's twelve years younger than me, and I always felt like her protector when she was little. We were close, especially after our brother died. But she can't take care of herself. Even now, as an adult. It's worse now. She's in the sanitarium back home. Father put her there when she started hurting herself. I didn't agree with that, abandoning her to strangers, to people who would rather drug her than deal with her, to put her in some dark room where she's kept restrained day and night, so she can't damage herself or others." For a moment, he didn't see the streets of the Iskandian capital, but the halls of that dreadful place. "I broke her out a few years ago." His lips twisted wryly, remembering the headline in the newspaper. Notorious Pirate Stages Raid on Home for the Mentally Disturbed. "I thought that maybe if she came with me, if she was in a better place, with someone who cared, maybe she'd improve."

Cas turned up a new street, one that sloped upward, with twin wrought-iron gates at the end. Tolemek doubted he had much time to finish his story.

"She wasn't any better. And my pirate life was no improvement for her. She wasn't safe with me, and I reluctantly returned her to the sanitarium. Temporarily, I told myself. Until I found the solution. I had, at least, found the reason for her problems."

Cas tilted her head toward him. "What?"

"Dragon blood. She was born with—*cursed* with—an affinity for magic. From my studies, I know that can manifest itself in a number of ways, and for her, it's made her... crazy. My only hope is to find her a soulblade to bond with, maybe one that holds the essence of a healer, someone who can help her and teach her to understand her abilities and come to terms with them." And not to be terrified of the world and herself. He sighed.

There was an alarmed—maybe even horrified—expression in her eyes when Cas looked at him, but all she said was, "That's, uhm, good of you to try to help her."

Magic was even less tolerated here than in his homeland, he gathered, but he needn't stay here once he found what he sought. He couldn't.

A boom sounded in the distance, back in the direction they

had come from. The harbor. A bright orange blaze had erupted from the waterfront. No, from out on the docks. From the very dock where they had landed? Even though they had climbed up a hill, there were too many buildings in the way and too much distance to be sure, but he certainly didn't see the balloon, partially deflated or otherwise, of a dirigible down there. Not now.

"One of your booby traps?" Tolemek asked, a numbness creeping over his limbs. He had given Goroth and the other pirates a sizable dose of that sedative. Chances were they were still on the deck in that cabin, or they had been. He closed his eyes. He hadn't meant to kill them.

"No. That shouldn't have happened." Cas sounded genuinely surprised.

"The hydrogen in the envelope must have ignited."

"A rip in the balloon shouldn't have caused anything more than a leak. The cabin was in good shape when we landed. There was nothing burning, no reason the gas should have been touched with fire."

Tolemek believed her. Crafty as she was, he didn't know how she could have set something like that up from the navigation area anyway. "Your port authorities then."

"That's hard to imagine. I could see them blowing up a pirate ship if it was out there far enough that it wouldn't damage anything else, but blowing up one of our own freighters just because it had some unconscious pirates on it? And when it was surrounded by privately owned vessels? The king would take more than their jobs over something like that."

"Hm."

"We'll have to wait and solve the mystery later," Cas said. "I have to report in."

Tolemek nodded, and they headed up the street again.

It turned out the army installation wasn't on top of the butte—it simply had a view of it from a hill overlooking the city and the harbor. It covered dozens of city blocks with a wall and razor wire marking the perimeter. The gates Tolemek had seen in the distance were guarded.

Cas stepped into an alley a couple of blocks from the entrance, waving for him to follow. "*I* can walk up to the guards and get in without... well, there will be questions asked, but they wouldn't be, so, who's your friend. Or so, which cell block shall we stick your pirate prisoner in."

The idea of him as the prisoner amused him, given that he was armed with weapons and the formulas and gadgets in his bag, while she wore little more than the parka he had given her. Still clad in those horrible cloth shoes, she didn't even have decent footwear.

"I anticipated this. You go ahead without me." Tolemek drew one of his leather spheres out of his bag, knowing she would recognize it. "I'll find my own way in."

Cas gazed up at him. Trying to read his face? To elicit a promise that he wouldn't hurt anyone? He thought about saying that he trusted her not to tell the gate guards which alley he was in and how many men they would need to subdue him, but decided it didn't need to be said at this point.

"Be careful," Cas whispered, then stood on tiptoes, resting her hands on his shoulder.

He wasn't expecting it, so he almost dropped his sphere when she kissed him. What a mess that would have made. Pirate and lieutenant believed to be dead found snoring and entwined in back alley, lips pressed together. Except they weren't entwined yet. Tolemek hurried to pocket the sphere so he could bend down, wrap his arms around her, and return the kiss. This would make it all the harder to leave, but he didn't care. In choosing her over Goroth, something had changed for her, and she was letting him know. With a soft, lingering kiss full of longing and... regret. Or maybe those were his own feelings. Still, when she drew back and he cupped the side of her face, his thumb found moisture on her cheek.

"You be careful too," he whispered. "I know you don't want to believe it, but if that sorceress *is* controlling your commander, he may not be the man you're expecting."

Cas snorted and walked out of the alley.

He wasn't sure why he had added that. Because he hoped it

was true? Because he wanted Cas to have faith in him instead of Zirkander? Idiot. He should have said, thank you for the sublime kiss and let's do it again sometime.

Chapter 13

Cas turned onto Griffon Street, her stride quick. The snow was falling more heavily, and the cold pavement pressed through the bottoms of her thin shoes. She had only the memory of the heat of Tolemek's kiss to keep her warm, something she couldn't, alas, spend as much time thinking about as she would have liked. The soldiers at the gate had recognized her—one of the perks of being a part of Wolf Squadron—and given her hearty thumps on the back and ushered her straight into the courtyard. It had been clear in their eyes that they wanted her story—especially since she still wore the ridiculous-for-this-climate prison smock beneath her borrowed parka—but a distant alarm had gone off, and they had all known stories would have to wait. Cas had to report immediately. She recognized the bong-bong-bongs and knew the alarm originated at one or more of the ocean watch towers beyond the harbor and were being relayed into the city. It wasn't the ear-splitting siren screech that would announce an all-out attack was imminent, but it did mean unfriendlies had been spotted in the sky, and it was strongly suggested that some fliers be sent out to check on them. *That* meant the colonel might be racing out his door right now.

Cas turned her walk into a run, watching the sidewalks of the officers' quarters ahead. There were larger houses on the left side of the street, for those who had families, but she looked right, toward a little cottage past a fountain featuring a dragon, its wings spread, ready to head into battle. The home's front window was shuttered, but a lantern glowed behind the slats. Good. Maybe he hadn't left yet. If she caught him, she might be able to go along in addition to briefing him. By the gods, she missed her work—and her team. And she would love to help Wolf Squadron finish off that pirate outpost. Tolemek could ask his questions about swords later.

She jogged up the sidewalk, slipping on the icy cement, its cracks thickened with snow. She missed her uniform and her boots too. She made it to the door without decorating her backside with snow and banged out a knock as hard and fast as the automatic gunfire on a flier.

"Colonel?" she called when seconds dragged by without a response. He usually answered a door knock with a "Yeah?" no matter what he was doing or who was calling. He could have left and forgotten to cut out the lamp.

But she heard footsteps, and a broad smile stretched her lips. Until the door opened.

A woman stood there. The wheels in Cas's wagon stuttered to a stop. It wasn't *unheard* of for the colonel to keep female company—though he didn't usually bring women back to the fort—but this woman appeared more regal than he usually went for. Oh, she was a beauty, with striking pale blue eyes and rich thick black hair held back from her face with combs, but she looked like someone who belonged in an upscale parlor rather than the dingy taverns Zirkander favored.

Tolemek's warning, the one Cas had dismissed with nothing more than a derisive snort, rushed to the forefront of her mind. This was not some sorceress who was—she refused to use the world controlling—*influencing* the colonel, was she? Surely sorceresses were old and gray with bent backs and canes. Or staffs. Or brooms. No, that was witches. Seven gods, this was superstitious nonsense. She was gaping at some poor woman in stockings who was being dusted with snowflakes blowing through the doorway. Did Cas even have the right house?

"Uh." She glanced past the woman's shoulder—she was taller than Cas, but who wasn't?—toward the combination kitchen, dining, living room. Yes, those were the colonel's pictures on the wall, a mix of fliers that had been his over the years and of pilots he had served with, along with a portrait of his world-exploring father standing arm-in-arm with his mother. That was *definitely* his tacky yellow-and-green plaid couch, a hand-me-down he had supposedly received from a now-deceased commanding officer and that he refused to part with—most of the pilots in the squadron were convinced he secretly adored it, or perhaps adored the appalled looks people had when they saw it. "Is, uhm, Colonel Zirkander here?"

The woman had been silently studying Cas even as she was studying the woman—and the couch—and said, "He's at a special meeting at the airbase. About you, I believe."

That made Cas's attention lurch back to the woman with the speed of a bullet. "What?" How could this woman possibly know who she was?

Because she was a sorceress and omnipotent...

Cas shook her head, suddenly wishing Tolemek were at her back with his bag full of concoctions.

"Lieutenant Ahn, isn't it?" The woman's voice was pleasant enough, melodious even, if oddly accented. Either way, it didn't make Cas feel any less uneasy. "He was stomping around, muttering and cursing all afternoon, waiting for a response from his commanders. His Captain Haksor thought he recognized you on a pirate outpost, and he's been trying to get permission to take his men back out. I believe this meeting might be about attempting to recruit people willing to go out whether permission has been granted or not. He was too agitated to unpack the details for me before taking off again." She smiled—fondly?

Cas pushed her hand through her hair. "I had wondered if anyone saw... I'm sorry, who are you exactly?" She hadn't been gone *that* long, and it seemed strange that the colonel had gone from not being involved with any women—the squadron gossip chain was quite up-to-date and accurate when it came to the personal affairs of its officers—to having one live with him in a few short weeks. Or... how long had he been back from his post in the mountains anyway?

"Sardelle." The woman brushed snowflakes out of her hair, stepped aside, and gestured toward the living area. "Would you like to come in? You seem agitated yourself."

"That's not a strong enough word. But, no. I have to find him. If he's—" Cas's mouth tumbled open. What if the colonel, thinking he needed to fly off to look for her, led the squadron out this very night and wasn't here for the pirate attack? The bong-bong-bongs drifting up from the harbor hadn't elevated to a more demanding alarm, but they hadn't gone away, either. "I haven't reported in anywhere yet. I have to find him. Or General Ort."

She backed up a step, debating between a polite goodbye and simply racing down the street to the headquarters building, but bumped into someone.

"*I'd* like to come in," Tolemek said. His expression was impossible to read, but his eyes had that determination he had accused her of. And maybe something of a lupine fierceness as well.

"Uhm, Sardelle," Cas said, feeling ridiculous doing introductions when she had barely met the woman herself. "This is Tolemek, the pirate who helped me escape."

"Pirate?" Sardelle's brows rose in mild curiosity, not the alarm one might expect from the announcement.

"He's retired now," Cas said, "though he hasn't turned in his garish wardrobe yet." She patted Tolemek's chest—the hide vest and trousers weren't so bad, since they displayed his physical attributes nicely, but the shark-tooth necklace and barbed-metal wrist bracers had to go.

Tolemek was keeping his eyes on the woman—maybe he was thinking of sorceresses too?—but he murmured, "Big talk from someone wearing a potato sack," and swatted her on the butt.

At first, the familiarity surprised her, but she *had* kissed him, not twenty minutes ago. He must have considered that an invitation to engage in other sorts of intimate exchanges. After a brief consideration, Cas decided she liked that and gave him a little grin. Of course, she would like it more after she reported in, and the world returned to normal.

"I have to go," she said. "Are you sure you want to stay here? Or that her invitation applies to you?"

Sardelle's face was hard to read. She wasn't armed, wearing only an attractive blue dress with a braided cord for a belt— no place to tuck knives or guns there—but she didn't appear alarmed by Tolemek's pirate garb—or the pistols holstered at his waist. Her arm was still out, extended toward the living area, and she tilted her head in that direction now too.

"Come in, Mister Tolemek. I don't imagine it's safe for you on the streets of this installation."

No, even if he weren't wearing such dubious clothing, with that Cofah bronze skin, he was clearly not an Iskandian soldier.

"Be careful," Cas whispered after him when he started inside.

He looked over his shoulder and nodded gravely to her. Cas had no choice but to leave him, but as the door shut and she ran back down the street, she wondered if she was making a mistake.

* * *

Tolemek's senses tingled. He was uneasy, yes, but there was more to it than that. It was almost as if he could feel... magic. Ridiculous since, aside from his sister, he had never been around anyone with otherworldly power, at least not to his knowledge, and his sister didn't make his nerves jangle like this. When the front door thumped shut, he almost jumped over the awful couch, so he could spin around, putting it between himself and the woman. The sorcereress. His hunches might not be scientific, but he trusted them.

The woman—Sardelle, wasn't it?—leaned against the wall. She wasn't armed, and she wasn't leering at him with a threat on her lips, but he nonetheless felt like he had walked into the dragon's lair unarmed.

"What brings you to Ridge's doorstep, Cofah pirate?" Sardelle asked, her eyes narrowed. Her tone might not be threatening, but it wasn't friendly, either.

Ridge—that was Zirkander's first name, right? Ridgewalker? Something like that.

"Originally, I'd thought to kill him." It might not have been the brightest thing he could have said, but he wasn't going to admit that he was here looking for her—or her sword. "He ruined my career in the army. I was in command of an infantry company defending an airship. He and his pilots destroyed it and almost everyone on it."

"Through chicanery or in honorable combat?" she asked, though the way she crossed her arms over her chest and gave him a frank stare suggested she knew the answer. Odd, he hadn't expected her to defend Zirkander. If she was truly controlling him for some ulterior motive, wouldn't she see him as little more than a pawn?

"I'm not sure I'd call your dragon fliers all that honorable when they zero in on airships," Tolemek said.

"Airships that have a long history of dropping bombs on our people."

"*Our?*"

It was a simple question, but she didn't respond right away. "Do I not look Iskandian?"

"It's not what you *look* like that's the issue. You feel..." Tolemek stopped himself before he could reveal information he should keep to himself. She would be warier if she knew he knew what she was. Better to have her think he was just a big dumb pirate.

"Interesting," she said and studied him from head to toe.

Too late. He had hinted at too much. Was she even now reading his thoughts? The sorcerers of old had been able to do that, but would some modern version be as strong? The histories said all of the major lines had been wiped out and that there were none left with substantial power, or even the faculty to teach. Unless one could find a soulblade.

But if she wasn't that strong, how had she defeated a jungle shaman? Those people, on their isolated and distant continent, had survived the purge of three centuries past, and were rumored to have power that nearly matched that of the old Iskandian sorcerers.

"Ridge was your original reason for coming, you say," Sardelle said. "What is your *current* reason for being here?"

Tolemek faced a wood stove in the corner of the room, as if he were deep in thought, though he only wanted his back to hide the fact that he was reaching into his bag. "Mostly... Cas. Lieutenant Ahn." He bypassed one of his leather spheres—that would affect him as well as her, not to mention starting a fight if it didn't work—and grasped a vial of his truth serum. He had no idea how he might convince her to drink it—did Iskandian sorceresses enjoy inviting Cofah pirates for wine?—but it seemed a far more viable way to get the answers he wanted than holding a knife to her throat. "We escaped from a Cofah prison together. I've come to care about her. I wanted to make sure she made it home safely."

"A feat that could have been accomplished by leaving her at the dock," Sardelle said. "You risked a lot to walk her to her door. And not even her door, at that. I believe she lives in the barracks."

Tolemek distracted himself by wondering if her room was still there or if her people, believing her dead, would have sent her things back to her family. It would be a shame if she had to keep wearing that canvas smock around.

Focus.

"I did risk a lot," he agreed, facing the woman again. She hadn't moved from the wall. "I heard an interesting story on the way back here, and I wished to check on the details." He gestured toward the little kitchen. "Perhaps we could discuss it over a glass of wine."

"And poison?" Sardelle arched a single brow.

Tolemek froze. Apparently he hadn't been as subtle as he had thought. This whole situation had him flustered. He had planned to stalk her down and speak with her. Why hadn't he prepared himself better?

Because it was Zirkander he had expected to run into here, not his sorceress.

"Poison?" he said, mouth dry. "No. If I meant to kill you, I would shoot you."

"You could try." Those pale blue eyes had taken on the temperature of ice.

Yes, he had found his sorceress. And what was he going to do about it? He supposed he could try to force the truth serum down her throat. But she looked confident about responding to a physical threat. Maybe she would simply answer his questions. No, she probably wouldn't, not when magic was so feared on this continent. It was hard to believe she was here, on an Iskandian military base.

Oh.

"They don't know you're here, do they?" Tolemek asked. "Or maybe they've seen you, but they don't know what you are."

Some of the confidence faded from the woman's face. Bull's-eye. She lifted her chin. "Somehow I doubt you, pirate, are going to be the one to tell them anything. Your word can't be any more trusted here than mine."

"How about I just tell *him*?" Tolemek waved toward the inside of the cottage to suggest Zirkander. "Or have Cas do it. He has no reason to trust me, but he'll trust her."

Sardelle's eyebrow twitched upward. "Ridge knows."

Tolemek rocked back on his heels. He knew some sorceress was controlling him? And he wasn't moving the world to try and stop that? He was just accepting the fact and letting her stay in his house too?

She's not controlling him, genius. She's sleeping with him.

Already on his heels, Tolemek stumbled backward, grabbing the wall for support when the voice sounded in his head. Yes, that had been *in* his head. And, dearest gods and demons, it hadn't even been her, had it?

"Who are—who was that?" he rasped, half to Sardelle and half to the empty room.

Sardelle didn't respond as he had expected. She dropped her face into her hand, shook her head, and groaned something that sounded like, "Jaxi."

Sardelle is too polite to root around in your thoughts. I'm not. Get to the point here and leave her alone. Trouble's coming, thanks to you. A lot of it.

Tolemek sensed the impatience of the other... voice, but he couldn't help but blurt, "Who are you?"

A sigh whispered through his thoughts. *If you must respond to me—and let me stress how optional that is—you can think the words. No need to look like an idiot for talking to yourself.*

By now Sardelle had lifted her head, but she was gazing out the window at something. At least that was the impression she gave; the shutters were still closed.

Tolemek silently repeated, *Who are you?*

Jaxi.

Jaxi?

I'm not giving you any more of my name. Not that you'd know what to do with it.

"We need to leave," Sardelle said, a hint of agitation—or maybe irritation—in her voice for the first time. "When you knocked out the guards, you left the way open for other unsavory persons to sneak onto the base."

She gave him a cool stare, but not a long one. She was busy striding into the little bedroom and, judging by the slamming of drawers and cabinets, packing. Tolemek turned out the lamp near the window and peeked through the gap between the shutters. The now-heavy snow made it tough to see farther than the street. If there were people out there, they weren't within sight yet. His heart clenched at the thought of Cas taking her flier up in this weather.

Huh. You do care about the girl.

Tolemek jumped, blurting, "Blind hedgehogs and bat spit."

"Does that pass for a curse in Cofahre?" Sardelle strode out of the bedroom carrying a wooden box tucked under her arm. She had also donned a thick cloak, fur-lined boots, and a weapons belt with a sword hanging in a decorative scabbard.

"In the presence of a lady, yes." Tolemek, realizing he had been clutching at his heart, lowered his hand.

Ladies, corrected the voice in his head.

It was only then, when he saw the sword on Sardelle's hip, that he realized who must be talking to him. He wasn't sure whether to be honored or terrified.

Both.

"Back door," Sardelle said. "Nobody's watching it yet."

"You're inviting me to come with you?" Tolemek asked.

She gave him a long look over her shoulder. "I'm inviting you to let me keep an eye on you. Regardless, you're not staying here to paw over Ridge's belongings. Or mine."

Also, she booby-trapped the house. There was a smile in the voice, as if the sword *wanted* him to stay here and trigger them.

Tolemek eased around the dining table and picked his way

toward the back door, walking gingerly as he wondered what magical booby traps might look like.

A tea kettle sitting on the cast-iron stove blatted a puff of steam. He kept himself from jumping again, though he was fairly certain there wasn't a fire stoked under the burners.

"I think your sword is teasing me," he whispered, stepping past Sardelle, who had paused to hold open the door for him. A half inch of fresh powder coated the neatly manicured lawn behind the cottage.

"Consider yourself lucky." Sardelle shut the door and locked it—without using a key. She simply waved her hand. "For a moment, I thought she was going to stop your heart, leaving me with the problem of explaining a mysteriously dead pirate on the living room rug."

Tolemek opened his mouth, but nothing came out. What was one supposed to say to that?

"I'm not quite caught up on who you are yet," Sardelle said, walking through the snow behind the cottage and slipping over to the backyard of the next house instead of using the pathway, "but she assured me Ridge would be pleased to have your head stuffed and mounted on his wall." She glanced at his face, or maybe his long ropes of hair. "I'd find that disturbing decor myself."

"You don't know who I am, but... your sword does?" Tolemek reminded himself that he had wanted this meeting. It just wasn't going at all how he had imagined.

"She doesn't need to sleep, so she has a lot more time on her hands to read the tabloids."

Please, I only deign to read scholarly periodicals and peer-reviewed journals.

They reached the last house on the block, and Sardelle angled toward an oak that had probably been there since the city was founded. Its thick, bare branches offered some protection from the snow, though the wind was picking up, swirling the flakes sideways as well as down.

"Do you hear what she says when she's talking in my head?" Tolemek asked.

Sardelle stopped behind the trunk and looked back toward Zirkander's house. "I make it a point to stay out of other people's conversations."

That hadn't been a no, he noted.

"They just broke the lock on the front door," Sardelle said. "Eight of them. Most went inside to search for whatever it is you people are searching for." She looked at him. An invitation to share?

"You're sure they're *my* people?"

"They share your suspect dress code."

Tolemek put a hand on the trunk of the tree and squinted into the snow, wishing he could see what she saw. Eight people. That was more than they'd had on the freighter. So, whoever was out there, it wasn't Goroth. But weren't all the other pirates supposed to be in the air, waiting to attack? Someone wasn't going along with the script.

A yelp of pain drifted across the yards, someone crying out from the house.

"Booby trap?" Tolemek asked.

"Yes. I'm not letting pirates, or anyone else, poke through my laboratory."

"Laboratory?" He eyed the wooden box under her arm, intrigued.

Sardelle didn't respond. She was staring intently at the house—or through the walls maybe.

A glint of orange appeared through the snow, and something sailed out of the night to land on the roof.

"Burning fuse," Tolemek said.

"I see it."

He thought she might snuff it out with her mind, or whatever sorcerers did, but the burning fuse turned to a blast of white and yellow light, with an accompanying boom. The snow muffled the noise somewhat, but dogs started barking somewhere down the street. Smoke shrouded the building.

Tolemek looked to the fort's big stone wall, the gray mass rising two blocks away. He had seen soldiers marching up there. It wouldn't be a secret that the base had been breached for much longer. Shouts rose in the distance, not from the nearby wall but from the direction of the front gate. The soldiers he had left sleeping must have awakened. He grimaced. When he had been coming up with a way to get in, he hadn't been worrying much about getting out. Of course, he hadn't been planning on setting off explosives either.

He checked on the house, expecting the smoke to clear to reveal little more than rubble, but it remained intact, not so much as a roof shingle torn free.

"It seems your ordnance team is ineffective," Sardelle said, her eyes gleaming.

"It's not *my* team."

"They've decided not to try again. They're heading toward the wall in the corner of the fort. I think they're planning to blow themselves a new exit gate." She glanced toward the top of the wall, much as Tolemek had done. "I intend to stop them."

"I'll help." Tolemek strode through the snow beside her. He doubted she needed his help, but if he could turn her into an ally, maybe she would help him with his quest, or at least point him in the right direction.

The flat look Sardelle gave him didn't suggest his help or company was appreciated, but he matched her pace anyway. She had invited him along, after all.

As they crossed the street near the wall, he spotted fewer soldiers than he would have expected running in step toward Zirkander's house. The bong-bong-bong of that alarm was still going off, so maybe men were being siphoned toward the harbor. Oddly, none of them noticed Tolemek and Sardelle crossing the street.

Tolemek spotted dark figures ahead, angling toward the corner she had mentioned. Hand delving into his sack, he jogged into the lead. He could deal with the men the same way he had with the guards, then tie them up afterward. Besides, he wanted to see who these people were, preferably before a sorceress obliterated them.

The bongs halted as he jogged toward them, trying to soften his steps so they wouldn't hear him coming. They were doing a lot of nervous pointing and gesturing. Already he had them pegged for lackeys. Goroth wouldn't have been stupid enough to hurl explosives and let everyone know he was in the compound. But *whose* lackeys?

When he was within fifteen meters, Tolemek thumbed the activator on his leather ball and chucked it into their midst. They had reached the wall, and two were crouching in the snow, setting something against its base. One noticed the ball hit the ground and jumped back, yanking a pistol free.

"Go ahead," Tolemek whispered. "Shoot it."

That would simply free the air-borne sedative more quickly.

The man didn't shoot the ball though. He kicked snow over it, tapped a comrade on the shoulder, and peered all around them. There was no camouflage to hide Tolemek except for the falling snow, but he had his next weapon ready. He had withdrawn and unfolded a collapsible blow gun, already loaded with special darts. He fired at the same time as the man—the pirate, yes, he wore the unlikely collection of stolen garments that so many of the Roaming Curse favored—spotted him.

Tolemek dropped, rolling to the side, expecting a shot. It never came. The man had dropped his gun to claw at his face. From his belly, Tolemek shot two more projectiles, glad the cold hadn't yet frozen his black cobwebs, as he called them. These darts were similar to the one he had fired at the guard back when he and Cas had been escaping that fortress. They expanded upon impact and stuck to the flesh like instant glue. A shot to the eyes or mouth was particularly effective.

After three shots, he was out, but by then, the sedating smoke from the leather ball had permeated the area. Though Tolemek couldn't see it from his spot on the snow, he saw the effects. Soon all eight men collapsed.

Rising to a crouch, he looked back to check on Sardelle. To see if she might be impressed, or at least pleased that he had dealt with these people so she hadn't had to incinerate them or turn them into frogs, or whatever her style was. She was only a few feet behind him, her gaze toward the wall, or maybe the harbor beyond it.

Before he could say a word, an ear-splitting wail started up. It seemed to come from the same amplifiers that had brought the bongs. It also seemed to say that whatever had been going on before was nothing compared to what was coming now.

"Attack," Tolemek whispered. What else could that alarm be meant to signal?

The aerosol from his ball should have dissipated, so he ran forward to the fallen pirates. He turned them over on their backs, checking faces. Two were covered with his black cobwebs, rendering the features indistinguishable, but a couple of the men seemed familiar, pirates he had seen around the outpost on occasion. He stared in surprise at the fourth man, recognizing him instantly. It was the Cofah corporal who had been seeking asylum.

"Guess you weren't on the *Burning Dragon* when it blew up," Tolemek muttered. "Was your captain, I wonder?" If Stone Heart had survived that attack but lost his ship... he would have a lot of new reasons to loathe Zirkander and the Iskandians.

Do you always interrogate unconscious men?

This time, Tolemek didn't jump at the voice in his head, but he doubted he would ever find it anything but jarring. *No.*

Good, because I can't imagine that with your skills you'd find it particularly effective.

"Your sword has gone from teasing me to insulting me," Tolemek said when Sardelle approached, carrying lengths of twine that he was fairly certain hadn't been among the items she took from the house. Unless they had come out of that box. He doubted it.

"That's how she bonds with a person." Sardelle tossed him four of the ropes, then knelt to tie the first of the downed men.

"Does she insult *you*?"

"Hourly."

Sardelle moved onto her second pirate, and Tolemek hurried to catch up. That siren wailing couldn't mean anything good. He wondered if Cas had found her squadron yet, and if she was even now preparing to go up into the gusting wind and heavy snow. She had sneered at the snail-like attributes of the dirigibles and airships, but being in one of those little fliers when nature was throwing a fit did not seem like a life-sustaining activity.

"She's not what I imagined in a soulblade," Tolemek said to distract himself from worrying. It wasn't as if he could do anything to help Cas, except maybe find out where Stone Heart was and what he was up to.

Sardelle paused in tying her third man. "You know what a soulblade is? That's not common anymore. Nor is talking openly about them." Her lips thinned and she glanced up at the wall. "Nor anything related to magic."

It occurred to him that she might be as much of an intruder here as he was. Well, no. She must be Zirkander's guest, but doubtlessly she was down on the books as girlfriend, not sorceress. So what would happen if the army found out?

By this point, he almost expected a threat from Jaxi, but the sword either wasn't paying attention to his thoughts or was chilled to silence at the idea of Sardelle being caught. Probably the former. From what little he had seen, he doubted much could chill the entity to silence.

"I've been researching them." Tolemek wondered if this might be his opportunity to broach the subject with her, to ask if she might know a way to help his sister.

But Sardelle was frowning down at one of the pirates—the former Cofah soldier. She couldn't have seen him and remember who he was, could she?

"He came to our outpost," Tolemek said, "blabbing about a battle in the mountains and a mine that Zirkander was guarding."

She met his eyes, her own blue ones sharp. "And of a strange woman with a glowing sword?"

"That might have been mentioned."

"I see." She looked like she might wish to cut the corporal's throat instead of merely tying him and leaning him against the wall for the soldiers to find, but she kept herself to using the twine. Roughly.

Then again, maybe it wasn't the time to ask for favors.

"They went this way," came a call from Griffon Street. The soldier raised his voice, "You men on the wall see anything?"

"No," someone responded from above, "but we're looking at..."

Tree branches stood in the way, and Tolemek couldn't see where the soldier might be pointed, but guessed the harbor. With the snow, he doubted any ships would be visible yet, but they had to know something was out there.

"Looks like the investigative team is approaching," Tolemek said, glad they had finished tying the unconscious men. "I'm presuming we don't want to be found here?"

"No." Sardelle pulled a rope out from under her cloak—there was definitely no way she had come out of the house with that. "Loop this around that dragon head up there, please. Climb up, then help me up. I'll keep the men on the wall distracted."

"As you wish."

Wondering when he had gone from thinking to interrogate the sorceress to taking orders from her, Tolemek made a loop of the end of the rope and tried for the indicated target, one of several dragon-head downspouts. It took him a few tosses, but he eventually lassoed one of the protrusions. He shimmied the fifteen feet up to the top, his vials clinking softly in his bag, then turned to help Sardelle.

"Catch," she whispered, and tossed the wooden box to him.

It wasn't heavy, and he caught it easily. His hands, wanting for mittens in the cold, were strangely warmed by the wood's touch. Something else magical? He was tempted to peek within, but Sardelle was nearly to the top. He helped her onto the walkway.

"Down the other side?" he asked, pointing to the street below.

She shook her head mutely, looking toward the harbor, not the street. "You know anything about that?"

When Tolemek turned, following her gaze, it was all he could do to keep from cursing. The snow had let up momentarily, and he could make out a layer of fog rising up from the harbor and curling through the streets of the city.

"No," he whispered. "I disabled the machine. Anyway, it was inside the freighter. The freighter that blew up." This couldn't be his doing. It couldn't.

Sardelle gave him a long, penetrating stare.

Tolemek dropped his face into his palm. Goroth might be dead or imprisoned, but his vision was going to come to pass. The fog and the snow were going to bury the city, and the armada was going to do its best to devastate it.

He peered through his fingers toward the butte, where the number of lights had doubled. Was Cas already there? Preparing her flier to go out in that mess? He groaned, wishing he could tell her to come back to him instead.

"Come on," Sardelle said, pointing to the street. "We need to get up there before they take off. I have something that will help them." Her voice lowered, and the wind almost kept him from hearing her next words. "If they'll accept it."

Chapter 14

Cas bounced from foot to foot, almost wishing she had run up the path to the top of the butte instead of taking the aerial tram. She knew from previous experience with bets and stopwatches that the tram was faster, but it didn't *feel* faster. The weather was getting worse by the minute, and she feared the squadron, wanting to deal with the threat before the storm began in earnest, would take off without her. It was only at General Ort's insistence that she had taken the time to sprint to the barracks and change into her flight uniform and grab her goggles, scarf, and cap. Granted the sturdy boots and fur-lined jacket were more appropriate to the winter weather, but if she missed catching up with the colonel and the others, and if they found trouble out there—trouble she might have advised them on—she would pummel the nearest target with bullets, whether it was something living or not.

"You're lucky you're heading up here at all, ma'am," the sergeant operating the tram said, the wind nearly stealing his words. It was gusting hard from the north, and the cabin, supported only by the cables above, rocked under the weather's influence. Taking off would be extremely challenging. He waved at her shifting feet. "I'm about to close the tram down for the night. Inclement conditions."

"Better keep it running. Pirates are coming to attack the city." Even as she spoke the bong-bong-bong alarm bell escalated to an undulating siren call.

The sergeant asked something, but Cas burst out of the tram cabin as soon as they reached the butte. She sprinted for the hangar, scarcely paying attention to the icy ground beneath her feet. She threw open the door and nearly crashed into someone's back. Two men were standing there, discussing something while controlled chaos—pilots and the ground crew racing to and fro, preparing the fliers—went on in the hangar in front of them. The man on the right was the only person who could wrinkle a leather jacket and scarf—and the rest of his uniform—on a consistent basis, so she knew him from behind: Captain Crash Haksor. The man on the left had his cap tilted at a familiar rakish angle.

"Lieutenant Ahn reporting for duty, sir," she said around a lump in her throat.

Cas had barely gotten her hand up for a salute before the two men spun toward her and she found herself engulfed in a hug. She wasn't even sure who it was, as she found her feet lifted from the ground and her face buried in the shoulder of a jacket, inhaling the scent of worn leather. Someone thumped her on the back, which was followed by the sound of boots pounding the cement floor, and a lot more thumps. And more hugs. And more time spent with her feet in the air. It was overwhelming, and as much as she appreciated the enthusiasm, she had to fight the urge not to wriggle free and escape for a gasp of fresh air. She reminded herself that they had all thought she was dead. The other women, Captain Blazer and Lieutenant Solk, were the only ones who didn't try to pick her up, though they did clap her on the shoulder. Blazer's usually-irritating head pat was a welcome expression of affection this time, due to its sedateness.

Cas was about to say something to the officers—her friends—gathered around when a straggler ran up, grease smearing his hair and snow dusting his shoulders. Lieutenant Pimples Averstash had been the youngest member of Wolf Squadron until she signed on, and he surprised her by pushing everyone aside to give her a fierce hug and a big kiss on the cheek. It actually might not have been on the cheek if she hadn't turned her head in time. That was surprising—they'd always been friends, but she hadn't known he had cared *that* much—and she couldn't find words for a moment.

"Cas, I lo—missed you," he blurted.

She tried not to look like the proverbial antelope in the hunter's sights as she stared at him, but doubted she managed.

"Lieutenant Averstash," came the colonel's drawl from the

side. "I know you're happy to see Ahn, but do you really think it's appropriate to kiss your fellow officers?"

Averstash released Cas's arms and skittered back, amidst stares, smirks, and chortles from the rest of the onlookers. Cas might have thanked Zirkander, but his brown eyes were glittering with amusement, and he wasn't bothering to hide his grin. She glowered at him. His grin broadened.

"Of course it's appropriate, sir," Averstash said, rubbing the back of his neck—it was flushed almost as red as his cheeks. "I'd kiss you, too, if not for the beard shadow. It looks itchy."

"I'll be sure not to shave anytime soon then."

"Donkey ass," Lieutenant Solk muttered to Averstash and elbowed him in the ribs.

"Sir?" one of the ground crew asked, jogging up to Zirkander's side. "Your flier is ready. Shall we get one ready for the L.T. too?" He nodded at Cas.

"Hells, yes," she said, relieved there was something in the hangar for her to fly. With poor W-48 at the bottom of the ocean, she had no right to a craft, but she had been praying Zirkander would deem her valuable enough to give her another without a long wait. "I didn't run across the city just to see these toad-kissers off."

"You heard the lieutenant, Grashon. Wipe the dust off W-5."

"Yes, sir."

"The rest of you cloud-hoppers, mount up," Zirkander called, his voice ringing in the hangar. "It's time to get these fliers in the air before the mosquitoes get here."

Cries of, "Yes, sir!" answered him, and men and women charged for their cockpits.

The colonel drew Cas aside, gave her a quick one-armed hug, and said, "It's fantastic to see you here alive. I didn't know if Crash had been delusional when he said he saw you on that pirate outpost. I want the whole story when there's more time, but I need as much intel as you can cram into two minutes now. This is a retaliatory attack from the pirates, we're guessing?"

"Yes, sir. They're bringing their whole armada."

"*Armada?*"

"All of the ships that were there for your attack and their big station too. You know that fog?" Cas searched his eyes, wondering how he had found the outpost in the first place, when the pirates' mobile location and their shroud of fog had kept the authorities from finding it for so long.

Zirkander nodded once, an odd hint of tension, or maybe wariness, entering his eyes at the question.

"The advance party, the ship they had me on, brought the machine for making it, and was planning to blanket the harbor so we'd have a hard time seeing them to fight and protect the city."

"Huh. That'll be as much of a hindrance for them as it is for us."

"I think their original plan was to have the fog going before the ships got here, so the soldiers in the watchtowers wouldn't see them coming, and we'd be caught completely unaware. But a pirate helped me escape and knock out the captain who thought everything up. He said he disabled the fog machine too."

The colonel's eyes narrowed. He couldn't possibly know who this pirate was who had helped her escape simply on that information, could he? Others could disable a machine... even if only by hurling it against a bulkhead a few times. She wanted to blurt out everything and try to explain how Tolemek had helped her and how he should be... if not exonerated at least not shot on sight. But there was no time. And if Tolemek stayed out of trouble, he might be able to finish his quest and escape before the army learned he was here anyway. So long as she didn't blab about it.

A rumble and a clank sounded as the big hangar doors were pushed open. Snow gusted inside, skidding past the wheels of the first flier, already in the queue, ready to roll out. Wind railed at the metal hangar roof, too, making it sound as if some giant were grabbing the corners and shaking and kicking at it. Outside, the night sky was utterly white. Cas swallowed. She liked to think of herself as fearless, or at least too focused to pay much attention to fear when she was out there, but this was going to be ghastly to fly in.

"Did they bring a snow-making machine too?" Zirkander asked dryly.

"No, sir."

"All right." He patted her on the shoulder. It was probably a gesture of dismissal, but he was looking toward the side door and chewing on his lip. "Hurry," he murmured, "we could use those devices more than ever for this one."

The words weren't for her, Cas knew, but she couldn't help but wonder at them. "Devices, sir?"

"My archaeologist friend is working on some communications devices from a recent Referatu excavation. I know the thought of magic will make everyone itch, but we've been waiting for the techs to figure out their wireless telegraph for ages, and it sounds like this could be a far better option for flier-to-flier communication anyway."

His *archaeologist* friend? Was that Sardelle? Magical communications? Cas couldn't imagine the general approving that for military use. Or any use. The colonel would be lucky if he didn't get shot for suggesting it. Well, no, maybe not. He was one of the few people in the army who could get away with... a lot.

Cas must have been gaping at him, for he added, "I've already spoken to the others about it. We're a superstitious lot, but the general consensus was that it would make us three times as effective to be able to speak to each other in the air." He grimaced. "For example, Crash could have told me he saw *you* on that outpost before we were all the way home. We could have gone back for you right away."

And gotten everyone mauled by pirates who had solidified their defenses by that point.

"Yes, sir. I was just shocked. I wouldn't think—"

"Colonel, you leading the way?" someone called from the hangar door. Wolf Squadron and Tiger Squadron were lined up, ready to leap into the white sky. Pilots secured in their cockpits stared down at Zirkander. They wanted him leading the way, Cas guessed from the concerned looks on those faces. Their goggles couldn't hide the fact that they were nervous about going out there in this weather.

Speaking of communications, Cas wished there had been a way to warn the city ahead of time. Would two squadrons be enough to defend the capital from that many pirates? If the general had been given advance notice, he could have called in the northern and southern continental air defenses for assistance.

Zirkander lifted a hand in acknowledgment and took a step toward his craft, but the side door banged open, snow swirling inside, along with a figure in a cloak and dress. Cas gaped. Given what Tolemek believed about Sardelle, and her own itchy instincts upon meeting her, Cas hadn't expected her to be wandering around the base. The sergeant from the tram was escorting her in, but he didn't have a hand on his pistol and wasn't restraining her in any way. Did that mean only Tolemek knew who she was? *What* she was? How could Zirkander have kept that hidden if she had been openly fighting with magic at that fortress battle? If a Cofah soldier had seen that, some of the Iskandians must have too. Of course, they were probably still stuck back at that mountain duty station. And Cas doubted there were any telegraphs, wireless or otherwise, snaking up into the Ice Blades range.

The colonel jogged over to the woman. She carried a wooden box under one arm. Something that might have been a sword poked outward under her cloak, but the garment covered it.

Cas watched the door, but nobody else came in. Not that she would have expected Tolemek to wander up here—or be allowed anywhere near the place without being shot at—but she couldn't help but wonder what had happened to him. If Sardelle had her sword with her, Tolemek certainly hadn't gotten his hands on it. It hadn't sounded like he wanted that specific blade, anyway, but what if he had ended up in a battle with the woman? And lost? She wasn't injured, nor was any of her hair even out of place after walking through the storm.

Zirkander met her a few steps inside the door, giving her a hug and a kiss. This earned numerous catcalls and whoops from the watching pilots. Cas looked away. She might have reconciled herself to the idea that the colonel was never going to be an option for her, but that didn't mean she liked watching him kiss other women. Especially not other *sorceress* women.

"That's one beautiful archaeologist," one of the ground crew muttered with longing as he walked past Cas.

Archaeologist, huh. She wanted the whole story—and to know if the colonel really knew what he was doing or if she was using him somehow—but there wasn't time. Zirkander knew it, too, for he kept his kiss short, traded a few words with Sardelle, and accepted the box from her with a wave.

He jogged to the end of the flier line, his hand delving into the box. It riveted Cas's eyes, because whatever was within emitted a soft blue glow. And Zirkander didn't seem to think anything of it. Crazy how much one's world could change in a few weeks away from home.

The colonel tossed a device—yes, that was a suitably vague word for whatever those things were—up to each pilot. Each of them caught it, but the faces ranged from slightly to extremely concerned. Nobody was as nonchalant as Zirkander. Even he might have been feigning it. Cas had always known him to be twitchy at the mention of magic. Before her time, he had lost a pilot because a military court judged the officer's skills to be too unbelievable for a mundane human being. He hadn't been sentenced to death, but there had been a lot of questions about the man's later suicide.

Zirkander tossed Cas one of the glowing devices as he ran by.

The little blue disk almost looked like a jewel. Or a crystal, Cas realized with a start. Like the flier power supplies. She had always assumed them the result of some secret government research—mundane, technologically based research, because that's what everyone always implied. But was it possible they were also artifacts from the time when sorcerers had walked the continent? And was that time as long past as everyone assumed?

Cas looked at Sardelle, standing near the door, watching the colonel. With concern? Cas couldn't tell. The woman's face might have been sculpted from ivory.

"Flying time, Ahn," Zirkander called, then lifted a hand

toward Sardelle and climbed into his flier.

Cas wrapped her hand around the blue object. She had no idea what she was supposed to do with it, but she would have to figure it out later. It was time to go.

* * *

As the snow flew in his eyes, the wind tugged at his cloak, the fog wrapped around his legs, and the cold chilled his bare arms, Tolemek thought of the warm, humid jungles of southern Cofahre. Had it only been three days ago he had been there, arranging to have himself captured and thrown into prison?

The wind snapped at his hood, and he grabbed it again, holding it over his eyes with one hand. Between the siren and the storm, the streets should have been empty, but there were squads of armed soldiers running to battle stations, horses and steam wagons charging about, and civilians of all ages standing in doorways, holding rifles or swords as they watched the gray sky. A pack of boys in an alley were gesturing with slingshots and clubs, making battle plans.

Any one of these people would be happy to shoot Tolemek if they saw his bronze skin. He hadn't considered wind when he had chosen the cloak to hide his features. Of course, he hadn't imagined himself skulking through the city, searching for the source of the fog, either.

Sardelle had promised to come help him after she delivered her box, and he could have waited in the shadow of the butte, but this was his responsibility. He had intended to disable the fog machine so it couldn't be used tonight. He should have destroyed it. That's what he would do now. One way or another. As soon as he found it...

The fog seemed heaviest down by the harbor, so he was slipping and sliding down the icy streets, heading in that direction. A baby squalled in a nearby building, reminding him that not just able-bodied fighters were in danger tonight. While he had been with the Roaming Curse, the pirates had occasionally raided small towns, but they had mostly preyed upon other ships and aircraft. Being down on the ground, where he would witness what their destruction wrought, he did not relish this.

"So, stop it before it starts, eh?"

Except he feared he was already too late. A boom rang out from some artillery station at the north end of the harbor. The first of the pirate ships must have been spotted. Not surprisingly, they were coming in on the opposite side of the city from the airbase.

Tolemek had been glancing in that direction often, expecting to see the fliers taking off—and also expecting Cas to be in one of them. The snow made it hard to see anything, but when he reached the waterfront, he was closer to the butte, and he spotted the first of the craft shooting over the edge of the butte, its bronze wings outstretched. Others followed on its tail, struggling to remain steady in the wind, but eventually gaining elevation and arrowing across the harbor toward the cannons firing in the north. From the ground, they truly did look like the dragons of old, or at least like the faded pictures in ancient books, even if their wings didn't flap and their movements were directed by propellers. According to legend, those old dragons had been gold, silver, and bronze, with the gold being the most powerful—physically and mentally. He wondered if the Iskandians had thought it would have been hubris to color their fliers gold, or if the metal had simply been in short supply.

An armored steam wagon clanked past, and Tolemek hugged the shadows. The fog helped hide him, but the wind was a constant enemy. Had the air been quiet, the gray murk would have risen higher and in greater density. Still, it was thicker down here by the water, so he knew he was heading in the right direction.

Following the line of the buildings on the main street, he jogged along, eyeing the docks stretching out into the choppy dark waters. Believing he might find clues there, Tolemek tried to remember which dock Cas had landed the dirigible on. He didn't see any sign of the big balloon and assumed he was looking for the remains of an explosion-riddled wreck rather than a gently damaged aircraft.

Out beyond the breakwater, the surf roared, competing with the booms from the cannons and the shrieking wind. A hint of something burning reached his nose, something that smelled of charred rubber, cloth, and machinery, not simply of the coal warming the stoves in nearby buildings. He squinted through the snow and down a long dock. Yes, there.

The envelope covering and frame had been destroyed, as had part of the dock—the metal remains of the cabin, the walls peeled back like warped flower petals, were half-sunken in the water. The surrounding merchant and fishing ships were also damaged, and in spots, nothing but a couple feet of the mast remained above the surface to mark their icy graves. Interestingly, the fog didn't seem to be coming from that spot. Had someone removed the machine before the explosion?

Tolemek waited for another armored vehicle to pass, then trotted down the dock. Halfway along, the boards grew warped, and some creaked ominously under his weight.

A boom sounded, not from the end of the harbor this time, but from overhead. The first of the pirate ships was visible now, a black shadow against the black sky, only a few running lights making it visible at all. It was hard to tell through the snow, but he thought it might be the *Night Hunter*. Goroth's vessel, leading the way, whether he was standing next to the helmsman or not.

Standing on the dock with nothing for cover, Tolemek felt vulnerable. He hustled along. Best to get this business taken care of quickly. He told himself that Maktu, the helmsman, couldn't pick him out from way up there, and wouldn't know he had turned against the pirates—and betrayed the captain—anyway, but his shoulder blades itched as he advanced on the remains of the freighter.

Spot fires still burned, on the dock and on wood that had been spat into the nearby water. All that awful wood paneling. Tolemek picked his way into the remains of the cabin, searching for clues. At first, he avoided looking in the navigation area or toward engineering, not wanting to see the bodies of the men he had knocked out, men he assumed had been killed in the explosion, but he couldn't search for clues without looking everywhere, and something soon became apparent: there were no bodies. Either they had been thrown free, or whoever had plucked out the fog machine had arrived in time to pull Goroth out too. Stone Heart? Most of the captains wouldn't risk themselves for each other, and would just as soon take over another captain's ship rather than help him return to it, but Stone Heart must have seen some value in saving Goroth. Which meant Tolemek had another enemy skulking around down here. Goroth wouldn't forgive his betrayal.

The wreckage didn't offer up a single clue, other than confirming that the fog machine was gone. Tolemek looked up and down the waterfront, then up at the sky. An airship could have come in and extracted everything, but not without the Iskandians noticing. It hadn't been snowing yet when that explosion had gone off.

With the broken boards of the dock threatening to drop out from beneath him, Tolemek scanned the harbor itself. The sky was less dim than it had been a moment before, for more pirate ships were appearing beneath the clouds, their decks lit, and the fliers were streaking out to meet them, their hulls burnished orange by the glow of their power crystals. Even so, Tolemek's gaze almost skimmed past the dark shape bobbing in the waves beyond the docks.

"Not an airship," he whispered. "A sailing ship."

The Roaming Curse *did* have some, though they might also have recently acquired this one. He couldn't see any identification—he could barely make out the ship—but who else would be foolishly sitting out there in the harbor on a night like this? Someone planning to lead the raid portion of the attack?

Realizing he might be visible to whoever was out there, thanks to the fires still burning around the wreck, Tolemek ran back up the dock, into the shadows and fog. He followed the waterfront, eyeing the smaller vessels tied up here and there, and finally selecting a yacht with a lifeboat. There was nobody about on the docks to complain about theft. He dropped the smaller boat, found two oars, and climbed in.

He hadn't rowed more than five meters when a cannonball screeched out of the sky and slammed into the yacht. Wood shot out in every direction. Tolemek dropped into the bottom of the rowboat as debris pelted its sides and flew overhead.

He gulped when he sat up, returning to the oars. The yacht was still upright, but he doubted it would be for long.

With the fog over his head, he didn't see how someone could be aiming for him, but it was hard not to think that way. He rowed into the harbor, regardless. If he had to swim over to that ship to disable the fog machine and deal with Goroth and Stone Heart, he would. It had occurred to him, as soon as he had seen the fog, that Cas might believe he had been lying to her, that he had never attempted to disable the machine in the first place and that perhaps he hadn't left his people behind after all. He did *not* want her thinking that.

Gunfire spat overhead, one of the fliers swooping low. Tolemek thought it might be diving toward the dark craft in the water, but it came up under one of the airships, scouring its belly with bullets. Was that Cas? He had no way to know. There were more than twenty fliers up there.

Though it took longer than he would have liked, he rowed north first, so he could come at the ship from the seaward side rather than from the city, where the lights might silhouette him, fog or not.

You're wasting your time.

Tolemek almost dropped an oar. Jaxi, again. After he and Sardelle had parted ways, he had assumed the soulblade wouldn't communicate with him further. He wouldn't have expected it to have such range—he was still surprised it talked to him at all. He had assumed that was something reserved for the relationship between blade and handler.

Sardelle isn't always chatty. I get lonesome.

What do you mean I'm wasting my time? Do you know who's out there? If it were a boat full of fishermen too cheap to pay the dock fees, he would feel idiotic for this long side trip.

Your people. And they know you're coming. Might as well go straight up to them.

And get shot?

They're not going to shoot you. They have something far worse in mind.

Tolemek went back to rowing. The waves and wind were trying to push him to the south, and he would shoot past the craft if he wasn't careful. *What might that be?*

Something that I'll kill you over if it comes to pass.

Given the soulblade's sense of humor—if one could call it that—Tolemek's first thought was that Jaxi was joking. But there was no follow-up to suggest that was the case.

Are you and Sardelle nearby? He wondered if he would need help—and if they would be willing to give it—in dealing with the pirates.

Not yet. A family was hurt. Sardelle stopped to heal them, ignoring the fact that if they figure out she used magic to do so, they'll turn around and accuse her of witchcraft, which will get her killed in this town, no matter who her boyfriend is.

The exasperation in Jaxi's tone made him think Sardelle might do such things often.

She was trained as a healer. She'd probably even heal you.

You wouldn't?

I wasn't trained as a healer, so I wouldn't have to make that choice. Besides, I know what you've done to my people.

With the side of the dark ship looming ahead of him, Tolemek had enough to worry about without wondering how a sword knew all of his secrets, but he caught himself breathing shallowly and rapidly anyway. His hands had been cold earlier; now he could feel sweat slicking the oar grips. Jaxi had bad timing.

What were you trained to do? Tolemek wasn't sure why he asked; he probably didn't want to know.

Pyrotechnics. Along with the word came a quick impression of a young woman, little more than a kid, with red hair in pigtails, grinning as she hurled streams of fire at an encroaching Cofah army.

A dark figure walking along the deck of the ship stopped and leaned against the railing. Yes, Jaxi was right. Whoever was out there had been waiting for him.

As the rowboat glided up to the larger ship, Tolemek dipped into his bag of vials and gadgets. He touched one of the leather balls, but bypassed it, fingers delving for a hard cylinder in the bottom with a pull-tab top. Several other shadows had joined the first. Given the roar of the sea and the buzz of the propellers overhead, it was amazing that he heard the loading of rifles, but the sound of bullets being chambered cut right across the water to him.

"Good evening, Mek," came Goroth's voice from the shadows, utterly calm, as if there weren't fliers and airships battling overhead. "Why don't you come aboard? We have something to chat about." It was a stranger's voice, nothing of the years of friendship in it. Tolemek knew he had made his choice, and he didn't regret it, but he also hadn't expected to have to face Goroth again a mere hour after sticking a needle in his neck.

"That might not have a salutary effect on my health," Tolemek said.

"Oh, we're not planning to kill you. We're planning to have you watch. From a distance. You'll have to let us know what distance would be suitable. And how long we have to wait before going ashore. We're here to loot, after all, not become victims of our own craftiness."

"What craftiness would that be?" Tolemek croaked. His mouth had gone dry. Goroth's allusions were obvious, though Tolemek didn't see how it could be possible. After seeing Tanglewood and hearing about Camp Eveningson, he had destroyed all of the canisters of the death gas. Very carefully. In a crematorium, with a device for delaying the dropping of them into the fire, to ensure he was far, far away when it happened. It had been a mistake to invent something so deadly that it terrified even him, but he hadn't truly understood that until that day.

"Stone Heart here was kind enough to see our freighter's distress and come pull us out before the authorities charged up. He even took care of those authorities with that explosion, so there wouldn't be any witnesses to his arrival. And I, though confused and betrayed, had the presence of mind to grab the bag I brought with me before he set the charges, the bag that I'd packed with a canister taken from your laboratory years ago."

"I destroyed all of the samples," Tolemek said. His rowboat had reached the larger vessel and was bumping against its side.

"Not all of them. I took one before you left to destroy them," Goroth said. "I couldn't let you make that much power disappear at a whim, not when I might one day need it."

"All this time, you had that canister in your cabin?" Tolemek choked at the idea, imagining a strong wind striking the ship and the canister being knocked over and activated in some cabinet, the poison blasting out to kill everyone aboard.

"Well insulated, I assure you. I'm not a fool."

"What about when the first *Night Hunter* was shot down last summer? Did you have it in your cabin then?"

"I did, and I retrieved it before we had to abandon the ship."

Tolemek pushed his hair away from his face, not caring that his hood fell back too. The past didn't matter. What mattered was... "You have it on this ship now?"

"No, my old friend. It's already been deployed in the city, the timer set. It's in a place where it can do maximum damage. You'll never find it."

"Maximum damage. You mean kill the most people."

"Yes," Goroth said. "Yes, I do. How convenient that it'll destroy all of the resistance, yet it will leave the contents of the banks and museums untouched."

"It won't destroy *all* of the resistance," Tolemek said, trying to sound calm, though inside he was alternating between quailing and raging. He looked up to the sky. The fliers, always conscious of the threat of ground fire, usually stayed high above their enemies. They should be high enough to survive the release of the death gas, but what would they come back to when they landed? A city full of dead, their organs boiled, their skin melted off from the inside out. And Cas... what would she think? That he had double-crossed her. That all along he had been working with Goroth.

"What use is a fighter squadron without a populace to defend?" Goroth asked. "They'll be too busy mourning to trouble our retreat. Our retreat with cargo holds full of loot. The Cofah might even give us a medal for destroying the capital city of their enemy, something they've failed to do in hundreds of years of war." Goroth propped his arm on the railing, leaning closer to Tolemek. "Climb aboard. As I said, we have questions for you. We want to make sure we don't get caught too close."

"Do you," Tolemek whispered. And then what? They shot him once they were safe? Some offer.

"Yes, and, believe it or not, I have no wish to see you killed this way, either. Come back to the *Night Hunter* with me. All will be forgotten. Or, if not forgotten, at least forgiven. So long as you continue to help make me a powerful captain with few who will contest my right to reign."

It sounded more like he wanted to be a king than a captain. Tolemek rubbed his face. He needed to figure out a way to locate the canister and stop the aerosol from being released. For Cas, for the people of the city, and... for his own sanity. He couldn't darken his soul with another Tanglewood. He just couldn't.

"Captains," came a terse call from the bow of the ship. "There's another boat approaching from the starboard side."

Two of the figures who had been aiming their rifles at Tolemek jogged to the other side, disappearing behind the cabin. Several remained, and Goroth would doubtlessly be armed, too, but it might be the best chance Tolemek would get. He traced the pull tab on his canister with his thumb. He could blow up the ship with the contents, but if everyone aboard was dead or unconscious, who would tell him where the canister was? The timer could be set for a maximum of an hour, so he didn't have much time. If they had already set it and returned to this boat...

"Friend of yours?" Goroth asked casually, though there was an icy layer to his voice, a suggestion that it had better *not* be.

"My only friend here is up there." Tolemek pointed to the sky.

"I see." Goroth's tone was even icier.

Perhaps saying "only" had been a mistake. Laying down the cards too early, letting Goroth know he refused the offer.

"It's dark," came the soft call from the other side of the ship. "Looks abandoned. No sail up, no oars. Like it's floating free, but, uh, it's coming straight at us."

A premonition tickled Tolemek's senses. He had never experienced any of his sister's talent for magic, and didn't think even she, in her more lucid moments, could speak into other people's minds, but he called out with his thoughts nonetheless: *Jaxi?*

He didn't receive an answer. Not surprising. It wasn't as if *he* were linked to the soulblade somehow, not the way its handler would be. Communication would always be per Jaxi's whims.

Still, he had to try, in some hope that the soulblade would check in with him first.

Jaxi, if you can hear me, don't hurt anyone on the ship, at least not the man in front of me. We need to know where the canister is and how much time remains on the countdown. We need—

The sky brightened behind Goroth's vessel. And then it turned to flame.

Tolemek had been standing in the rowboat, half convinced he had to climb onto the ship with Goroth, but he stumbled back now, raising a hand to protect his eyes from the sudden light—and the heat. A man on the other side screamed. Splashes sounded—people diving or falling overboard?

In the rowboat and on the other side of the now-flaming cabin, Tolemek didn't face the full intensity of the attack, but he scrambled to the far side of his little vessel, the heat forcing him to back up.

Jaxi, he tried again, his mind filled with that image of the soulblade—or maybe who the spirit had been before she turned into a sword—hurling streams of fire. *Don't kill them. I'm not just being sentimental. We need the location of the—*

Rifles fired—the men on the boat shooting at whoever was attacking them. Shooting at something anyway.

A second fireball struck on the heels of the first. The crackling of flames and the snapping of wood rose over the clamor of the battle going on above the harbor. The heat seared Tolemek's face. He was tempted to row away, to put distance between himself and the burning craft, but he had to find out where the canister was located.

Goroth was crouching, somewhat protected by the cabin, though flames were leaping from its roof and sides.

"Goroth," Tolemek called, intending to offer the man refuge on his rowboat.

Throw the grenade, a voice in his mind ordered. Jaxi.

What? Tolemek stared down at the cylinder in his hand. Goroth had turned to face him. He couldn't hurl a grenade at the man.

Sink the ship before these murderers cause any more trouble. If you don't, I will.

Tolemek lowered his hand and stuck the cylinder back in the bag. *I can't. And you shouldn't, either. We have to find out—*

Goroth had his foot lifted to the railing, prepared to leap overboard, or perhaps to jump for Tolemek's rowboat, but he was too late. Something struck the ship with the power of a bomb. It exploded from within.

The shockwave hurled Tolemek backward, almost knocking him out of the rowboat. As it was, he landed hard on his back, the air blasted out of him. The explosion lit the sky, and for a moment, the fliers and the airships were highlighted overhead, and he could see the faces of the men on one of the airships, none of them looking as afraid for their lives as they should have, given the fliers swooping all around.

Blinking, Tolemek pushed himself to his elbows. He stared at the spot where the sailing ship had been. There was nothing except flotsam now, boards burning on the dark, choppy water. Neither Goroth nor any of the other men aboard were anywhere to be seen, but something that looked like a severed arm floated by. Tolemek swallowed hard. He hadn't meant... when he had chosen to walk away from his old friend, he hadn't meant for it to end like this.

The black shape of a yacht rose from the water on the other side of the flotsam. It was wreathed in fog, the city lights hazy beyond it. Presumably Sardelle was somewhere on that dark ship and had been as much a part of that attack as her soulblade.

"What have you done?" Tolemek whispered. In a city of hundreds of thousands, how would he find that timer before it counted down to destruction?

Chapter 15

Cas watched Apex and Beeline on the runway before her, picking up speed as they headed for the edge of the cliff and the harbor beyond. She was inching along, waiting for the route to clear, and trying not to be alarmed by the rocking of the flier as gales swept across the butte, tugging at her wings. The snow flying sideways through her vision and sticking to her goggles wasn't nearly as alarming as the wind. The fliers might appear to be made of bronze, but that was just a coating. They were as lightweight as the engineers could make them, with the machine guns and the pilots being the heaviest part of the load. Taking off without crashing was going to be almost as challenging as landing without crashing. The number of propellers on the bottom of the harbor attested to the fact that countless pilots had stalled the engines or run into other trouble even on normal days. The squadron didn't usually fly at night, much less in storms. This was madness.

But the pirate ships had come into view, veering in from the north and angling toward the city. A massive dark shadow on the horizon had to be the outpost. The pirates were just as mad as the Iskandians for flying in these conditions.

Cas reminded herself that she had been eager to come out here—no one would have faulted her for staying on the ground tonight—and she tried to ignore the fact that her hands were already sweaty in her gloves. The flying had never come as naturally for her as the shooting—in flight school, she had thrown up more than once learning maneuvers with names like the zoom loop or the corkscrew—but she had never been scared of being in a craft, either.

"Might have something to do with the fact that you *crashed* last time," Cas muttered.

"That you, Ahn?" came Zirkander's voice... out of her pocket.

Her hand flinched, and the wings responded with a dubious wobble. Her pocket—that was where she had stuffed the little blue crystal.

"Uh, yes," she said, regaining control of the stick.

"Everything all right?"

"Yes, sir."

"Good," the colonel said. "I need you up here, second point. Wolf Squadron, we're heading for the outpost. Lance, you and Tiger Squadron clean up the rest of the riffraff in the sky."

The responding yes sirs came not only from Major Lance but from a dozen other mouths as well. Could *everyone* hear and speak to each other through those crystals? Wonderful. Cas made a vow not to talk to herself as much as usual. Before, the squadrons had always communicated with each other through hand signals and dips of the wings. She could see where this additional option would be useful, but it would take some getting used to. Nobody better start blathering in her ear—or from her pocket—when she was concentrating on a target.

She patted the side of the cockpit, hoping someone had thought to wedge a Mark 500 in there. She was the only pilot she knew of who used anything other than the guns mounted on the flier, but there were times when a sniper rifle was perfect for her. It wouldn't be *her* rifle, lovingly zeroed to her eye, since that was at the bottom of the Seven Tides Strait, but it would do for the night. And, yes, there was the familiar outline of a Mark 500, strapped in as securely as she was.

Cas took a deep breath, drove the stick forward, and accelerated toward the cliff. As soon as the flier left the ground, the wind pummeled it, tearing at the wings as if they were frail kites. The nose sank, the choppy black waters below filling her view. Cas forced herself to ease back gently, making subtle movements, finding as much equilibrium as she could with the icy northern gale pushing her back toward the cliff. Snow blasted against her goggles and frosted her cheeks. It felt like they were flying at fifteen thousand feet instead of scant meters above the harbor. With the propeller roaring in front of her, she couldn't hear the creaks and groans of the cables, but felt them through the stick, sensing the craft straining against the air currents. She skimmed above the water for a moment—the wind was calmer down there—then climbed up, angling for the position to W-83's left, to join the others in formation above the nearest airships.

"Does anyone else think it was bloody inconsiderate of these pirates to attack during a snow storm?" someone asked.

People's voices sounded tinny through the crystals, and Cas didn't recognize every speaker immediately. She thought that was someone in Tiger Squadron.

"We'll have to punish them for their impudence." That must be Apex. Nobody else used words like impudence while concentrating on flying.

"Gonna be hard punishing anyone if my wings are scraped off all over the cliff. That wind is rough."

Cas was glad she wasn't the only one who'd had trouble. Even now, flying straight was a challenge.

"Please, Duck, you can barely make that takeoff when the conditions are perfect. It's becoming obvious why Goat Squadron transferred you."

"It's not my fault so many cliffs and so much water are involved here. Everyone knows, a flier is meant to take off from a field. All you have to look out for then are the ostriches and llamas."

"That's one rural field."

The chitchat was relaxing Cas, though she still wasn't sure how she felt about having the mess hall conversations going on when they were on their way into battle. She used her scarf to wipe her goggles and looked toward 83. Zirkander glanced over his shoulder in her direction—to make sure she was there? Of course she was there. She wasn't going to let him down by falling apart after one stupid little crash. That hadn't even been her fault. The battleship's guns never would have caught her if the engine hadn't stalled. She gave him the two-fingers-up salute. She was ready.

"We're going in," Zirkander said. "Mission essential talk only from here on out. Speculation on what Duck was doing in that field there to attract all those llamas and ostriches will have to wait until we land."

Cas smirked. She had started to mind the wind beating at her wings a little less.

"Masser, Blazer, Crash, you're with me," Zirkander said. "We're gunning for the balloons. The new ammo is in, incendiaries every fourth round. I don't care how reinforced that material is; it shouldn't stand a chance."

"Yes, sir."

"Ahn, you know your job. Take out the gunners and the brass. Thasel and Pimples, watch her back."

"I didn't notice much brass on the pirate captains' hats," Cas said.

"Then look for the ugliest brutes on the platform. Those are probably the leaders."

"Will do, sir."

"Everyone else, take your opportunities and watch our asses from above," Zirkander said. "You know I don't like having pirates sniffing around back there."

"I'm not keen on *anyone* sniffing around my ass," someone muttered.

"I might not mind the colonel's archaeologist."

That drew snickers from the men, but everyone knew to fall silent after that. Zirkander dipped his starboard wing twice, then led the way into a dive. They had reached a spot a couple of miles from the shoreline and were flying over the six parallel balloons of the outpost. Other airships dotted the nearby skies, some closer to the city, but Tiger Squadron was forming up to deal with them.

In the beginning, Cas followed Zirkander and the others, then she dropped lower for access to the massive platform. The ships that had been docked there the day before were all flying independently now, or had stayed out at sea, leaving this insanity for others to partake in, so she had little trouble seeing the guns, the propellers, and other key targets. The gunners would have little trouble seeing her too. Thasel and Pimples weaved behind her, trying to draw some of their attention.

Cas charged in head-on to start with, using the twin guns

mounted at the front of the flier. The shots rang in her ears, even louder than the churning propeller. She targeted two grim-faced pirates crouched behind the giant gun mounted on the corner. They were aiming for her even as she blew rounds at them. One went down, but the other used the artillery weapon to hide behind. Shells shrieked past the cockpit, invisible in the night sky. She weaved unpredictably to make a harder target, then arced in, finding the angle to take down the second gunner. When he collapsed, she pounded the gun itself, followed by the propeller below it. Impressive streams of black smoke flowed from that corner of the outpost.

She was close enough to see faces on the platform—men with rifles waited, in addition to those manning other artillery weapons—when she pushed forward on the stick, diving below the outpost, almost scraping her cap off on the framework below. Guns fired behind her, her escort adding to the damage. Cas glanced back, making sure Thasel and Pimples had both dived below the platform too. They skimmed along the bottom behind her. Cas eyed the blocky shadows, the hint of pipes and vents, and wondered if any crucial targets might lie down there. But it was too dark to see much. And the colonel had given her a different assignment.

"Thasel, Pimples," she said, still feeling silly for talking toward her pocket, "I'm going to parallel the outpost to look for the colonel's brass. I'm pulling out my rifle."

"We're with you," Thasel said, his voice calm, professional, and as humorless as always.

Pimples, on the other hand, responded with, "In other words, you're going to be flying with your knee for the next five minutes, and we should stay back so you don't crash into us. Thanks for the warning."

Cas snorted but couldn't come up with a suitable comeback, since it was essentially true. If she thought her flier was quaking in the breeze now, this would be a true challenge. And a challenge of her aim as well.

She had flown out from beneath the platform and circled back, gaining in altitude, so she could come in from above the balloons and not risk her craft until she was ready to start firing.

"Nice shooting, Colonel," someone said.

Cas saw why the compliment had been thrown when she swooped back toward the outpost. One of those balloons had been damaged. *More* than damaged. Flames were leaping from a hole in the top, like a volcano erupting.

"Just demonstrating the new incendiary rounds," Zirkander drawled.

"And lighting a real nice candle too. 'Preciate the light."

When the squadron hadn't destroyed any of the outpost's balloons the day before, Cas had feared they might be reinforced somehow, so she was relieved to see the damage. The extra light might help her identify targets too. She unstrapped her rifle as she sailed in, paralleling the big platform. She wiped her goggles with her scarf one more time, clearing off a gray sludge made of snow and engine oil, then lifted her weapon, bracing an elbow on the side of the cockpit. She kept the stick as steady as she could with her knee and picked her targets. Gunner, gunner, ugly face bellowing orders, gunner—damn, clipped that one—and another ugly.

"Four o'clock, Ahn," came Thasel's detached voice at the same time as Pimples barked, "Look out, Ahn!"

His shout startled her, and her knee slipped. In theory, the flier was supposed to continue straight and level when there weren't any hands on the stick, but the wind was blasting theories to dust tonight. Her craft pitched to the side alarmingly, and she almost lost her rifle. A stream of bullets screeched past her, several tearing into her upward-tilted wing. Cas jammed the rifle to the side of her seat and took the stick.

"You all right, Ahn?" Zirkander asked.

"Fine." Cas righted herself, using the bottom of the outpost for protection, though the tufts of flaming material raining down on either side suggested it might not be a good hiding spot for long. "Apparently pirates don't like being shot at."

"Not just *at*," Pimples said. "Shot dead. Another pass on the other side, and they won't have anyone at the guns."

"I'm sure they can find reinforcements," Cas said, though she did intend to go back and attack the other side. By now, she had come out from under the outpost. She circled back, the lights of the city visible through a lapse in the snow. Interestingly, the big station hadn't moved much closer. She spotted burning wreckage down in the harbor. One of the airships down most likely. Good.

"Somehow I don't think they'll get many volunteers," Pimples chortled.

"Better not look so impressive, Ahn," someone said, "or you'll get kissed again when you and Pimples land."

She shook her head, thinking of the kiss she had shared with Tolemek and hoping he was staying out of sight down there. She dug out her rifle and lined herself up for another attack. Another balloon was up in flames. Also good. Sinking the outpost would get rid of a lot of pirates at once, something sky *and* sea freighter captains would thank them for.

"Going in again," she announced, then did so, propping her elbow on the side of the cockpit again. She could simply use the machine gun, like everyone else did, but she had always preferred perfect accuracy to flinging a slew of bullets and hoping to get lucky. Her father's influence, doubtlessly. Besides, the delay from the synchronization gear that kept the bullets from hitting the propeller always irritated her. Everyone else said they couldn't tell, but it was apparently her one thing to be hypersensitive about. She blamed her father for that too.

She eyed the city lights for a moment, wondering if he was home. His work took him out of the capital, and sometimes to other continents altogether, so she had no idea. If he *was* there, would he thank her if she and the other fliers were successful in keeping the pirates out of the city? He might not fear for his own life, unless bombs were dropped high up into the hills, but he had a lot of valuables at home that might attract looters. She wouldn't hold her breath for a show of gratitude, though; he hadn't sent one yet.

On her second pass at the outpost, she knocked out three more gunners and three gesticulating older men she hoped were captains giving orders. Nobody came close to hitting her flier.

Between the flames from the balloons and the smoke wafting from propellers and other crucial areas, the outpost didn't have much ability left to fight. It might have been different if Tolemek's fog had blanketed the entire harbor and stretched up into the sky, but these pirates had been outmaneuvered from the start. Cas secured the Mark 500 again, then switched to strafing the remaining balloons with the rest of the squadron.

"That snake nest is about to drop out of the sky," someone crooned.

"Don't get cocky," Crash said. "The weather's getting worse. Just finish up so we can get out of here."

He was right. The snow had let up somewhat, but the howling wind had picked up its intensity. There was a crosswind coming in from the sea too. Cas struggled to control her flier.

"One more balloon should do it," Zirkander said. "Focus fire on the aft one. And give your neighbors some distance. We're being bobbed around like buoys out here."

"Is anyone else wondering why they haven't started bombing the city?" someone from Tiger Squadron asked.

"I am," Zirkander said. "It's like they're waiting for something."

"Maybe they're enraptured with us," Pimples said.

"I believe the word you're thinking of is enthralled," Apex said, "though neither seems likely."

"Thanks," Pimples said. "I'd be lost without your guidance."

"What's the word for it when an officer kisses another officer in front of a whole bunch of other officers?" someone asked.

Cas winced, imagining Pimples' embarrassment. This wasn't the time for squad-wide mockery. W-83 was busy blowing flaming holes in the balloon he had selected for targeting.

"How long before everyone forgets about that?" Pimples asked.

"I don't know, but it's sure going to take more than an hour."

"Enough, Wolves," Zirkander said as his craft flew out of the flames leaping from the balloon. The platform sagged, the aft end dipping down at an impossible angle, and pirates tumbling over the side. Others clawed their way into buildings and hung from lampposts. "We'll mock Pimples thoroughly once we're on the ground with beers in our hands."

"Gee, thank you so much, sir," Pimples said.

Several quieter moments passed, with nothing except the thrum of the propellers and the bangs of the guns speaking to the night. Cas focused on the shooting and tried to relax, though the wind had her whole body tense.

"Look out," several people cried at once.

Cas glanced in all directions, thinking the warning might be for her. But two Tiger Squadron fliers had clipped wings or crashed in some other way. Both craft were spiraling toward the harbor. There was no chance for the pilots to pull up—they'd lost all control. The fliers plunged into the water, the wings ripped off by the impact and hurled free. Cas stared in horror, reminded that nature was every bit as dangerous as enemy bullets.

* * *

Zirkander's house. That was the only place Tolemek could think of to check for the canister. Those pirates had been searching it, but they might have done more than that. Perhaps the attempt to blow it up had been a ruse. Or maybe they had placed the device nearby and had wanted to cover their tracks.

As he pondered this, Tolemek rowed toward the other vessel. A great screech of metal sounded overhead, and the sky lit up. Until then, he had been more concerned about his own problems than the air battle in the sky, but seeing two fliers plummeting from the clouds had a way of riveting a man's attention. Several of the pirate airships had already crashed, but nearly a mile away, at the north end of the harbor. These fliers would strike down much closer to him. Even before they smashed into the water, he doubted there were survivors—and then the wings were torn off by the impact, and the cockpits disappeared beneath the waves. One of the torn pieces of wing flew in his direction, and he lifted a hand—as if that would do any good—but it bounced down with such force that it skipped off the water again and flew over his head before landing.

Tolemek rubbed his face, staring. For the most part, the pilots were strangers to him, indeed he would have considered them enemies mere hours ago, but he stared in horror at the froth and bubbles, having no way to know if Cas had been in one of those fliers.

"Pirate," came a soft call from ahead of him.

Sardelle crouched in the shadows, on the sailboat he had been rowing toward. It had drifted closer now—or he had—and he could make out the figure on the deck.

"Tolemek," he said, not that it mattered at the moment.

"There's little time. One of the pilots lives. I have to help."

"The whole city is in danger if Goroth told me the truth, but I don't know where—"

"Jaxi does." Sardelle shifted her weight, then tossed something to Tolemek—her sword scabbard. "I'll catch up." Her requisitioned yacht was gliding past him, heading unerringly toward the spot where the closest flier had disappeared.

When Tolemek caught the weapon, he stared at it for a moment, before laying it on the floor of the boat and rowing for shore. "You wanted a soulblade..." He looked down at the weapon in its scabbard, no hint of glowing or magic about it. "You're going to talk to me, right?" Because otherwise he had no idea where to go.

Yes, I'm done arguing with Sardelle now.

About healing people?

About tossing me into some pirate's hands. Especially a pirate who came here with the intention of stealing me.

That wasn't my exact intention. Tolemek threw his back into the rowing, not knowing how much time they had or how far they had to travel.

Up to the butte. The device is going up and down the side of the cliff, attached to the bottom of a tram cabin.

The tram on the airbase? Tolemek slapped the oars into the water with more vigor than the task required. *You saw that in Goroth's mind?*

Yes.

The airbase. How am I supposed to get past the soldiers guarding the gate? Not to mention riding their manned tram without being spotted.

How did Goroth even get it up there to start with?

The captain hadn't been here any longer than Tolemek. And he had been unconscious half the time. How had he managed so much?

He has men to order around. You seem to be lacking in that area.

Yes, it's hard to get people to defect en masse with you. The rowboat bumped against the dock, and Tolemek climbed out, not bothering to tie the craft.

Do you not have more of your devices for knocking humans unconscious?

One. How's your magic? Any chance you'll let me use it if I get stuck?

I'll use it if I get stuck. It would inconvenience Sardelle if she had to retrieve me from some military research facility.

In other words, I'm on my own, and you're only here to guide me to the device.

There's the swift thinking that leads me to believe you might actually have the brainpower to be an evil inventor.

Just... an inventor.

The device kissing the bottom of the tram cabin gives validity to my adjective.

Tolemek wished he could object more meaningfully, but if the sword was in his head and knew everything he knew...

He reached the head of the dock and turned onto the waterfront street, tugging his hood over his head again. With Goroth's ship destroyed and the fog machine on the bottom of the harbor, only the snow remained for cover, and the wind was blowing most of that away. The street was busier than ever with soldiers and armored vehicles, many with artillery weapons mounted on them, stationed every block or two. Their focus was toward the sky, but they might notice a suspicious figure running along the street. Tolemek did his best to use the shadows of the buildings to hide his travel. He was about to cut through an alley and hope the next street over was less populated—and paralleled the waterfront so he wouldn't get lost—when a pair of cavalrymen on horseback trotted out of the alley toward him, their rifles resting across their thighs.

Keep going, Jaxi instructed.

Though he had his reservations, Tolemek did so, hugging a stone wall in hopes that the soldiers would assume he was just a helpful soul out for a walk and ready to beat down pirates with his sword if need be.

The men didn't so much as look his way.

You're welcome.

You can keep them from seeing me?

You're not invisible, but they were distracted, and probably won't remember your passing unless someone brings it up.

Handy.

Yes. I hope my obvious versatility isn't making you think of stealing me again.

Tolemek turned onto the street that he hoped paralleled the waterfront. With the butte looming ahead, he shouldn't be able to lose his way. *I was never thinking that. I just wanted to ask—*

I know what you want. If there are other soulblades out there still—and I hope that is the case, because you don't know how depressing it is to be the last of your kind—we haven't located them yet.

"Oh." Though Tolemek's priority was finding the canister before the timer ran out, he couldn't help but feel disappointed. *You said yet. Does that mean—*

It's not our priority.

What is?

At the moment, keeping Sardelle's new soul snozzle alive.

Tolemek curled a lip, more at the idea of Zirkander as anyone's 'soul snozzle'—whatever that was—than because a sorceress might fall in love.

Listen, Jaxi said, *no soulblade would want to bond with a crazy girl, anyway.*

Tolemek clenched his fist as he ran. *She's not crazy. She just needs help understanding her powers.*

Maybe so, but there were always so few soulblades in the world that we could be highly selective with who we chose.

The statement sounded perfectly reasonable, but it was perfectly frustrating as well. Another wasted research trip.

No, not wasted. He gazed up toward the sky, praying that Cas was still up there and still healthy. Even if there was no future for them, he wouldn't regret anything that had happened this past week. He would only regret having to leave her. Or losing her. He frowned at the harbor, though he couldn't see where the fliers had crashed.

That much I can give you. She's fine.

It was probably only in his imagination that the sword sounded apologetic. But maybe Jaxi actually regretted that she had to say no to his hopes for his sister.

We're not gods; we can't be the answer to everyone's problems.

The gates of the airbase came into view, and Tolemek slowed down, pressing himself against a wall and digging into his sack. He still had the one knockout ball and the grenade as well. He squinted past the gate, where snow swept along the dark vertical wall of the butte. The tram cabin looked to be at the top rather than the bottom. Not good. His aerosol was heavier than air, so even if the rocket element wasn't activated, the gas would descend upon the houses at the base of the cliff, probably drifting farther out into the city as well.

He patted the leather ball. He would have to use it on the guards and try to sneak over to the tram without anyone noticing him. And then he had to hope he could remove the canister and disarm it, also with nobody noticing. Unfortunately, he hadn't brought tools for fine work.

I don't suppose you can disarm it from here, Jaxi? That would certainly save some trouble.

I can sense that it's fastened to the bottom of the cabin. Disarming it... I would rather leave that task for you. It looks complex, inside and outside. Better to have its creator handle that. He doubtlessly has a steady hand and a familiarity with the contraption.

I see, you're all compliments now. Tolemek imagined himself hanging out of the cabin, trying to disarm the device while fumbling in the dark under the floor.

I don't want to be the one to slay half the people in the city, Jaxi thought.

I don't, either.

Good, because I was going to threaten to kill you if you weren't enthusiastic enough in disarming your contraption.

I'm glad you're not interested in being stolen, because you would make an abysmal teacher for my sister. Tolemek crept closer to the soldiers guarding the gate, until they spotted him, at which pointed he lifted a hand, as if to greet them, then feigned a slip on the ice. He rolled the leather ball along the street toward them, and dropped to his hands and knees, hoping they would be too fascinated by his fall to notice the ball.

"That's the same man who knocked out the gate guards at Fort Marsh." The speaker flung a hand in the direction of the other installation. Ah, the word had gotten around quickly.

"Watch out for that ball." The second man kicked it before the sides peeled back to emit the smoke. It bounced up the street and didn't start emitting the gas until it was out of their range.

The first man leveled a rifle at Tolemek. He rolled to the side, expecting a barrage of bullets. He wasn't disappointed. They skipped off the cobblestones, near his head. He gave up on rolling and jumped to his feet, sprinting toward the closest building. He was still armed and could have shot at the guards, but he didn't want to leave a trail of blood behind him. How could he attempt to save the city on one hand, but kill everyone in his path on the other? He raced toward a brick two-story building, fearing he would take a bullet between the shoulder blades before he reached cover.

But the guards had fallen silent, neither yelling again nor shooting.

You're welcome.

Tolemek slowed and turned. The guards lay on the ground, unmoving. Impossibly, his leather ball had rolled back to them, and vapors drifted up to kiss the soldiers' nostrils.

Thank you. Tolemek ran for the gate, hoping nobody on the walls was paying too much attention. Most of the men, little more than shadows visible through the snow, appeared to be clustered around the artillery weapons mounted at the corners of the installation, focused on the sky. Every now and then, one fired, though the airships were still hugging the north side of the harbor and staying over the water. Tolemek was surprised none of the ships were trying to bomb the city.

He nearly tripped as a realization struck him like a bullet. Standing in the middle of the street in front of a military installation full of enemy soldiers wasn't the place for realizations, but his feet wouldn't move until the gears in his mind finished spinning. The pirates knew. They knew that his canister had been placed and that it wouldn't be safe to come in and attack—and loot—until the toxin had been disseminated into the city. There was no way Goroth could have communicated with the incoming airships and accomplished all this after Tolemek had betrayed him. No, he had put this in motion from the beginning. At least as far back as the day before, when Tolemek and Cas had been hiding in those ducts, and Goroth had been wandering around, plotting and planning with the other captains. With Stone Heart.

Those men who had sneaked onto the freighter and attacked them? What if they had been trying to stop this madness? What if Tolemek had helped kill the only men on the outpost with consciences?

"Goroth planned to use my weapon on the city from the beginning," Tolemek whispered. The whole story about the fog machine being what would help the pirates take the city, it had been a lie, a ruse that Tolemek had believed. Fool.

Jaxi gave him a mental prod. *It doesn't matter now. Go.*

She was right. Tolemek shelved the thoughts for later consideration. He wiped snow out of his eyes and bent before the unconscious men, thinking he would have to pat them down and hope one had keys. The iron gate creaked open of its own accord. He slipped through without hesitating.

Thanks. He trusted Jaxi had handled that as well. *You're handy.*

An incalculable treasure.

And modest.

Yes. Now, take a right, then go up the street to the base of the tram. You'll have to figure out how to get that cabin down here to visit. I could do it, but the soldiers standing up there might notice and find it odd.

Tolemek ran past machine shops and warehouses built in the shadow of the butte. There weren't offices, barracks, or houses like at the fort—this installation seemed to be dedicated to supporting the fliers. When he reached the shack squatting beside the landing pad at the bottom of the tram, Tolemek peeked inside, thinking an operator might be waiting. It was empty and dark. Whoever's job it was to move the cabin up and down had taken a break—or was, more likely, on the wall with the other soldiers, ready to defend his homeland.

Inside the shack, there was a simple control mechanism: two levers. He couldn't read the labels in the dark room and dared not light a lantern, but took a guess, pulling the one on the left toward him. He leaned through a window—there wasn't any glass, and he had to stick his head out and crane his neck to see to the top of the cliff. In calmer weather, and with less gunfire in the distance, he might have caught the creaking and clanking of the cabin if it were descending. He didn't hear or see anything. He tried the other lever.

It's moving. But there's a soldier in the shack up there. He noticed. Is he alarmed?

No. He probably thinks his counterpart called it down. Though if it doesn't eventually come back up...

Understood.

Tolemek verified that the cabin was descending, battered by the wind and swaying like a puppet on a string. He bared his teeth in horror. If Goroth, or whatever peon he had sent, hadn't secured that canister well...

For the first time, it sank in that he could die that night. A victim of his own creation. Was that irony? There had been a time when he might not have cared, but he still had to find a solution to help his sister. And then there was Cas. He wasn't sure what there might be for them yet, but he didn't want to die before he could find out.

"Focus on this," he muttered and poked around in his bag. He pulled out his one and only tool from the middle of the canisters and vials. The multi-function device came from an Iskandian tinkering family famous for the tools, and he had thought it terribly clever when he had traded for it, but now, as he unfolded and held up the one-inch-long, cross-tip screwdriver, he had to fight down a wave of panic that threatened to wash over him. "I need finer tools for this, Jaxi," he whispered, envisioning the countdown timer and mechanism that protected the four glass ampoules inside. Their ability to kill thousands depended on detonation in the air, but if any one of them dropped out and broke at his feet, it would not only kill him but everyone downwind. He eyed the soldiers on the walls.

You might want to stop the tram before the cabin lands, so you can access the device.

Tolemek, a vision of the canister smashing down onto the landing pad, lunged for the control lever. A second later, he realized that the cabin had probably gone up and down a few times since the detonator had been planted. The canister must be tucked under a beam or something that kept it from being pressed into the ground. Still, Jaxi was right. He needed access to it.

He leaned out of the shack and found the cabin swaying in the wind, its bottom a few feet off the ground. Swaying. Great, that would make his task even more fun.

"I don't suppose you can make the wind stop for a while?" he muttered.

Sorry, I never studied weather. The usually sarcastic Jaxi sounded contrite, even regretful. *Anyway, controlling nature is beyond the capability of all except the most powerful of sorcerers. There may not be anyone left in this time who can do it.*

With a look of disgust for the multi-function tool, Tolemek strode to the cabin. It would be worth hunting in one of the machine shops for finer tools, if there was time. He needed to check the clock first.

A good idea. As I said, the inside appears very intricate.

It is. An engineer friend had designed the vessel for him. He had the nickname of Precision for a reason.

Tolemek peered under the cabin, though the gloom made it difficult to see anything. He slid his hand along one of two support beams that crossed beneath the floor and found a familiar cylinder nestled against one. Even though he had expected it, his heart rate must have doubled or tripled at the irrefutable evidence.

"I'm going to have to risk a light," Tolemek said. And hope none of the soldiers on the wall found it strange that a man in a cloak was bent over under their tram cabin.

Take me out of my scabbard, and I'll provide it.

Somehow I suspect whatever light you emit will be even more suspicious to these soldiers.

I'll be incognito.

More because he was afraid he didn't have much time than anything else, he removed the sword from the scabbard and, since there was nowhere close by to lean it, thrust it into the packed earth beside the cement landing pad.

You better volunteer to clean and oil me later.

If I survive this, I'll do it in a most loving way.

Save the love for the girl. I just want to be clean.

A soft yellow glow that simulated lantern light arose from the blade. It was enough to make out the details of the cylinder, including the clock ticking down on the outside.

Tolemek closed his eyes and blew out a shaky breath. "There's not going to be time for tool shopping."

Less than eight minutes remained.

Chapter 16

Once the pirate outpost was nothing more than a carcass floating on the dark water below, Cas and the rest of Wolf Squadron flew in to help the others. With their giant base destroyed, she assumed the airships would give up and head back out to sea, but they lingered, their gunners pounding rounds toward the fliers swooping in and out of their scattered ranks.

"Strange that they're putting up this much of a fight," Zirkander said over the crystal.

"And not attacking the city," Blazer responded. "What do they win by shooting at us?"

"Besides our deaths?" Pimples asked.

"They might find our deaths satisfying, but that won't earn them any money or treasure."

"The colonel's head might," Pimples said. "I hear the bounty has gotten big in Cofahre."

"That true, Ahn?" Zirkander asked. "You see any wanted posters with my mug on them while you were held prisoner over there?"

"Papered on every tree, table, and tent post," Cas said, though she wasn't paying much attention to the banter. She had her next target picked out, a small airship that had moved into the harbor after the crash. She couldn't know its intent for certain, but there was no way she was letting them drop hooks to pull up the fliers—or their power crystals.

"Huh," Zirkander said. "Guess the Cofah are too cheap to pay for real wallpaper."

By then, Wolf Squadron had closed the distance to the remaining pirates, and everyone fell silent, concentrating on their work. Those manning defenses on the black airship saw Cas coming. It had a row of cannons bristling from the hull on either side, like in the nautical warships from generations past. She kept her eye on them as she swept upward to attack from above.

Wreckage floated in the harbor down below, some of it still aflame. Cas spotted a figure on a personal yacht, struggling to pull something—someone?—out of the water. One of the downed pilots? She couldn't imagine anyone surviving that crash, but then again, she had survived *her* crash. Granted, she had pulled up the nose and skidded across the water instead of dropping straight into it, but she hoped whoever it was had made it.

Cas popped a few rounds into the balloon, being careful with her ammunition. She had already fired a lot of rounds, and there were numerous targets left floating in the sky. She got the incendiary bullet she wanted, and it pierced the dirigible, hydrogen going up in flame.

"Those new bullets are effective," she observed. Usually they just had to punch as many holes into the envelopes as possible, target the engines, or drop explosives.

"Yes," Zirkander said. "Enjoy it now. We just got some intel that the Cofah are coming up with countermeasures."

"They can't reinforce their balloons any further, or they'll be too heavy to achieve lift," Apex said.

"No more balloons. They've already launched a number of experimental craft akin to dragon fliers. Short-range, since they still don't have a fuel source equivalent to our power crystals, but they're building special ships to carry them to their destinations."

"That'll make things interesting," Blazer said.

"Something to worry about another day," said the Tiger Squadron leader. He and his men hadn't been vocal on the communication crystals much since their two fliers went down.

"Agreed," Zirkander said.

A few cannonballs whistled past Cas before the airship drifted downward, narrowly missing the yacht, but they weren't close enough to worry about. She climbed back up to join the others, only to realize that most of the airships had disappeared from the aerial battlefield. More had gone down in the harbor and the rest were finally retreating. Limping back out to sea.

"Let them go or give chase?" someone asked.

Zirkander hesitated a moment—he might be renowned for all of the aircraft he had taken down, but he wasn't a bloodthirsty man at heart. Still, pirates were pirates, most of them cutthroats as well as bandits, and Cas wasn't surprised when he said, "Take them down. We don't need them making repairs and harassing Iskandian ships another day."

"Yes, sir."

Fulfilling the orders didn't take long, though the storm made the flying a challenge regardless, as the snow was gusting sideways again, the clouds thicker than ever overhead. When they turned for home, she could barely see the city or the airbase. Landing was going to be tricky. Her shoulders had been bunched into knots for the last half hour, and the thought did nothing to relax them. She wondered if Tolemek was the kind of friend—or more than friend—who could be convinced to give a girl a massage. Or would she even find him again when she landed? Maybe he had already gotten what he sought from Sardelle and was on his way out of the city, using the chaos to disappear before anyone noticed a criminal in their midst.

Cas found that thought depressing.

* * *

The snow had turned to hail. It was pelting the landing pad all around Tolemek's feet, and bouncing off his bare arms. The wind whipped his cloak about him like a flag on a pole. He kept waiting for someone to notice him—and the glowing sword. He had no idea what he would do when that happened. Seven minutes remained on the timer.

It wouldn't be easier to work on it inside the shack? On a table? Then I could glow in the shack, and it would be less obvious to onlookers.

"I'm trying to get it off," Tolemek said, his back twisted and bent awkwardly, so he could look up at the cylinder. "The morons nailed it—" he couldn't help but make a strangling noise at the idiocy, "—to the floor. They may have damaged some of the wiring inside. In fact, I'd be shocked if they hadn't. I have to be very, very careful." Thus far, between the screwdriver and the file pieces of his tool, he had managed little more than to pry the end open. "If I can get to the wiring that connects the clock, I should be able to stop the countdown. That's the most important thing."

You may want to stop talking aloud. Most of the pirate threat has been dealt with and the fliers are returning to the base. Some soldiers are coming down off the wall as well.

In other words, his odds of being caught had gone up. And Cas was on her way back to the base. To land right in time for his fatal invention to go off? He groaned. How could this night get worse?

"Watch out on base," someone shouted from the wall. "The gate guards were knocked out. Intruders inside."

"Sound the alarm!"

"That's how," Tolemek muttered. He tried to make his fingers work faster, but they were numb and clumsy from the cold. He had already dropped his tool twice.

Jaxi dimmed her light, probably trying to avoid notice, but that only made it harder for him to see. And he very much needed to see right now. The wire he needed to disconnect threaded through a nest of other wires and between two of the ampoules.

Nails or not, he was going to have to risk removing the canister. He needed better conditions for working on it—better conditions located in a place where the soldiers wouldn't spot him. Where he could find such a place in the next seven—no, damn it, six—minutes, he couldn't guess.

Holding his breath, he slid the first of the two nails free. The end of the canister drooped down, but nothing happened to the innards. And now for the second nail...

The tram cabin lurched.

Tolemek dropped his tool. "What are you—"

The operator up top is calling for the cabin.

"No, he can't. Not now. That'll be even worse. The pilots—"

But the cabin was already rising. Tolemek snatched up his tool, stuck it in his mouth, and leaped. He caught the edge of the cabin bottom with his fingers. For a moment, he stared at the cylinder, now dangling from a single nail and being battered by the wind. This would *not* end well.

He debated on grabbing it and simply trying to tear it the rest of the way free, but he dared not. For all he knew, that nail was snugged up against one of the ampoules, and jerking it to the side would break the glass.

Tendons straining, Tolemek pulled himself into the cabin by his fingers. He turned and flopped onto his belly, hanging halfway outside, hoping he could reach the canister. Now he could barely see it. The soft glow of the soulblade, still stuck in the dirt below, faded as the cabin rose, creaking and groaning on its cable. Not to mention that he had left Jaxi behind for any passerby to pick up.

Reason Number Two why nobody in your family will be trusted with a soulblade.

Tolemek pressed his feet into the sides of the cabin to brace his body, then folded himself in half, bending under the floor. He found the canister by touch, though without being able to see what he was doing, he was terrified he would detonate it. Or drop it. With the cabin being pulled toward the top of the cliff, the ground growing farther and farther away, it became a certainty that a drop would break the ampoules. Or maybe even detonate the dispersal mechanism. His father had once told him that men didn't cry, but he was on the verge of tears of frustration.

You can do it. Also, Sardelle is coming.

I wish I knew how that could help me. Tolemek had levered the other nail out a millimeter or two, and he switched to the tool's pliers. Keeping an iron grip on the canister with his free hand, he pulled at the nail, being careful not to wiggle it. Engines roared overhead as fliers landed on the top of the butte. *Can you stop this thing?* There was no time to try and explain to the soldiers up top what he was doing and that they had to let him continue.

The cabin lurched to a halt. Tolemek's feet slipped an inch, and he almost lost his tool again.

Thanks. Hail beat at his face, and his leg muscles quivered from holding up his weight. He pulled the nail out, letting it drop, and lowered the canister. Carefully, so very carefully, he eased it and himself back into the cabin.

I can't even see how much time is left on the clock. I need a light, Jaxi. Is there anyway—

Something blurred through the doorway, and a clank sounded on the floor beside him. Before he could guess what it was, the soulblade lit up, its glow a brighter yellow this time. He might have asked how she had levitated herself up here, but his eyes were riveted to the now-visible clock.

Sardelle is down there. She threw me.

Tolemek finished opening up the outer casing, but his shoulders were slumped. Two minutes. There wasn't time, and the fat tip of the screwdriver wouldn't work for the small, inner casing. He opened the knife blade. He would simply cut the wires holding the ampoules inside. If he lucked out and didn't trigger the bomb, maybe he could separate the poison from the detonator.

She says she'll teach your sister if we all survive this.

At another time, *any* other time, Tolemek would have found the news wonderful, but in his heart he knew there was no chance. Not enough time. Sweat dripped down his brow. His fingers kept moving, but they couldn't move fast enough, not with the clunky multi-tool.

He glanced at the sword. It seemed magic should have some kind of solution for this. Had science surpassed the old ways and become the more powerful? If only—

Tolemek froze. "Jaxi, pyrotechnics."

Yes...

Thinking of the explosion on the boat, he asked, "How hot of a fire can you make? And can it instantaneously be that hot? Or does it warm up slowly?"

No, I can burn something instantaneously. But the temperature? I don't know. I've never measured it.

"I need hot. The melting point of iron. Can you do that?"

Easy.

Tolemek lifted the canister, the wires and half-removed ampoules threatening to spill out like fish guts. "You're positive?"

There were only thirty seconds on the timer.

Yes. What do you want me to do?

"Burn these ampoules with as much heat as you can make."

That won't... release the toxin?

"Not at the melting point of iron. The gas will be vaporized. Hurry," he whispered, his eyes like cantaloupes as he watched the clock ticking down.

A strange tickle went through his mind. Jaxi reading his thoughts? He hadn't sensed her before, but maybe she was tearing through his mind at some deeper level, making sure he wasn't lying. As if he would lie when he was fifteen seconds from dying too.

Can I just vaporize the whole thing?

"Yes!"

Throw it outside, so I won't burn you.

Tolemek would gladly take some burns if they succeeded, but he chucked the canister into the storm anyway. It disappeared into the snow and hail, at least to his eyes. Just throwing it from him wouldn't do anything to save him though. He needed...

"Now, Jaxi. *Please.*"

A small flash of orange lit the sky for a moment, then disappeared. Tolemek held his breath, not that doing so would make an iota of difference if he had been wrong.

Well, Jaxi said after a moment, during which nothing happened and Tolemek's heart remembered to start beating again. *That was anticlimactic.*

Tolemek flopped back onto the floor and laughed. Magic trumped science after all.

The cabin lurched and started moving. His humor faded. He was about to be delivered to a pack of soldiers. After what he had just gone through, he supposed it didn't matter much.

Sardelle was in earnest when she promised to teach my sister?

Yes.

If I am unable to do so, will she find a way to extricate her from the sanitarium too?

A pause followed, Jaxi relaying the message perhaps. *Yes. Sardelle has been lonely for her own kind and had planned to seek out others with dragon blood, regardless. After this, she says she'll even teach you.*

Tolemek snorted. *What would she teach me? I don't have dragon blood.*

Jaxi snorted back—an impressive feat for a soul without lips or a nose. *Blood is hereditary, genius.*

But I never—

Please, you think science *accounts for all of the things you've made?*

Tolemek found himself gaping at the ceiling in stunned silence when the cabin clanged to a stop.

* * *

Cas had never appreciated the feel of pavement under her feet more than she did after climbing out of her flier. Her landing had been better than expected, with the wind easing up for her, though she had chewed on her nails, watching some of her comrades land. Lieutenant Solk had nearly gone over the edge of the plateau, with one wheel hanging off when the craft came to a complete stop. Her face had been whiter than the snow around her when the ground crew had thrown cables around the craft, pulled it fully upright, and hauled her out of the cockpit.

Mishaps notwithstanding, everyone in Wolf Squadron had made it, though there would be drinking later to honor the fallen Tiger Squadron men. She had gotten the names. Both officers had been well-liked.

When Cas, walking beside Captain Blazer, Crash, and Apex, noticed a holdup at the top of the tram, she slowed down, a hint of unease returning to her stomach. Several people were leaning over the edge of the cliff and pointing downward. Had some airship slipped in to do some damage? Or... this couldn't have anything to do with Tolemek, could it? No, she had left him at the other installation, chatting with Zirkander's "archaeologist." Of course, Sardelle had made that appearance to deliver the communications devices. What if Tolemek was around too? Around where people might spot his Cofah skin and pirate garb?

"What's going on?" came the colonel's voice from behind them.

"Unknown, sir," Apex said.

Cas chewed on her lip. Zirkander fell into step beside her, and they soon joined the group.

"It's moving now." The tram operator waved an apologetic hand. "Not sure what the delay was, but it'll be up in a few seconds."

"Good," someone said. "There's drinking to do."

Cas would settle for a meal and a bunk with lots of warm blankets, though she did want to know what had become of Tolemek. She considered the colonel out of the corner of her eye. Sardelle hadn't seemed alarmed by the pirate, but she also hadn't seemed to know who he was. Zirkander would be a different matter. Even if Tolemek was hiding somewhere, Sardelle might have to do nothing more than describe him to the colonel for the recognition to kindle.

The tram cabin came into view over the edge of the cliff. The pilots, noticing Zirkander, stepped aside, offering to let him go first. Thus, since Cas was standing next to him, she had a clear view of the cabin interior when the operator opened the gate.

Tolemek sat on the floor, his arms draped over his knees, his cloak having fallen back to reveal his skin, his hair, and far too much of his face. A rather dazed face, as if he had been struck on the side of the head and was still trying to recover. A sword in a scabbard lay on the floor in front of his feet.

In the first second, Cas hoped nobody would recognize him. By the time the second second was upon them, no less than six people had their pistols out, including Zirkander.

"Wait," Cas blurted, stepping forward. "That's..." *A retired pirate who isn't a threat? A man not holding a weapon in his hands? Someone who looks like he needs a stiff shot of vodka?* "That's my prisoner," she said.

"What?" Zirkander asked. He wasn't the only one. But he was the only one who mattered, at least for the moment.

"Your *prisoner* is armed," Crash said, waving to the sword.

Zirkander's gaze followed that wave, locking onto the weapon. His face grew hard and unreadable as he looked back and forth from it to Tolemek. *That wasn't Sardelle's soulblade or whatever it was called, was it? Surely he wouldn't have stolen it,* would he have?

Tolemek found her in the crowd, meeting her eyes. He didn't say anything with so many people looking on, but he gave her a small smile and a shrug that seemed to say, "It's a long story."

"Yes," Cas said, answering Crash's objection, "because he gave me his parole. He turned on his own people to help me escape from the pirates. I didn't make him any promises, in light of his past crimes, but I'd appreciate it if no one shot him full of holes until we figure out what's going on." She looked at the colonel as she said this, but his face hadn't grown any more amiable. It was as hard and unfriendly as granite. An unusual expression for him. Cas had only seen it once before, when he had been defending her from that pompous, groping Cofah diplomat. Seeing it again now could not be a good thing.

Zirkander stalked into the cabin, his pistol still pointed at Tolemek, though Tolemek's hands were clearly empty of weapons, and picked up the sword scabbard. "Get in, Ahn. I have to report to General Ort anyway. You can explain your story—and why you feel this murdering criminal shouldn't be shot immediately—to him."

In the minute it took the cabin to reach the base of the cliff? And here she had thought she had faced all of the tough challenges of the day already. She joined the two men inside, relieved when Zirkander didn't invite anyone else in.

The gate clanged shut, and the cabin started descending. Cas opened her mouth, but she didn't yet know what she intended to say. She wanted to ask what Tolemek was doing here, but at the same time, she wanted to try to explain everything to the colonel. If they took Tolemek to Ort, it would be all over. He would be in front of a firing squad by dawn, if not before. The colonel... he would be more reasonable. She hoped.

Before she got any words out, Zirkander grabbed Tolemek by his vest, hauled him to his feet, and shoved him against the metal wall. The cabin swayed and groaned.

"Sir," Cas said, raising a hand, though she could barely see the men in the dark. The only lit lanterns were back on the butte and in the compound at the base of the cliff.

"If you've done anything to Sardelle," Zirkander growled, "I'll shove you out that gate *right* now."

At a loss for anything intelligent to say, Cas went for the inane. "Colonel Zirkander, meet Tolemek, retired pirate. Tolemek, this is Colonel Zirkander."

"Yeah," Tolemek choked out, his airway restricted, "we've met in the air. He's almost killed me a couple of times."

A clang sounded—Tolemek being shoved against the wall again? "Sardelle," Zirkander repeated. "Where—"

"At the bottom of the tram, waiting for you. Or so the sword told me."

Cas stared at him. The *what* told him?

For a long moment, nothing sounded except the moaning of the wind and the creaking as the cabin swayed, descending slowly toward the bottom. Then Zirkander stepped back. They were the same height, Cas realized—a stupid thing to notice then, but as the gas lamps of the base approached from below, she could make out their silhouettes as they faced each other.

"We'll see what she has to say then," the colonel said, his voice softer now, though the warning hadn't disappeared from it. For Tolemek's sake, Cas hoped Sardelle would appear as soon as the men stepped out of the gate.

The cabin clanked down on the landing pad. An operator rushed over to open the gate.

"Welcome back, sir. Great flying up there. You, too, L.T."

"Thank you, Borscot," Zirkander said, though his gaze was roving all along the lighted area in front of the tram.

Cas scooted forward, trying to see around the men. There was no sign of—wait.

Sardelle stepped out of the shack, her cloak wrapped around her. "Ridge." She smiled, the expression full of genuine warmth. "Did the communication devices work?"

"Infallibly, but we have something to discuss."

Sardelle's smile turned dry as she nodded at Tolemek. "Yes, I imagine so."

"Sir, ma'am?" The soldier frowned at Tolemek, not knowing how to address him. "I need to send the cabin back up for the next group."

The colonel walked toward Sardelle. When she looked toward Tolemek again, he tossed her the sword scabbard. The tram operator jerked his arm up, looking like he meant to intercept the weapon, but it couldn't do much damage while sheathed. He seemed to realize that, too, and lowered his arm, though he gave Sardelle an odd look when she attached it to her belt and draped her cloak over it. Civilian archaeologists probably weren't supposed to have swords on base.

Cas stepped out of the cabin with Tolemek and drew him to the opposite side from Sardelle and Zirkander. She dared not drag him far until there was a modicum of resolution with the colonel, but she didn't want everyone in the squadron coming over to interrogate him—or her—when they walked off the tram.

"Why do I have the feeling you two have had adventures?" she asked, deeming it a more tactful question than the what-by-all-the-gods-in-the-universe-are-you-*doing*-here one that was bubbling up inside of her.

"I hope you never know the details," Tolemek whispered, then surprised her by drawing her into a hug and burying his face in her neck.

Cas was beginning to think he'd had a worse night than she. "I hope you'll tell me a few of them at least. Or Zirkander if not me. I'm trying to figure out how to save you from General Ort and a firing squad."

"You smell like engine oil, guns, and leather," he said, sounding bemused—and not in the mood to worry about firing squads.

"Not the usual combination you get from women you spend time with?"

"No, but I like it."

His lips brushed up her neck, to her jaw, and then to her mouth. The kiss he gave her made her earlier one seem chaste and sweet; this one was heated with passion and more... the sort of relief and fire one felt after saving something invaluable that had almost been lost. Cas was breathless by the time he lifted his mouth from hers, and she couldn't remember where she was, what she was supposed to be doing, and why they weren't scurrying off to find a bunk to share.

"Lieutenant?" Zirkander asked from a few feet away.

Cas flushed, her cheeks so hot that she was sure she was melting snow for several meters in every direction. "Sir?"

A group of her fellow officers walked away from the tram cabin, chatting and trading shoves as they headed for the base gate. Fortunately, they didn't look over to Cas's shadows. She wasn't even sure if that was the first group that had departed. She didn't remember hearing the tram in operation. She touched her lips, blushing all over again. Tolemek stood at her back, his hand on her waist.

"I'm going to go talk to the general," Zirkander said. "You... find a rack. Get some rest. Or... whatever." He flicked his hand toward Tolemek. He didn't sound approving, but he wasn't threatening to kill her pirate, either. That was an amazing turn around.

"I wonder what Sardelle said," Cas mused as Zirkander walked away.

"I don't know," Tolemek said, his arms wrapping around her waist, and his mouth returning to her throat, "but I vote for whatever."

Cas shivered and leaned back into him. "My vote... depends on whether you're taking those awful bracers off."

He chuckled softly. "I'll take off anything you like."

"Enticing."

"I certainly hope so."

Epilogue

Tolemek shifted his weight in the saddle, wincing at sore muscles. Pirates didn't spend a lot of time on horseback, and it didn't help that Zirkander had picked the biggest, orneriest horse in the stable for him. Tolemek had been thrown three times during the two-hour trip, which had caused the women to look at him with surprise and concern while Zirkander apologized heartily for the beast's temperament, then smirked into his scarf. Bastard.

At least they had turned off the road and, judging by Sardelle and Zirkander's enthused chatter, come to their destination. Given the revelation that the cabin was someplace Cas had once dreamed of being invited, Tolemek was expecting a bit more. A quarter mile down the path, the log structure perching next to the frozen lake and blanketed with six inches of snow, scarcely looked big enough for two people much less four people. Four people who barely knew each other and two of them men who might come to blows at any moment.

Five people.

Tolemek flinched, almost falling off the horse again. Jaxi hadn't spoken into his mind since the night of the attack, and he had assumed, with the emergency past, she was done communicating with him. *Are you actually considered a... people?*

I'm as much of a people as you are, Deathmaker. You're fortunate Sardelle has agreed to train you. Assuming you pass her tests this weekend and prove trainable at this point in your life. You're awfully old.

A centuries-old sword was calling him old? How bizarre. *Do you jump into Sardelle's head unannounced like this? Or am I special?*

You're definitely special, but, yes, Sardelle and I have no secrets. It's part of the joy of being bonded with a soulblade.

Maybe it was just as well that he had finagled magic lessons for his sister without acquiring an actual soulblade. Tolemek tried to imagine what it must be like having one's night of amorous passions interrupted by the commentary from a snarky sword. Then he decided he didn't want to imagine anyone having amorous passions with Zirkander and pushed the thought from his mind.

He's equally displeased by the idea of you having amorous passions with his lieutenant, Jaxi put in brightly.

"You're looking thoughtful over there." Cas, who was riding beside him on a docile mare, gave him a smile.

"Am I?" Tolemek decided not to mention the conversation. When he had alluded to the fact that Jaxi not only had a name but could communicate with people, her face had assumed that expression it did when magic was mentioned, a mixture of disbelief and horror.

"Apex would call it dyspeptic. That's one of his words. He usually reserves it for General Ort."

In the week since the pirates had been turned away, Tolemek hadn't met many of her pilot friends. He hadn't been allowed to wander the city and meet many people at all, but he couldn't complain overmuch, nor did he consider himself dyspeptic about anything except having a sarcastic sword sauntering through his thoughts. He had expected the firing squad, but instead, thanks to Zirkander's influence, he had been invited to stay in the city and had been given the full use of an immaculate laboratory that was technologically superior to anything he had ever seen. Indeed, he had spent far more time playing with the fancy centrifuge than was dignified for someone of his age and expertise. Until Cas had walked in and caught him at it. She hadn't seemed to believe he was doing "important experiments to further your people's war efforts," either. But then he had given her the tour, including the compact living quarters that had come with his lab, and they had grown delightfully distracted. For quite some time. He still grinned at the memory—and the realization that she *liked* being distracted with him. He hadn't caught her giving Zirkander so much as a thoughtful gaze in the time they had been together, so Tolemek was beginning to believe that any feelings for her commander that Cas had admitted to under the truth serum had been replaced by feelings for him, or perhaps her confession had been nothing more than a tale of a fleeting infatuation to start with.

He would have left the pirates years ago if he had known he could have such a life here. Granted, his lab assistant was obviously a spy, soldiers followed him whenever he left the building, and the Iskandians hadn't been subtle in stating that they expected their new scientist to make them useful things. But it was far more than he had expected. They might loathe him for his past, but they wanted his talents for their future. He hadn't foreseen that. They had even wanted him when he'd said he was out of the weapons, poisons, and biological-agents creation business—both on principle and because he didn't detest his homeland to the point where he wanted to harm its inhabitants. The general overseeing him had been delighted at the demonstration Tolemek had given him of Healing Salve Number Six. He had promptly ordered five hundred ounces worth, and, yes, Tolemek could have more lab assistants if he needed help fulfilling the order. It was a good beginning.

"I'm actually rather contented with the situation and the good company." Tolemek smiled at Cas, so she could make no mistake as to whom he meant. "I'll be even more contented when I figure out a way to get my sister over here. My understanding is that I'm to be treated well, produce lots of militarily significant formulas, and never leave the continent, especially not to go back to Cofahre where I might be tempted to blab Iskandian secrets."

"That's your understanding, or that's exactly what some general said?" Cas asked.

"Actually the general was more blunt than I. And I gathered he was paraphrasing your king. Who was even blunter."

"Ah. Well, in a few years, when you've proven yourself, they might allow you some travel privileges. After all, it's barely been a week, and you're already being permitted to see the country." Cas stretched an open palm toward the small and extremely rustic cabin.

Tolemek kept himself from pointing out that it was only

because two trusted officers were escorting him that he had been allowed this excursion out into the world. He also kept himself from suggesting that being in a tiny cabin wasn't exactly seeing the country, not when its owner was in earshot. Besides, Cas looked tickled to be out here. With him. Tolemek smiled at her again. "This is true."

"And I'm sure we can find a way to retrieve your sister. Even if *you* can't leave, you have friends here now."

Zirkander had dismounted, and his eyebrows twitched at this statement. Sardelle smiled back at them with more enthusiasm.

"I have some ideas for getting her over here," she said. "We can discuss them this weekend."

"We're here to relax," Zirkander said. "Not discuss work." He looked at Tolemek again. "Or schemes."

"Don't be ridiculous, Ridge. This is the one place I feel I can speak openly. On your base, your houses are so close together that I'm scared I'll slip up and alert some nosey neighbor that I'm more than an archaeologist."

"Are you truly accusing Lieutenant Colonel Ostraker of being nosey? He's the most proper example of a military officer you'll ever find. He's far too busy ironing his uniforms and polishing his boots to wander over and peep through our windows."

"His grandmother isn't," Sardelle said, dismounting near the cabin's small porch. "Not only is she so old that she was probably alive when I was walking the continent the first time, but she's always over in your yard, trimming your shrubs and filling your bird feeder."

Tolemek hadn't quite gotten the story on where Sardelle had come from, but for whatever reason, she didn't seem to worry about keeping her secrets around him or Cas. Maybe because they had already suspected her of being a sorceress when they showed up on her doorstep.

"Well, the shrubs shouldn't need trimming now that the snows have come." Zirkander rubbed his jaw and took the reins to Sardelle's horse. "But the birds do enjoy their suet in the winter."

She dropped her hand to his forearm. She managed to look

sweet, earnest, and determined all at the same time. "We must have a discussion. And some planning. That's what I'd like to do while we're here. We have to convince your people that magic can be useful, perhaps to finally free this continent from its would-be oppressors. Those communication devices are a start, even if your people don't know they were made a week ago and not centuries in the past, and they gave me an idea about perhaps making a few more indispensable items for the military and then letting the news slip that they're magical."

"I'm willing to discuss those things," Zirkander said as he led their two horses back to a lean-to against the back of the cabin that was out of the wind. "So long as it's in a relaxed state."

"Besides," Sardelle went on. "It's more than wishful thinking that has me bringing this up. The pilot I healed, the one who crashed..."

"The one who would have died without your intervention?" Zirkander returned from the back and pulled her into a hug, burying his face against her fur cap for a moment.

"Yes," she said, her voice quieter. "He said something... I tried to disabuse him of the notion, but he was quite convinced that he had been the beneficiary of a miracle and that I had the powers of a goddess. His words, mind you."

Zirkander frowned thoughtfully.

Tolemek was considering how to dismount from his beastly horse while this conversation was going on. For the moment, it was standing quietly, but he swore it was watching him out of the corner of its eye.

"Perhaps nothing will come from it," Sardelle went on, "but perhaps I may not have the luxury of remaining incognito for long. Things may get more complicated."

"No," Zirkander said. "This is my cabin in the woods. Things don't get more complicated at my cabin in the woods. It doesn't work that way. It just doesn't." He sounded like he knew he was being petulant—maybe he was intentionally being petulant to make a point—and sighed in the end, releasing Sardelle. "We'll think of something." He smiled and touched her face. "*After* our relaxing weekend together. This cabin is for enjoying the wilderness and appreciating the quiet time away from the city. That's what this cabin is for. Fishing. Hunting. Star gazing. Long walks with a loved one..."

Sardelle considered the frozen lake and the snowy branches of the trees. "It's cold for such activities, don't you think?"

"Snuggling by a fire with a loved one is also an acceptable form of relaxation." Zirkander gave Sardelle an eyebrow wriggle and a leer.

"Excellent. Snuggling is the perfect time to discuss agendas."

The leer turned into an exasperated sigh, though his eyes held a share of humor.

"I think you were right," Cas whispered to Tolemek. "She does control him. Not magically perhaps..."

"Does that mean you don't believe there will be much relaxing this weekend?" Tolemek replied.

Cas was dismounting, so he decided he had better do so too. He threw his leg over his horse, and it chose that moment to shake the snow off its fur. Vigorously. Its timing was precise. Tolemek lost his balance and ended up on his backside again.

Zirkander grabbed the reins. "No horses in Cofahre?" he asked mildly.

Tolemek glowered as he pushed himself to his feet, noting that Cas had dismounted without trouble. "No horses that have been trained by enemy commanders to torment new allies, no."

"Huh. Odd country." Zirkander took Cas's reins as well and led the two horses back to join the others.

At least he wasn't the sort to foist chores on someone else. Tolemek had wondered if Cas, as lowest ranking military person present, might be turned into an errand girl.

"You should try to get him to like you," Cas whispered, dusting snow off Tolemek's clothing.

"What if I don't like him?"

"You only feel that way because he's treating you like an enemy right now. If he starts to like you, he'll be roguishly charming instead of devilishly disagreeable."

The idea of Zirkander using roguish charm on him was more alarming than the notion of a firing squad. Cas was beaming up at him with hopeful eyes though. Ugh, speaking of women being in control...

"Any suggestions for how I might accomplish this?"

"Perhaps you could challenge him to a snowball fight."

"As if we were ten-year-old boys?" Tolemek asked.

"He's known to have a playful side."

"Not by the Cofah."

"That's because they insist on chucking grenades and cannonballs at him instead of snowballs," Cas said.

"I doubt there's anything they *haven't* tried throwing at him at this point."

Cas scooped up a big handful of snow and packed it into a ball.

"Are you volunteering to be on my team if a snowball battle should break out?" Tolemek imagined he could take anything Zirkander and his sorceress could hurl his way if he had Cas's arm at his side. And he wouldn't actually mind smacking Zirkander in the face with a heavy pile of snow. Having the other man shove him up against the wall in that tram cabin had rankled, but Tolemek hadn't dared defend himself then. He had been so exhausted that he probably couldn't have even if he tried.

"Not exactly."

As soon as Cas grinned, he knew he was in trouble. Up on the split-log deck, Zirkander was in the process of unlocking the door and holding it open for Sardelle, leaving his back to Tolemek. And Cas. She threw the snowball with the speed and accuracy of a sniper's daughter. It smacked Zirkander in the back of the neck and exploded. It would be shocking if icy chunks of snow didn't make their way down his shirt.

When Zirkander spun around, Cas, still smiling, pointed at Tolemek.

"What?" Tolemek blurted, stunned by this betrayal. Thus, he wasn't prepared when a cannonball-sized snow missile was launched at him.

He tried to dodge, but it caught him in the shoulder, spattering his face with slush. Tolemek wasn't close to the cabin, the trees, or any conveniently placed cover to hide behind, so he did the only thing that made sense. He snatched up a wad of snow, hurrying to pack it into a ball. But he paused with it held aloft. Who to hit? Zirkander, for striking him? Or Cas for *causing* Zirkander to strike him?

In that second while he was deciding, two snowballs slammed into him from different directions. Betrayed—on all accounts. He spun, hurling his weapon in the direction of the deck. He should have checked first. Sardelle had climbed the steps, apparently to usher Zirkander inside and stop this silliness. Tolemek's snowball exploded against her arm. Her expression wasn't so much angry as startled. As if she couldn't believe that he had dared strike her—well, actually he hadn't dared... He'd misfired.

At first, Zirkander looked like he meant to leap over the railing and pummel Tolemek for targeting his lady, but she caught his arm, whispered something, then plopped a snowball into his hand.

"Oh?" he asked, then launched it.

Tolemek would have dodged, but he was busy gaping because the snowball grew in size as it sailed toward him. It wasn't an illusion. It was bigger than his head by the time it slammed into his chest. Fortunately, it spattered into a slushy mess without hurting him, but it did cause him to step back to brace himself. That was the intent, anyway. Unfortunately, his heel slipped on something hidden beneath the snow, and he landed on his back in the white fluff.

"You're right," came Zirkander's voice from the deck. "That *was* more satisfying."

Cas snickered. Loudly. Tolemek hadn't heard her laugh often, so he supposed this was worth it, so long as she decided to give tender attentions to his grave injuries later on.

She appeared over him, her impish face framed by the cloudy sky. She had another snowball in hand—how *did* she make the things so quickly?—but didn't throw it, perhaps considering a downed man an unworthy target. "It's a good thing you can make potions, because I don't think the Iskandian army would accept you based on your fighting prowess."

Tolemek decided the proper reply to such mocking was to grab her ankle and pull her off her feet. She squawked a startled curse. She might have fallen into the cold snow beside him—surely a suitable punishment—but he tugged her so she landed atop him instead. He wasn't sure if he wanted to use her for a shield, keep her from tossing more snowballs at him, or employ the maneuver to encourage the pressing of her body parts against his body parts. "One would hope that Iskandian army recruits are taught to assist their comrades in battle rather than to set them up for enemy assaults."

"You obviously haven't been along on any academy combat drills." Cas still had her snowball in hand—alarming—but rested her chin against his chest instead of pulling away or mashing it into his face. That was promising.

"Lieutenant Ahn?" Zirkander called from the deck. "Is that dastardly pirate using you for a shield? Or are you canoodling?"

Cas turned her head over her shoulder to respond with another grin. "Yes, sir."

Encouraged, Tolemek readjusted her so that her face was in line for a kiss. He was vaguely aware of Zirkander and Sardelle going into the cabin and shutting the door.

Sardelle has announced that your training will not begin until the morning.

Tolemek managed to receive this mental intrusion without being overly distracted from his physical activities. Or perhaps he was too focused on those to care about the comment.

Just relaying information. Also, I suggest you don't enter the cabin for a while. Jaxi did the soulblade equivalent of sighing. *Humans. As randy as bonobos.*

"Looks like we'll be stuck out here for a while," Tolemek murmured, not moving his lips far from Cas's lips, though he managed to tilt his head toward the closed cabin door.

"You better keep me warm then."

"I can do that."

THE END

Printed in Great Britain
by Amazon